THE WORLD IN MY POCKET

James Hadley Chase

CHIVERS
THORNDIKE

This Large Print book is published by BBC Audiobooks Ltd, Bath, England and by Thorndike Press®, Waterville, Maine, USA.

Published in 2005 in the U.K. by arrangement with Hervey Raymond Esq.

Published in 2005 in the U.S. by arrangement with David Higham Associates Ltd.

U.K. Hardcover ISBN 1–4056–3430–8 (Chivers Large Print)
U.K. Softcover ISBN 1–4056–3431–6 (Camden Large Print)
U.S. Softcover ISBN 0–7862–8012–3 (British Favorites)

The text of this Large Print edition is unabridged.
Other aspects of the book may vary from the original edition.

Set in 16 pt. New Times Roman.

Printed in Great Britain on acid-free paper.

British Library Cataloguing in Publication Data available

Library of Congress Cataloging-in-Publication Data

Chase, James Hadley, 1906–
 The world in my pocket / by James Hadley Chase.
  p. cm.
 ISBN 0–7862–8012–3 (lg. print : sc : alk. paper)
 1. Robbery—Fiction. 2. Organized crime—Fiction. 3. Large type
books. I. Title.
 PR6035.A92W67 2005
               2005016550

THE WORLD IN MY POCKET

CHAPTER ONE

I

Four men sat around a table on which were scattered playing cards, poker chips, a couple of loaded ash trays, glasses and a bottle of whisky.

The room was in semi-darkness except for a green, shaded light that fell directly on the table. A smoke haze hung overhead and spread out, drifting away into the shadows.

Morgan, a big man with cold, restless eyes and a thin mouth, laid down four kings and sat back, drumming gently with his finger tips on the table.

There was a pause, then with grunts of disgust the other three men threw in their cards.

Gypo, born Giuseppe Mandini, a fat ball of a man with black curly hair, going grey at the temples, a swarthy complexion and a small beaky nose, flicked his chips across the table to Morgan and grinned ruefully.

'That cleans me,' he said. 'What luck! Nothing better than a nine all the evening!'

Ed Bleck fingered his neat stack of chips, removed four of them and pushed them over to Morgan. He was tall, fair and heavily sun-burned. He had a vicious handsomeness that

1

appealed to women but made men wary. He wore a neatly pressed grey flannel suit and his tie was hand painted: yellow horse shoes on a bottle-green background. Of the four men, he was the best dressed.

The fourth man was Alex Kitson. He was the youngest of the four, around twenty-three. He was solidly built, dark, with high cheekbones, a flattened nose of a professional fighter and dark, uneasy eyes. He wore an open-neck shirt and a pair of black corduroy trousers. He tossed the last of his chips over to Morgan, grimacing.

'Me too,' he said. 'I had four queens. I thought . . .' He broke off, aware the other two were looking intently at Morgan and not listening to what he was saying.

Morgan was making the chips he had received into three neat piles. A cigarette hung from his thin lips, and the other three men listened to his quick, steady breathing. When he had arranged the chips to his liking, he looked up. His black snake's eyes moved slowly from face to face.

Bleck said impatiently, 'What's on your mind, Frank? Something's been biting at you all the evening.'

Morgan continued to drum on the table with his finger tips for some seconds, then he said abruptly, 'How would you boys like to pick up two hundred thousand bucks?'

The three stiffened. They knew Morgan

well enough by now to be certain he wouldn't kid about a thing like that.

'What was that again?' Gypo asked, leaning forward.

'Two hundred thousand bucks *each*,' Morgan said, emphasizing the last word. 'It's there for the taking, but it'll be a tough one.'

Bleck took out a pack of cigarettes. He tapped a cigarette out and then began to roll it between his fingers while he regarded Morgan thoughtfully.

'You mean the complete take is eight hundred Gs?' he asked.

'A million,' Morgan said. 'There'll be a five-way split if you three want to come in on it.'

'Five? Who's the fifth?' Bleck asked sharply.

'We'll get to that,' Morgan said. He pushed back his chair and stood up. Putting his hands flat on the table, he leaned forward. His thin white face was tense as he said, 'This is the big one. It's tough, but it yields a million bucks in hard cash: money you can stick in your pocket without your pocket catching fire. Nothing bigger than a ten-dollar bill. But make no mistake about it—it's a tough one.'

'Two hundred thousand bucks?' Gypo was gaping. 'There ain't that much money in the world!'

Morgan grinned at him. The expression on his face made him look like a hungry wolf.

'It's the big one,' he repeated. 'With that amount of dough, you'll have the world in your

3

pocket!'

'Let me guess, Frank,' Bleck said. 'It's the Rocket Research Station's pay roll.'

Morgan sat down. He nodded, grinning.

'You're smart, Ed. That's the one. How do you like it? The pay roll is worth exactly a million: all in small bills. It's there to be had.'

He looked directly at Kitson who was staring at him, a startled expression on his face.

'You heard me, kid,' Morgan said. 'It's there to be had.'

'Are you crazy?' Kitson said, his big hands turning into fists. 'That's one job we don't do, Frank, and I know what I'm talking about.'

Morgan smiled at him, the way an older man smiles at a younger man who has said something stupid. His eyes moved to Bleck, knowing that if Bleck had a feeling for the job, something might be done about it. Bleck was the one with the brains. This kid, Kitson, had guts, was fast with his fists and could handle a car, but there was nothing in his head. If Bleck said it couldn't be done, then he might have to think again.

'What do you say, Ed?'

Bleck lit the cigarette, frowning.

'It's the one job I wouldn't pick in spite of the size of the pay off, but if you have an angle, I'm willing to listen.'

That was like Bleck. He never expressed an opinion unless he had all the facts.

4

Gypo moved his fat body uneasily, looking from Kitson to Morgan, a puzzled expression on his face.

'What's so tough about the job then?' he asked.

Morgan waved his hand at Kitson.

'You tell him, kid. You should know. You worked for the outfit.'

'Yes,' Kitson said. 'I do know. This is the one job no one swings. Anyone who is crazy enough to try to grab that pay roll is yelling for trouble.' He looked around the table at the other three, uneasy to be talking this way to three men much older than himself and unsure of himself. 'I'm not kidding. The Welling Armoured Truck Agency is really organized for trouble. I should know. As Frank said, I worked there once.'

Gypo rubbed his face with his hand and frowned at Morgan. 'But you have an angle, haven't you, Frank?'

Morgan ignored him. He continued to stare at Kitson. 'Go on, kid,' he said. 'Keep talking. Tell them how tough it is.'

Kitson picked up one of Morgan's poker chips. He began to turn it over and over between his thick fingers while he stared at it, frowning.

'Before I quit the agency,' he said, 'they got delivery of a new truck. Before this truck arrived, they were using a sardine can with four outriders to protect it. This new truck

5

doesn't need outriders. It's really the tops. They're so sure it is foolproof they don't even insure the load any more.'

'What's so special about it?' Morgan asked.

Kitson ran his thick fingers through his hair. It embarrassed him to talk but he was determined to prove that this time Morgan was wrong to suggest such a job. He had had, up to now, a lot of faith in Morgan. The four of them had been working as a team for the past six months, and they had pulled several pretty good jobs. The money hadn't been much, but there had been no risk, and each one of these jobs had been Morgan's brain child. Kitson was willing to admit that two hundred thousand bucks was real money, but what was the use of thinking about it? Morgan had said it was to be had. But he was wrong! He just didn't know what he was talking about!

'Go on, kid,' Morgan urged, a jeering expression in his eyes. 'What's so special about this new truck?'

Kitson drew in a deep breath.

'You won't get near it, Frank,' he said. He was so anxious to make his point, his voice shook. 'This truck is made of a special armoured plate alloy. You can't cut into it. Maybe it would melt under continuous and intense heat, but the heat would have to be applied for hours, maybe days. The strongest part of the truck is the door. There's a time lock on it. When the truck is loaded, they fix the lock. It takes the truck three hours fast driving to reach the Research Station. The lock is set to operate four hours after it has left the Agency. That gives the driver time in hand to take care of traffic blocks or a breakdown.' He put the poker chip down and looked at the other two who were leaning forward, listening, intent expressions on their faces. 'There's a push button on the dashboard that controls the time lock. If there is any sign of trouble, the driver has only to punch the button and the time lock cancels out.'

'Then what happens?' Morgan asked jeeringly.

'Once the button is punched, no one opens the door until the time lock is reset, and that's an expert's job.' Kitson lit a cigarette and let the smoke drift down his wide nostrils. 'Then there's another thing: they carry a short-wave receiving and transmitter set in the truck, and from the moment they leave for the Research Station, they are in continuous radio communication with the Agency.' Aware now that Morgan was grinning derisively at him, he turned his attention to Gypo and addressed him directly. 'Look, suppose some nut tries to hold up the truck. Suppose this nut blocks the road and stops the truck. The driver and the guard automatically go into their routine. The driver punches the button that scrambles the time lock and the guard flicks down a switch that slams steel shutters over the windshield and the windows, turning the truck into a box that just can't be bust open. Then the guard flicks down another switch on the transmitter which sets up a continuous signal. Any cop radio car can home on to this signal, and no matter where the truck is, the radio car will find it. Once they've operated the three switches, all they have to do is to sit tight in their steel box and wait for help.' He tapped ash off his cigarette, his hand shaking from nervous excitement. 'Like I said: no one is going to hi-jack that truck. They are really organized for trouble.'

Gypo scratched the back of his neck, a sudden bored expression on his fat face. Bleck had picked up a deck of cards and was shuffling them aimlessly, his light-coloured eyes on Morgan.

'How about the driver and the guard?' Morgan asked. 'Couldn't they be got at?'

Kitson waved his hands.

'Got at? Those two? Are you that crazy? Who's been telling you what?'

An ugly glint came into Morgan's eyes.

'I asked you a question,' he said. 'Don't flap with your mouth, and don't ask me if I'm crazy. I don't like it.'

Seeing his angry expression, Bleck said smoothly, 'Take it easy, Frank. The kid's doing all right. At least he seems to know what he's talking about.'

Morgan sneered at him.

'Yeah. Well, we'll see.' He looked at Kitson. 'Go on. Tell me why these two can't be got at.'

Kitson was beginning to sweat. Tiny beads of perspiration made his flattened nose shine in the hard light.

'I've worked with them,' he said, staring hard at Morgan. 'I know them. The driver's name is Dave Thomas and the guard is Mike Dirkson. They are tough and keen and quick with a gun. They know if they defeat a holdup, they will get a two thousand-dollar bonus each. They know there's no way of busting open the truck to get at the payroll so they wouldn't be that crazy to throw in with us and lose a regular job that pays off. These two are on the beam. You'll find that out fast enough if you start something with them.'

Gypo broke in, 'If it's going to be that tough, I don't want anything to do with it. Okay, two hundred grand is fine, but no money is big enough if you ain't alive to spend it.'

Morgan smiled.

Gypo was a defeatist. He had his qualities, but guts and staying power weren't his strong points. He was a technical man. There were few locks that his sensitive fingers couldn't master. He had opened many impossible locks in his time, but he had always worked in an atmosphere of quiet. He had never been called on to work under pressure, and Morgan knew this job would be working under the greatest

9

possible pressure. He wondered if Gypo would make the grade. He had enough confidence in himself to be sure he could talk Gypo into tackling the job, but that didn't mean much. When the time came: when the cards were down and the pressure was on, everything would depend on Gypo's skill. If his nerves blew up, then the job would blow up too.

'Relax,' he said, putting his hand on Gypo's shoulder. 'Since we four ganged up, I've steered you all into good jobs. Right?'

Gypo nodded while the other two stared at Morgan, waiting.

'Not big stuff,' Morgan went on, 'but you all had some dough. But sooner or later the cops are going to get wise to us. We can't go on and on pulling little jobs for peanut money without getting a rumble. So I figure we should try the big one, collect the dough, break up the mob and go our own ways. Two hundred thousand can buy a lot of fun. The world is in our pockets with that kind of dough. This job can be done. It's just a matter of working on it. I know it's tough. Kitson has given you most of the dope. What he says is right, but he's forgotten one thing.' He looked at the three men, seeing Gypo was uneasy, Kitson obstinate and scared, Bleck still indifferent, still waiting to be convinced. 'What he forgot to tell you is that this new truck has been on the hoof now five months, week in and out, and everyone believes it is foolproof.

Everyone, including Kitson, is sold on the idea that no one in his right mind would try to grab the truck. When you get that kind of idea into your head, you lower your guard and your chin's uncovered. It only needs a quick right-hand punch, and you're licked.'

He deliberately used the parlance of the ring because he wanted to catch Kitson's interest. He had to have him as well as Gypo on his side. He saw he had been successful. Kitson was now looking less obstinate and more interested.

'Everything Kitson has told you about the truck I read in papers months ago,' Morgan went on. 'These guys were so cocky about their truck they gave it wide publicity. They are certain no one can bust into it, and they figure the more details they give out about it, the tougher they make it sound, the more business they'll drum up for the agency. Ever since I read about that truck, I've had it at the back of my mind to bust it. We can do it if you guys have the guts to work with me. It'll need guts, but don't forget the pay-off is two hundred grand each.'

Bleck crushed out his cigarette and immediately lit another. He was staring at Morgan, his pale eyes narrowed.

'And you've got an angle?' he asked.

'Yeah.' Morgan lit a cigarette, blowing smoke across the table towards Gypo. 'I've got an angle. At least we have plenty of time to think about it. That truck is going to deliver a million bucks to the Research Station every week now for five years, and maybe longer. I admit they are organized for trouble, but as the weeks go by, they are going to get less watchful, less alert, and that's when we step in and sock them.'

'Now, wait a moment,' Kitson said, leaning forward, his face flushing. 'This is a lot of crap. How long does it take a guy, even if he is half asleep, to press a button? Two seconds? Certainly not more. Six seconds to press three buttons, then the truck turns into a steel tortoise and there's nothing you nor anyone else can do about it. Do you imagine you can stop that truck, break open the door and handle the driver and the guard in six seconds? Talk sense! This is a goddamn pipe dream!'

'You think so?' Morgan said jeeringly.

'I know so! Stop that truck, and before you can get within a yard of it, the steel shutters will be down, the time lock scrambled and the radio screaming for help!'

'Sure?' Morgan said and his jeering smile made Kitson itch to hit him.

'I'm sure, and nothing you can say will convince me otherwise,' Kitson said, controlling his temper with difficulty.

'Suppose you pipe down and let Frank give us his angle?' Bleck said. 'If you think you've got better brains than he has, then why the hell don't you run this outfit?'

Kitson flushed scarlet, shrugged angrily and tilted back his chair. He looked sullenly at Bleck and then at Morgan. 'Okay, but I tell you it can't be done,' he said.

Bleck looked over at Morgan.

'Go ahead and tell us how you figure to work it, Frank.'

'Yesterday I took a look at the route from the Agency to the Research Station,' Morgan said. 'It's quite a trip: ninety-three miles by the clock. Seventy of these miles are on the highway, twenty on a secondary road, ten on a dirt road and three on a private road leading directly to the Research Station. I was looking for a place where we could stop the truck. The highway is out. The secondary road is out too. The traffic on both these roads is continuous and heavy. The private road is guarded night and day so that's out too. That leaves us with the dirt road.' He flicked ash off his cigarette, screwing up his black eyes as he stared around at the three men facing him. 'Ten miles of road. Four miles from the secondary road and up the dirt road, there's a branch road leading to Highway 10. Most of the traffic, and it isn't heavy, uses the road past the Research Station gates because it is a better road and two miles shorter than the other dirt road. A couple of miles before you get to the Research Station gates there's a bottle-neck made by two big rocks either side of the road. Besides the rocks, there are a lot of scrub bushes. It's a pretty good place for an ambush or an accident.'

Bleck nodded.

'That's right,' he said. 'I've been over that road myself and I very nearly had a pile-up there. If you take the bend too fast you're on this bottle-neck before you know it. They've put up a sign now because of the number of accidents.'

'That's right,' Morgan said. 'Well, imagine those two guys in the truck. In this weather it'll be damned hot in the cab. They've driven over the same route dozens of times, and what with the heat and the boredom of the ride, they'll be down on their heels. They come to the bottle-neck. As they turn into the bend, they'll see a car, smashed up against the rock, but off the road. Lying in the middle of the road will be a woman, with blood on her and looking pretty bad.' He leaned forward, staring directly at Bleck. 'You tell me something: what are those two guys going to do—keep going and drive over the woman or stop and find out how badly hurt she is?'

Bleck grinned. He looked at Kitson.

'Are you listening, stupe?' he said. 'Some pipe dream!'

'What are they going to do?' Morgan repeated as Kitson shifted in his chair, his face turning red.

Bleck said, 'They'll stop. I guess one of them will get out of the truck and the other

14

will use the radio to get help. That is if they are as security minded as Kitson says they are.'

Morgan looked over at Kitson.

'What do you say? What do you think they would do?'

Kitson hesitated, then grudgingly shrugging his shoulders, he said, 'I guess Ed's right. Dirkson would get out of the truck and Thomas would stay where he was. Dirkson would find out how badly hurt she was, move her off the road, go back to the truck, radio for help, and then they'd go on, leaving her for the ambulance to pick up.'

'Okay. That's what I think too,' Morgan said. He didn't bother to ask Gypo his opinion. Gypo seldom expressed an opinion that was worth listening to except when it had to do with the busting of a safe or the opening of some tricky lock. 'So we have this situation,' Morgan went on: 'we have one guard out of the truck and the other guard inside the truck. Now tell me something else.' He was looking directly at Kitson. 'Would the driver scramble the time lock and drop the steel shutters across the windows and the windshield in a situation like that?'

Kitson took out his handkerchief and wiped his face. 'I guess not,' he said sullenly.

Morgan looked over at Bleck.

'What do you think?'

'Of course he wouldn't,' Bleck said decisively. 'From what Kitson says if the time-lock is scrambled, it takes an expert to fix it, and this guy wouldn't start a thing like that unless he thought the truck was in danger. He wouldn't operate the shutters because he'd be curious to see what his pal was doing and how badly hurt the woman was.'

Morgan nodded.

'Well, at least we're getting somewhere. The truck has stopped and the buttons haven't been pushed.' He pointed a finger at Kitson. 'That's the situation you said wasn't possible. You said it was crazy talk and a pipe dream. What do you say now?'

'Where's it going to get you anyway?' Kitson said angrily. 'Okay, so I was wrong, but for all the good it's done you, I could have been right.'

Morgan blew a thin stream of smoke towards the ceiling. He now looked as if he were enjoying himself.

'All the same I haven't done so badly,' he said. 'I've stopped the truck and I've got the guard out into the open. Now imagine this bottle-neck. That's where the truck will be stopped. On each side there's thick cover where two or three guys can hide. The guard gets out of the truck and walks to where the woman is lying. Don't tell me in this heat those two drive for ninety-three miles with their windows shut. Do you imagine the driver will close the windows when the guard leaves him?'

Kitson again hesitated, then reluctantly

shook his head.

'I guess not.'

'I'm damned sure not. It'll be hot enough in that steel box without him closing the windows. Well, then, we have the truck at a standstill, close enough to the shrubs where two men can easily hide. The driver is watching through the windshield what his pal is doing. His pal is moving towards the woman. They're not expecting trouble. This is an accident spot. There have been five bad smashes there within six months. I'll be in the shrubs. I'll have about ten feet between me and the truck. I'll come out behind the truck as the guard bends over the woman, and I'll come up to the driver's window and stick a gun in his face. At the same time the woman sticks a gun in the guard's face.' He reached forward and crushed out his cigarette. 'Now, tell me something. What are these two birds going to do? Make heroes of themselves?'

'They could do,' Kitson said soberly. 'They're good men.'

'Okay, so they are good men, but they're not crazy. It's my bet they'll give up.'

There was a long, heavy pause, then Gypo said, a slight quaver in his voice, 'Suppose they don't give up?'

Morgan looked over at him, his black eyes glittering.

'The take is a million bucks: two hundred thousand each. If they don't give up, they'll get

17

hurt. You can't pick up that kind of money without someone getting pushed around a little.'

There was another pause, then Gypo said, 'I don't like it, Frank. Maybe it's too big for us.'

Morgan waved his hand impatiently.

'What are you worrying about? You won't be there. I've a special job for you and it won't be too big for you. I promise you that.'

Kitson leaned forward.

'How about me? I'm not crazy enough to get tied up in a murder rap! Count me out!'

Morgan looked over at Bleck who was lighting a cigarette.

'I've heard these two chickens: how about you?'

Bleck pursed his lips as he flicked the dead match across the room.

'It's my bet those two will give up. If they don't, then it's going to be just too bad.'

'That's the way I feel about it,' Morgan said. 'Okay, then you and me and the girl will handle it. Gypo and Kitson can handle the soft end, but their cut will come lower. We take the risks so we get more dough. That's fair, isn't it?'

Kitson frowned uneasily. Already the thought of what two hundred thousand dollars would mean to him was beginning to take a hold of him.

'Well, maybe. It depends what my cut would be,' he said.

18

'A hundred and twenty-five grand,' Morgan said promptly. 'Because Gypo's a technical man, he'll get a hundred and seventy-five grand. The hundred grand you two don't get would be split between Ed and me.'

Kitson and Gypo exchanged glances.

'If those guys act tough, one of us or maybe one of them could get killed,' Kitson said, breathing heavily. 'I don't like it. Up to now the jobs we have pulled have been small and sweet. The worst we could have drawn could have been a year in jail, but this is a murder rap. Count me out.'

'That's right,' Gypo said. 'Count me out too.'

Morgan smiled wolfishly.

'Okay. Let's vote on it. The rules of this outfit are that we always vote on a job. So let's vote.'

'We don't have to vote,' Kitson said sharply. 'It's a tie anyway even if Ed throws in with you. Your rules say if it's a tie we don't do the job—remember?'

'Sure, I remember,' Morgan said, grinning. 'Let's vote all the same. Let's keep this outfit business-like. Whatever the decision, we stick to it—right?'

Kitson shrugged.

'Yes, but why waste time?'

Morgan pushed back his chair and stood up. His big muscular frame threw a black shadow across the table.

'Get the voting slips ready, Gypo.'

Gypo, his moon-shaped face puzzled, produced a notebook and tore a page from it. He cut the page into four strips with a penknife and dropped the strips of paper on the table.

'There you are, guys,' he said. 'Help yourselves.'

Morgan said softly, 'Why only four, Gypo?'

Gypo stared up at him blankly.

'It's always four, isn't it?'

Morgan smiled.

'This is a five-way split—remember? The girl has a vote too.'

He walked to the door, threw it open and said, 'Come on in, Ginny. They want to vote on this job, and I need your vote.'

II

She came out of the darkness into the hard light from the overhead lamp and stood beside Morgan, looking at the three men who stared back at her.

She was young, not more than twenty-three, and slightly above average height. She had copper-coloured hair, piled to the top of her head. Her eyes were large and greenish-grey and as expressionless and as impersonal as a cupful of sea-water. Her mouth was over large, her lips full and sensual, and there was an arrogant, determined tilt to her chin.

She was wearing a blood-red silk shirt tucked into a black over-lap skirt. Her body was full breasted and narrow waisted. Her full hips tapered down to long, slim legs. It was a body made fashionable by Italian film stars, and it caught the three men's attention the way a hook catches a fish.

Morgan's black eyes roved around the faces of the three men, and he grinned. He knew the girl would make an impact on them and it interested him to see just how great the impact would be.

Gypo's hand had gone to his red string tie, adjusting it, while he peeled his thick lips off his big, dazzling white teeth in a leering smile.

Bleck, frankly startled, lifted his eyebrows and pursed his lips in a soundless, appreciative whistle.

Kitson looked as if someone had hit him on the head with a hammer. He stared at the girl the way a tortured bull stares at a matador the moment before the *estocada*.

Morgan said, 'This is Ginny Gordon.'

Bleck got to his feet. After a moment's hesitation, Gypo also got to his feet, but Kitson sat there, his big hands into fists on the table, his eyes a little glassy, his expression still stunned.

'Reading from right to left,' Morgan went on, 'is Ed Bleck who takes care of the gang when I'm out of the way. Gypo Mandini, our technical man and Alex Kitson who handles the car when we need a car.'

Kitson suddenly lumbered to his feet, nearly upsetting the table. He continued to stare at the girl, his hands still in fists.

The girl's eyes moved quickly from face to face, then she pulled out a chair beside Morgan and sat down.

'I've given the boys an outline of the plan,' Morgan said to the girl, standing over her. 'Two of them think it's too big for us. Our rules are if there's any disagreement about the job, we vote on it. So we're going to vote.'

The girl frowned, her face suddenly puckering into a puzzled frown.

'Too big for them?' she repeated. 'You mean two of them don't want to pick up two hundred thousand dollars?' Her voice was cold and incredulous.

'I wouldn't say that,' Morgan said and grinned. 'They think someone might get hurt and that bothers them.'

The girl looked at Gypo, then her greenish-grey eyes moved to Bleck, then flickered over to stare at Kitson.

'I thought you said your outfit was good,' she said.

The sudden scorn in her voice made Kitson flinch and turn red.

'That's what I said.' Morgan's grin widened. 'But this is the first job we've planned that's really big and two of us aren't too happy about it.'

'This is the big one,' the girl said, her voice tense. 'It pays off a million dollars. You said your outfit could handle it and I believed you, otherwise I wouldn't have come to you. Now you are taking a vote. What is all this?'

The three men were startled. The contemptuous, reckless note in the girl's voice angered them.

Bleck, who had the reputation of treating his women rough, said, 'You sound a little loud, baby. Suppose you relax a little?'

The girl pushed back her chair and stood up. Her pretty face was cold and hard.

'I guess I've come to the wrong address,' she said to Morgan. 'We'll skip it. I'll peddle this idea to a mob who has blood in its veins. I'm not going to waste my time talking to a bunch of powder puffs.'

She swung around on her heels and started towards the door.

Still grinning, Morgan reached out and caught hold of her arm, checking her.

'Take it easy!' he said. 'These boys are okay. They've just got to adjust themselves. Gypo here is the best safe man in the business. Ed has nerves as good as mine. Kitson can handle a car the way no one else can. Just take it easy. You've caught us on the wrong foot. Maybe I shouldn't have got around to the facts so fast. These boys are technically good, but they're scared someone is going to get hurt.'

23

She stood staring at each man in turn.

'Hurt? Who's the dumb cluck who imagines we can pick up a million dollars without getting hurt?' Her voice was harsh as she looked at the three men. 'It's a million dollars! For that kind of money I wouldn't give a damn what happened to me or to anyone else!'

She shook off Morgan's restraining hand, moved back under the hard light.

She looked directly at Kitson.

'Are you scared to get your pretty skin bruised when there's two hundred thousand dollars for the taking?'

Kitson had to make an effort to meet her steady, scornful eyes.

'The job can't be done,' he said sullenly. 'I know. I've worked for these people. This could be a murder rap and I don't go for that.'

'All right, if that's the way you feel about it,' the girl said, 'we can do without your help. If you don't want the money, now's the time to pick up that beautiful, muscular body of yours and get out of here!'

Kitson's face darkened and he pushed back his chair.

'Who do you think you're talking to? I tell you this job can't be done! It's a pipe dream!'

She flicked slim fingers towards the door.

'And you are a pipe dream too. Run away, powder puff. We can handle this without you.'

Slowly, Kitson got to his feet, his breath snorting through his broken nose. He walked slowly around the table towards the girl who pivoted on her heels so she faced him.

The three men at the table watched. Bleck looked worried. He knew Kitson's temper was unreliable. Gypo was frowning. Morgan still grinned.

'You and nobody else talks to me that way!' Kitson said as he confronted the girl.

They made an incongruous couple. Her head scarcely reached to the top of his shoulder, and standing in front of her, he seemed at least three times as broad as she was.

She looked at him, her expression still scornful.

'Then in case you didn't hear, I'll repeat what I said,' she said quietly. 'Run away, powder puff. We can handle this without your help.'

Kitson made a low growling noise and he lifted his hand, threateningly.

'Go ahead and hit me,' the girl said. 'I'm not scared of getting hurt!'

Morgan laughed.

Kitson dropped his hand and stepped back. He muttered under his breath and then started for the door.

'Kitson!' Morgan's voice rapped out. 'Come back here and sit down! We've got to vote. You walk out now, and you're through with this outfit for good!'

Kitson hesitated, then turning slowly, his

face confused and sullen, he walked back to the table and sat down.

Morgan looked at Gypo.

'Another slip.'

Gypo took out his notebook and cut another slip of paper.

Bleck said, 'Before we vote, Frank, I want to know more about this job. How does she get mixed up in it?' He jerked his thumb towards Ginny.

'For the past five months I've been trying to figure out how to knock over this truck,' Morgan said, 'and I couldn't figure an angle. Three nights ago, she came to me and dropped the whole thing, sewn up, into my lap. It's her idea, that's why it's a five-way split. She's worked out all the angles, and I'm satisfied her plan will work.'

Bleck looked at the girl.

'And where do you come from, baby?' he asked. 'What put the idea into your pretty head?'

The girl opened her cheap, shabby bag and took out a pack of cigarettes and a book of paper matches. She lit a cigarette while she regarded Bleck, her gaze cool and impersonal.

'It's no business of yours nor any one else's where I come from,' she said curtly. 'I thought up the idea because I want the money. While we're on the subject, I don't like being called baby, so drop it, will you?'

Bleck grinned. He admired a woman with

spirit.

'Sure, I'll drop it. What made you pick on this outfit to help you with a job as big as this one?'

She pointed to Gypo.

'Because of him. I asked around. They said he's the best man with a lock in the district and that's what's needed for this job. They said you had a lot of nerve, that Morgan had a flair for organization and Kitson was the best get-away driver on the coast.'

Gypo was smiling now. He thrived on flattery. The girl is dead right, he thought. There is no better man in the lock business.

Kitson had lost his sullen expression. He now looked embarrassed, and he kept his eyes down, staring at the wet ring on the table made by his whisky glass.

'They said . . . who said?' Bleck asked.

'That's neither here nor there. We're wasting time,' the girl said. 'I asked around because I had to be sure I was coming to the right outfit, but it seems I could have made a mistake. If I have, then I'll try elsewhere.'

Bleck lit a cigarette while he stared at her.

'Well, you've certainly picked the toughest end of the job if you're the one who's going to lie in the road. Was that your idea?'

'Of course.'

'Let's look at what you are taking on. You'll be lying in the middle of the road. You'll have a gun under you. When the guard comes up to

27

you you'll stick the gun in his face . . . correct?'

She nodded.

'It could be rugged,' Bleck said. 'Two things could happen: either the guard tosses up his hands and quits or else he won't take you seriously and makes a grab at your gun. From what I hear about this guy, he won't give up. He'll make a grab at your gun. Then what?'

The girl let smoke drift down her nostrils.

'This is a million dollar take,' she said in a cold, expressionless voice. 'If he makes a grab at the gun, he'll get shot.'

Gypo took out his handkerchief and wiped his face. The tip of his tongue moved over his lips as he looked uneasily at Morgan and then at Kitson.

'This is the big one,' Morgan said. 'You've got to face up to it, guys. If you don't like it, you can always quit.'

Bleck was studying the girl.

She's no bluffer, he was thinking. Sweet Pete! She's as hard as a diamond. She'll kill the guy if he starts anything. With any luck, he'll see it in her eyes when she shoves the heater in his face. If he does, he won't make a move. If I were he, and found myself looking into a gun held by her, I know damn well I'd stop breathing let alone make any sudden move.

'Okay. I just want to know which way we're heading,' he said, reaching for a cigarette and tapping it on the table. 'Let's have the rest of the plan.'

Morgan shook his head.

'We don't get the rest of it until we vote,' he said. 'That's the arrangement. She tells me she's taken care of all the details and ironed out all the snags. What I've told you just now is a sample of it. If we agree to work with her then we hear the rest of it, but if we don't want the job, then she's free to peddle it elsewhere. That's fair enough. What do you say?'

'But has she really ironed out all the snags?' Bleck asked. 'It seems to me there're a hell of a lot of them. We've stopped the truck and we've fixed the driver and the guard. That in itself is something we didn't think possible. But from what you tell me the truck is in continuous radio communication with the Agency. As soon as the truck goes off the air, a search for it will be started. They know where to look for it, and what's more, not only the cops will come a-hunting, but the army as well, and that means hundreds of men, aircraft and cars. They have only ninety-three miles of road to check. An aircraft can cover that in a few minutes. The truck will stand out on any road like a boil on the back of your neck. We will have less than twenty minutes to get it out of sight. It might be possible if we didn't have to stop the truck at the bottle-neck. Beyond there and the other side of it is as bare of cover as the back of my hand. We'll have to travel twenty-five miles to reach any good cover and they'll know it and that's where they'll look for us. I can't see how we can hope to stop the truck, bust it open, get the money and get away before the cops and the Army arrive.'

Morgan shrugged.

'I thought that too.' He nodded at the girl. 'She says she has taken care of that angle.'

Bleck looked at Ginny.

'Is that a fact? You really know the answer to that one?'

"Yes,' she said in her cold, expressionless voice. 'That's the hardest part. I've taken care of it.'

She spoke with such assurance that even Kitson, who was listening cynically, had a sudden feeling that she might swing this job.

Bleck spread his hands and shrugged his shoulders.

'Okay, I'll take your word for it, but you've certainly dreamed up a miracle. There still remain two more problems. The first is when we've stopped the truck what's to prevent other traffic coming up on us just when we're fixing the guards? This road isn't over-used, but there is traffic on it. We could be surprised.'

The girl's face became wooden and her eyes bored as she leaned back in her chair, her scarlet shirt tightening across her full, provocative breasts.

'That's an easy one, isn't it? There are two roads, both linking up with Highway 10. All we have to do is to put a diversion sign at the

30

bottom of the road after the truck has passed and the rest of the traffic will use the other road. What's so hard about that?'

Bleck grinned.

'Yeah, that's a fact. Now, bright eyes, solve this one: we have the truck and we get it under cover somehow. How do we bust it open? According to Kitson, it's the toughest thing made. We'll have to work fast. Have you solved that one?'

Ginny shook her head.

'That's his headache,' she said and pointed to Gypo. 'He's the expert. I've fixed it he has the truck. There's no hurry. He can work on it for a month or even two months if he has to.' Her sea-green eyes moved to Gypo. 'Could you open that truck if you had a month's uninterrupted work on it?'

Gypo, inflated by the flattery he had already received, nodded eagerly.

'I could bust into Fort Knox if I had a month's work on it,' he said.

'That's what he'll have,' Ginny said. 'At least a month; more if he needs it.'

'Okay. We've talked enough,' Morgan said. 'She's really worked this thing out, and I'm satisfied she can handle it. Let's vote. What you've got to make up your minds about is whether you are ready to get hurt or if you are prepared to hurt, and by that I mean, someone, either on our side or on the other side, could get killed. If the other side gets killed, then we all face a murder rap. Whatever happens, if no one gets hurt, and we make a slip, we face from ten to twenty years in jail. Against that, there's the pay-off. Each one of us will have two hundred thousand dollars, and that's quite a slice of money. That's the position. Let's vote, unless anyone else wants to ask any more questions.' He paused, looking at the three men. 'Once we've voted, we go ahead on the decision. You all know the rules of this outfit. Whoever is out-voted, if there is a majority against him, works with us or quits for good. Don't rush at this. The take is two hundred grand. If we make a mess of it, we land in jail for maybe twenty years or if we make even a bigger mess of it, we land on the hot seat. That's the set-up. Do you guys want a little time to think about it?'

He looked first at Bleck who was relaxed, looking at Ginny, genuine admiration in his eyes. Morgan then looked at Gypo who was staring thoughtfully down at the table, his face puckered, his thick, black eyebrows drawn down in a frown. Then he looked at Kitson who was staring at Ginny, his breath coming in short, sharp snorts through his broken nose.

'Let's vote,' Bleck said and, reaching forward, he picked up one of the slips of paper.

Ginny picked up another.

Morgan picked up the three remaining slips, tossed one in front of Gypo and the other in front of Kitson and then taking a ball pen from his pocket, he scribbled on the remaining slip, folded it and dropped it in the middle of the table.

Ginny borrowed his pen, scribbled on hers and laid it beside his.

Bleck had already written on his slip with a gold-capped fountain pen. He waved the slip in the air, then folded it and put it by the other two slips in the middle of the table.

Gypo spent two moments staring down at his slip. Finally, with a stub of pencil, he scrawled something on his slip, folded it and placed it with the other slips.

That left Kitson, who looked worried as he stared at his slip.

The girl and the other three watched him.

'Take your time,' Morgan said, the jeering note back in his voice. 'We have all night.'

Kitson looked up, stared at him, then his eyes moved to the girl. For a long moment they regarded each other, then abruptly he picked up Morgan's ball pen, scribbled something, folded his slip and tossed it on top of the other four.

There was a pause, then Morgan pulled the five slips towards him and unfolded one.

'Yes.'

He unfolded another.

'Yes.'

His fingers moving fast, he unfolded the remaining three slips.

'Yes and yes and yes.'

He looked around the table, his thin mouth curving into its wolfish smile.

'So we're going to do this job. That's the way I hoped it would work out. Two hundred thousand bucks each! Some job, but some pay-off!'

Kitson looked across the table at Ginny.

She stared back at him, her chin tilted, then suddenly her expression softened and she smiled at him.

CHAPTER TWO

I

A little after eight o'clock the following morning, a black, dusty Buick Century slid to a standstill a few yards from the entrance to the Welling Armoured Truck Agency.

On either side of the broad street were parked cars, left overnight, and the Buick immediately blended in the scene as just another parked car.

Morgan sat at the wheel, his greasy stained hat tilted over his nose, a cigarette hanging from his thin lips. Ed Bleck sat at his side.

The two men looked over at the high wooden gates of the Agency. There was nothing to see except barbed wire tangled on the top of each gate, a glittering brass knob that was the bell-pull and the big sign screwed to one of the doors on which was printed in bold red letters on a white background the following legend:

THE WELLING ARMOURED TRUCK AGENCY
You want security—We have it
The Safest and Best Trucking Service in
the World

'They seem to think a lot of themselves,' Bleck said when he had read the sign. 'Well, they're due for a surprise.'

'Or we are,' Morgan said with his jeering grin.

'I have a hunch we're going to get away with this job,' Bleck said. 'This frill has really worked it out, hasn't she?'

'Yeah.' Morgan took his cigarette from between his lips and stared at the glowing tip. 'The plan's right, but all depends on the way it's carried out. There're a number of weak links. Gypo bothers me. It's crap for the girl to say we have all the time in the world to bust open the truck. We haven't. Okay, we have a certain amount of time, but that's all. Once they start searching for it, the heat will be on good, and the quicker we bust it, the safer for us it's going to be. So Gypo will have to work under pressure. That's something he's never

35

done. It'll be nervy work. He could flip his lid.'

'Then it's up to us to see he doesn't,' Bleck said. 'I'm not worrying about him.' He glanced at Morgan, his pale eyes hard and restless. 'The more I think about the setup the more obvious it becomes we'll have to kill these two guys. If we don't, they'll have a description of us, and that could cook us.'

Morgan shrugged his shoulders.

'Yeah, I know, but you don't have to spread it around. The other two are jittery enough already.'

Bleck looked at him.

'She isn't.'

'That's a fact.'

'Who is she, Frank?'

Morgan shrugged his shoulders.

'I don't know. She doesn't belong to this town. It's my bet she's worked with some outfit before.'

'That's what I think.' Bleck glanced at his wrist watch. 'Know what? I don't believe she worked this plan out herself. I don't believe a kid of her age could dream up all the answers the way she claims to have done. It wouldn't surprise me some mob has already worked on the job—a mob she was in with—and they either got cold feet or they're going to pull the job and she's stolen their plan and is trying to beat them to it. Maybe they wouldn't give her a big enough cut. We've got to watch her, Frank. It wouldn't do for another mob to move in at the same time as we do, and it wouldn't do for them to beat us to it.'

'Yeah.' Morgan pushed his hat to the back of his head irritably and frowned. 'I've thought of all that. We've got to take a chance. We can't do it before Friday week, if then. There's a lot to be done. How's the time?'

'Just on half-past eight.'

'The bus is due then.'

'Yeah.'

They looked down the road to the bus stop where a group of people were waiting.

'She's a sexy piece, isn't she?' Bleck said, staring through the windshield. 'She's got a shape on her like a roller coaster.'

Morgan stiffened. His flat, black eyes moved on to Bleck's face.

'Since you've dragged up the subject, let me tell you something,' he said, his voice harsh. 'This girl's to be left strictly alone. There's going to be no monkey business. She'll be with us for a couple of weeks; probably longer. The way we'll be living could make it tricky. She's going to be right bang in the middle of us for twenty-four hours of the day. I don't want any of you to get wrong ideas about her. No monkey business. Let's get that straight from the start.'

Bleck lifted his eyebrows, a cynical expression on his handsome face.

'Have you reserved her for yourself, Frank?'

Morgan shook his head.

37

'No. I'm telling you: this is strictly business. This setup is much too important and the take much too big for us to have woman trouble as well. There's going to be no monkey business, and I mean that. Whoever tries to start something with her is going to walk into a belly-load of trouble from me.'

Bleck met the cold, snake's eyes and grinned a little uneasily.

'Have you talked to Kitson? He's the boy to watch. He was staring at her last night like a stricken bull.'

'You all three want watching,' Morgan said curtly. 'You're no plaster saint yourself nor is Gypo.'

A little gleam of anger appeared in Bleck's eyes.

'Did you polish your halo this morning, Frank?' Morgan started an angry retort, but then stopped short as he saw the bus coming around the corner.

'Here it is,' he said. 'Keep your eyes skinned.'

Both men leaned forward to stare through the windshield.

The bus pulled up at the stop and two men got off. One of them was short and skinny; the other was around six foot tall, broad-shouldered, narrow-waisted and he held himself stiffly upright. He was wearing the buff blouse and slacks of the Welling Armoured Truck Agency's uniform. Set squarely on his head was the peak cap with its glittering cap badge. His shoes had been polished until they looked like patent leather, so too had his pistol belt and holster. He walked with a quick, springy step, and his movements were those of an athlete in training.

The two men in the Buick watched him pull the brass bell knob at the gate.

'That him?' Bleck asked.

'Yeah.' Morgan's eyes were running over the man and what he saw gave him a little stab of uneasiness. 'That's Dirkson. Thomas will be on the next bus, coming the other way.'

'He could be a sonofabitch,' Bleck said, also not liking the look of the guard. 'He'll be as quick as a snake, and he's got guts. Look at that chin!'

Dirkson had turned and was looking indifferently towards the parked Buick, not seeing it. He was around twenty-five or six. He couldn't be called good-looking, but there was strength and character in his face that Morgan was quick to recognize.

'She'll have to kill him,' Bleck said and he felt sudden damp patches under his arms. 'Has she seen him yet?'

'Yeah. She saw him yesterday. He doesn't scare her. She says she can handle him.'

The gates had opened and Dirkson disappeared from sight, the gates closing behind him.

'A fast, determined joker with a lot of guts,'

Bleck said soberly. 'I guess Kitson was right. This guy isn't going to cry quits, Frank. We'll have to take him.'

'That's going to be your job. We can't leave it to the girl. He'll probably be much too fast for her,' Morgan said, not looking at him. 'I'll take care of the driver. You'll be out of sight with a rifle. When he leaves the truck, you've got to have him covered all the time. If he starts anything with the girl, you've got to kill him. Understand?'

Bleck felt his mouth turn dry but he nodded.

'Sure. I'll take care of him.'

'Here comes the other bus,' Morgan said. 'Here comes my piece of meat.'

Thomas, the driver, was a tall, rangy man with a fiddle-shaped face, widely spaced, cold eyes, a jutting chin and a thin, tight mouth. He was immaculate as Dirkson had been and carried himself upright the way Dirkson had carried himself. He looked the older man: around thirty or thirty-three. He moved with an assurance that impressed Morgan, who screwed up his snake's eyes, wrinkling his nose.

'He's another,' he said in disgust. 'They've certainly picked two bright boys to handle their truck, haven't they? Both of them spell trouble. I'll have to kill this beauty. I'm not kidding myself about that. He's not going to quit.'

Bleck took off his hat and wiped his

forehead. His heart was thumping unevenly.

'If we queer this, Frank, we'll be in a hell of a jam.'

'The take's a million dollars,' Morgan said. 'The way I see it is this: I'm forty-two. Fifteen years of my life have been spent in jail. The other years were just another kind of jail. The only thing in life that means a damn is money. Without money, you're nothing. With money, you're somebody. It's as simple as that. Two hundred thousand bucks in my pocket means I'll be alive. Without it, I might just as well be dead. So what? That's the way I look at it. No one; no smart, tough guard is going to stop me getting my hands on that amount of dough. So okay, we slip up and we're in a jam. That's a fact. I'm not disputing it, but can't you see we're in a am right now—all of us? Who cares if any of us is dead? Who cares if any of us is alive? Who cares about us anyway? But if each of us has two hundred thousand bucks in his pocket, then that's another story. We suddenly become people, and that's what I'm going to become. That's what you're going to become too—right?'

Bleck put on his hat.

'I feel that way too, but know what I think? I think Kitson and Gypo were influenced by the girl. I think they didn't want her to think they hadn't the guts to go through with this job. I think that's why they voted with us.'

'So long as they voted why should we

worry?' Morgan said. 'Now, they've got to go through with it.'

'If their nerve lasts.'

'It has got to last.'

'I hope you're right,' Bleck said and made a gesture. 'If those two . . .'

'If we get the truck,' Morgan said, speaking slowly and distinctly, a threat in every word, 'we'll bust it open with or without the other two. You don't imagine I'd get so far and then quit?'

Bleck nodded.

'Okay. Then there's another thing. Looks like we'll have to raise at least two thousand bucks to finance this thing. That was something we didn't go into last night. How do we raise the dough?'

'We'll have to do a job,' Morgan said. 'A small one, something that won't get us into trouble. I'm thinking about it. With the big one ahead of us, I've got to watch it not to pick on something that'll put the cops on our tails.'

Bleck sucked at his cigarette.

'How about the filling station on Highway 10? The one on the left as you leave Dukas.'

'Maybe,' Morgan said. 'It could be knocked over for two thousand, but I'd rather pick on something a little quieter, not on the highway. I was thinking of that all-night café on Maddox Street. After the theatres it gets pretty full and the people who go there have money. We might pick up a lot more than two thousand

42

if we have any luck. It would be a straightforward heist job. I'm working on it now.'

Bleck grimaced.

'It could be rugged, Frank. I don't like that kind of job. You never know if someone's going to turn hero.'

'It'll be good training,' Morgan said with a grim smile. 'We know for sure these two will be heroes. We may as well get used to the idea. That café could be worth three grand if we're lucky. Besides, we'll take the girl along with us. I want to find out for sure if her nerve is as good as she makes out it is.'

'Who else will be on the job?'

'Kitson will handle the car. You and me will handle the heaters and the girl collects the dough.'

'Gypo on the easy end of it again?' Bleck asked with a sneer.

'Look, Ed, you're always making those cracks about Gypo. We don't want him on a job like this. He's our technical man. He's no good on a caper like this and you know it. He is going to bust open the truck. No one else in this outfit can do it, so he's going to be reserved for that job and that job alone. Get it?'

'Oh, sure. One of these days I'll learn to be a technical man myself,' Bleck said shrugging. 'Where are we going to get the caravan from?'

'There's a place that sells them at Marlow.

43

As soon as we get the dough I'll send Kitson and the girl there. Their story will be they're going on honeymoon together.'

Bleck smiled.

'Watch out Kitson doesn't try to kid himself that's what he is really going to do.'

'Will you skip it?' Morgan snarled. 'We've enough on our plates without woman trouble. I'm telling you once and for all: there's going to be no monkey business. Kitson's the youngest of the four of us. It's his job to act the husband, but that doesn't mean a thing. If he thinks it does, then he has me to talk to.'

'How about the frill?' Bleck asked. 'Have you consulted her on how she's going to conduct her sex life?'

Morgan drew in a slow, deep breath.

'I saw this coming,' he said, his voice low and savage. 'As soon as I saw her with that body of hers, I knew you three punks would try to reach for her. I told her: if she starts any monkey business, she's out.' His lips twisted into a hard smile. 'It would have surprised you if you had seen her when I said that. Make no mistake about this: there's only one thing in that baby's life, and it's not sex. It's money. Don't kid yourself otherwise. Neither you nor Kitson nor Gypo are going to get anywhere with that girl. It's money first and last with her. If Kitson tries to start trouble with her, he's in for a shock. That goes for you and Gypo too. So get your mind adjusted. She says no monkey business. I say no monkey business, and that means no monkey business. Now do you get it?'

Bleck laughed.

'Sure. It sounds to me there's going to be no monkey business.'

Morgan put his cold, thin fingers around Bleck's wrist and tightened his hold. Startled, Bleck looked quickly around and met the glittering black eyes.

'I'm not fooling, Ed,' Morgan said softly. 'This is my big chance to break out of the prison that's been my life. This is the big take. If you imagine you can queer my show because you've got hot pants for a twenty-year-old girl, you have another think coming. I'll put a slug in your back if I think you're going to foul up this job. Remember that. This is the once-in-a-life-time chance, and I'm not having it put on the skids because you or Gypo or Kitson gets a sex itch. Is that understood?'

Bleck's smile was forced as he said, 'What's the matter with you, Frank? I was only fooling.'

Morgan leaned forward slightly. His tobacco-tainted breath fanned Bleck's face.

'You'd better be fooling.'

There was a long, tense pause as the two men stared at each other, then Bleck, making an effort to speak lightly, said, 'Think this car can tow the caravan? It'll be as heavy as hell.'

'It's got to tow it,' Morgan said, relaxing

back in his seat, his nicotine-stained fingers drumming on the steering-wheel. 'There're no really bad hills. The first half-hour will be the toughest. We've got to get as far away from the bottle-neck as we can in that time. After that it'll be easy. I want you to check this car, Ed, and I mean check it. If we have a breakdown when we have the truck we'll really be in trouble.'

'Sure. I'll give it a thorough check over. You can leave that to me. We'll have to knock off a car for the girl. When do we do that?'

'A couple of days before we do the job. You and Gypo will have to get new plates for it and Gypo must do a body spray job on it. We mustn't take any chances of the car being spotted when she's handling it.'

Bleck gave Morgan a sudden nudge as he saw the big wooden gates of the Armoured Truck Agency swing open.

'Here it comes . . .'

Through the gateway came the armoured truck. They were seeing it for the first time, and both of them stared at it, photographing it in their minds.

Bleck was surprised to see how small it was. He had expected something much bigger. It was like a steel box on wheels, plus the driving cab. They could see Thomas and Dirkson through the windshield. Dirkson was sitting upright, looking ahead. Thomas had that easy stance of a born driver, his hands at two o'clock on the steering-wheel. He edged the truck out into the flow of traffic as Morgan turned on the ignition of the Buick and moved it out into the traffic, two cars behind the truck.

'I thought it was going to be bigger,' Bleck said, trying to get a view of the rear of the truck, around the Lincoln that was in front of them. 'It doesn't look so tough.'

'Yeah? Maybe it's small, but don't make any mistake about it not being tough,' Morgan said.

He saw a gap in the traffic, touched the gas pedal and slid in front of the Lincoln. Ahead of him now was a low-slung sports car, and both men could get a clearer view of the rear of the truck.

Painted across the rear door was a sign that read:

THE WELLING ARMOURED TRUCK SERVICE
You are looking at the safest truck ever invented. If you have anything of value to transport, make use of us. The safest and best trucking service in the world.

Bleck found he was breathing heavily as he stared at the truck that moved smoothly and fast through the morning's traffic. It looked like a cube of solid steel on wheels. Instinctively he felt that this moving cube of

47

steel not only offered a challenge to his future but also to his life.

'On your right,' Morgan said suddenly.

Bleck's pale eyes swivelled to his right.

A traffic cop, sitting astride his motor-cycle, had just started his engine and had steered his machine into the traffic.

'Time we shoved off,' Morgan said. 'They'll have this joker with them now until they leave town. If we hang on to them, he'll want to know why.'

He swung the wheel and steered the Buick out of the flow of traffic and into a side street.

The last glimpse Bleck had of the truck was its steady movement forward with the speed cop riding at its side. He had a feeling of relief when he had lost sight of the truck.

Morgan slowed, swung to an empty parking space and pulled up.

'Well, you've seen it now . . .'

'Yes: a steel box. Seeing it doesn't mean much. Did you get the exact time it left the Agency?'

'Yes: eight forty-three.' Morgan took out a cigarette and lit it. 'Three hours from now, it should go through the bottle-neck. I bet Gypo and Kitson are sweating it out there in this heat, waiting for them.'

'Seeing the truck and the two guys brings the job to life,' Ed said, shifting lower in his seat. 'You're right, Frank: this is the big one and it's going to be tough.'

'If we get the breaks, it'll be okay,' Morgan said. 'We'll take a look at that all-night café now. I want to see what the escape route's like. We may have to leave fast. This is the one job, Ed, where we mustn't make a mistake.'

'This and the big one,' Bleck said, half closing his eyes. 'From now on—no mistakes, huh?'

Morgan nodded, then moved the car out of the parking space and headed up town.

II

A little after eleven-thirty a.m., Kitson and Gypo arrived at the bottle-neck two miles from the entrance to the Research Station in Gypo's battered Lincoln.

Kitson was driving and because Gypo loathed walking, he stopped at the bottle-neck to let Gypo out, and then drove on for a quarter of a mile to a wooded thicket where he could hide the car.

Leaving the car out of sight from the road, he walked back to the bottle-neck.

The sun was hot and blazed down on his unprotected head, and, pretty soon, he was sweating.

He was wearing an open neck, navy blue shirt, a pair of jeans and sneakers. He moved easily, swinging his big fists, his head up, his breath coming in sharp snorts through his broken nose. He welcomed the chance to stretch his long, powerful legs, and as he walked, he examined the terrain either side of the dusty, rain-parched road.

It was certainly rugged country, he thought as he strode along, kicking up the dust and hunching his shoulders, taking a pride in the way his muscles rolled under the sweat-soaked shirt. But there was plenty of cover, and this bottle-neck was a cinch for a pile-up.

Coming upon the bottle-neck, he paused to examine it.

The road sharply narrowed at this point, hemmed in by two gigantic rocks that had come down off the sloping hill either side of the road. Either side of these rocks were shrubs and scrubland, offering excellent cover.

Looking over the ground, he could see no sign of Gypo, although he knew he was right there watching him.

The fact that Gypo was able to conceal himself so well bolstered Kitson's sagging confidence a little.

He was scared of this job. He was sure that before Dirkson and Thomas gave up someone was going to get hurt.

For the past six months, since he had quitted the ring, Kitson had been under Morgan's influence. Morgan had been the only one who had stayed with him in his dressing-room after his ignominious beating by a man half his size and seventeen pounds lighter, but whose fighting brain was much superior to his own.

That was when Kitson's manager had tossed two ten-dollar bills on the rubbing table and had told Kitson he was through. His manager had walked out and Morgan had walked in.

Morgan had helped him dress and had led him, half blinded still and stunned from the beating he had taken, out of the Stadium to Morgan's car. Morgan had even taken him home.

'So you're through with getting your brains bashed into a pulp,' Morgan had said when Kitson was flat on his back on his bed in the sordid little room he called his home. 'So what? You and me could work together, kid. I've seen the way you can handle a car. I'm getting together a small mob: boys who can do a job sweetly and quickly and make themselves some money. What do you say?'

At twenty-three, Kitson realized he had reached the bottom of his ladder of ambition. He had hoped to become the Heavyweight Champion of the World, but this beating told him, as nothing else could, that this was now a pipe dream and he was just one more fighter in the trash bin. He had twenty dollars in his pocket, no friends and his future looked bleak. Even at that he hesitated.

He knew Morgan by reputation. He knew Morgan had served fifteen years in jail, that he was violent and dangerous. He knew that he was asking for trouble if he joined Morgan's mob, but he was more scared of being left on his own, to try to make a future for himself than of being hooked up with Morgan, so he had thrown in with him.

The five jobs he had done with Morgan's mob had earned him enough money to live fairly well. They were jobs without much risk: small and carefully planned, and he knew, if he had been caught, he would have had to serve only three to six months in jail as a first offender.

But he was intelligent enough to know that these jobs were merely a rehearsal for a big job. He knew enough about Morgan to realize that Morgan would never remain content to continue on such a small scale. Sooner or later, Morgan would plan a big job that would carry a twenty-year sentence, and Kitson would be involved.

While he had been trying to make a name for himself in the fight game, Kitson had worked as a driver for the Welling Armoured Truck Agency. He had lasted exactly ten days. The discipline of the Agency had defeated him. His shoes had never been as well polished as those of the other drivers. His driving had been just that shade more careless to earn him bad marks. His punctuality lagged behind. His shooting practice had made the instructor bitter and sarcastic. It came as no surprise to him when the foreman had given him his pay and told him not to come back.

But he had, in those ten days, learned enough about the Agency's methods and their men to realize that Morgan was taking on a world beater. It was as if he himself had had the audacity to get into the ring with Floyd Patterson. He might perhaps have a million to one chance of beating the champion, but the chance was so small as to be laughable.

He knew that neither Thomas nor Dirkson would quit, and that meant a gun fight. Someone would get killed. If he were caught, he faced a twenty-year sentence or the electric chair.

He had made up his mind as soon as Morgan had outlined the plan not to touch it. Rather, he would walk out on the mob. He would have done exactly this if it hadn't been for the copper-haired girl.

No girl had ever spoken to him nor looked at him as she had done. Up to the moment when he had faced her and seen the contempt in her eyes and realized her complete lack of fear of him, he had imagined that he had had power over women. Granted, he did have some kind of animal power over the women who were the camp followers any fourth-rate boxer will find tagging along behind him, but this copper head had shown him for the first time that the power he had been so proud of was strictly limited. She had made an impact on him that had badly shaken him, and now he was so acutely aware of her that he could think of little else.

So it was because of her, and only because of her, that he was going ahead with this job. He knew he was moving into something that was too big for him, that could be his finish, but he hadn't the moral courage to face her contempt.

He stood looking around the scrub land that surrounded the bottle-neck, but he failed to see Gypo.

'Okay, so you're good,' he called.

'Where are you?' Gypo's moon-shaped face appeared from behind two boulders, and he waved to Kitson.

'Here, kid. Pretty good, huh? Me and the invisible man like this,' and he held up two fingers pressed tightly together.

Kitson walked off the road and joined him.

'This is some place for an ambush,' he said, squatting down beside Gypo. He looked at his watch. 'They should be along in twenty minutes if they're going to have a fast run.'

Gypo stretched out on his back. Taking a splinter of wood from his pocket, he began to explore his teeth while he stared up at the brilliant blue of the sky.

'See that sky, kid?' he said. 'It reminds me of my home town. No sky like it in the world.'

Kitson glanced at him. He liked Gypo. There was a kind, sympathetic streak in the fat man that made companionship with him worth

54

having. Gypo wasn't like Ed Bleck who was always boasting of his conquests with women, who was always ribbing people, picking on them and playing practical jokes. Ed was smart, and had plenty of nerve, but he wasn't the man to go to if you were in trouble, whereas Gypo was. Gypo would lend you his last dollar with no questions asked, but you'd never get anything out of Bleck unless there was a string tied to it.

'Where's that, Gypo? Where's your home town?' Kitson asked, stretching out on his stomach and lifting his head so he had a clear view of the road.

'Fiesole, near Florence in Italy,' Gypo said, screwing up his small eyes and wrinkling his fat nose. 'You been to Italy, kid?'

'No.'

'No country like it in the world,' Gypo said with a heart-felt sigh. 'I haven't been there for twenty years. That's too long. Know what I'm going to do when I get my share of this dough? I'm going out there. I'm going to take a first-class passage in the ship. I'm going to buy an Alfa Romeo as soon as I arrive, and then I'll drive to Fiesole. That's going to give my old ma a hell of a bang. I'm going to buy me a little villa on the hill that looks down on Florence. My old man died about ten years ago, but my ma will be there, waiting for me. I'll get married and I'll settle down and have a lot of kids. Money can fix anything. Like Frank said: we'll have the world in our pockets. He's right. That's what I'll have: the world in my pocket.'

Unless you get shot, Kitson thought. Unless the cops catch up with you before you get on that ship.

Gypo looked at him, rolling his head on his arm, grinning.

'What are you going to do with your dough, kid? Thought about it yet? What are your plans?'

Listening to Gypo, Kitson thought, was like listening to a child talking.

'I guess I'll wait until I get it,' he said. 'It's too early to make plans. Maybe we'll never get it.'

Gypo pulled a face.

'You know something, kid? Making plans is the nicest thing in anyone's life. Maybe they don't ever jell. Maybe something goes wrong and the plan goes pooh! But the fun is in making the plan. I like to look ahead and plan things. I've been doing it for years. Okay, I admit it: none of the plans I've made so far have jelled, but this one might. Two hundred thousands bucks! Think what you could do with all that money!'

Kitson shrugged his shoulders.

'Yeah,' he said. 'I've thought about it, but we haven't got it yet.'

'I bet you'll buy a big car,' Gypo said, digging his fat fingers into the sandy soil and lifting a handful of it and letting it trickle through his fingers. 'That right? I've never known another guy handle a car the way you do. You deserve a fast, big car, the way you drive, then you'll find yourself a girl: a car and a girl, and maybe some sharp clothes.' He shook his head, grinning. 'What about this Ginny Gordon: some dish, huh? What did you think of her, kid? That shape, huh? I'll tell you something: that's the way the best Italian girls are built with that solid behind, the narrow waist and the water-wings. I guess she's a little young for me, otherwise I'd think about her, but she's okay for you, kid. She and you would look right. You don't have to worry about the way she acts. That's just on the surface. When a woman has her build, she's made for love. You could melt her down. All that hardness, those eyes of hers; it doesn't mean a thing: it's her heart you have to talk to.'

Kitson listened, feeling the hot sun burning down on the back of his neck. If anyone but Gypo had talked to him like this, he would have told them to shut up, but Gypo was different. Gypo said exactly what was in his mind, and thinking about what he had said, Kitson wondered about the girl. Maybe Gypo was right. Maybe she was made for love, but when he remembered the cold, impersonal sea-green eyes he doubted it.

'Look, kid, you talk to me,' Gypo said, his eyes closed and his moon-shaped face offered to the sun. 'You tell me what's in your mind. I'm interested in you. Maybe that strikes you as funny, but I mean it. Last night, after I had made up my mind to do this job, I thought about you. I knew you were like me. You didn't want this job, did you? I didn't either, then suddenly you said yes. Why did you do it, kid?'

Kitson wiped his face with the back of his hand.

'Why did you, Gypo?'

'There was something about that girl,' Gypo said. 'When she came into the room, looking the way she looked, and when she came out with her plan, I got a feeling of confidence. When Frank explained the job, I didn't want anything to do with it. Then when that girl came in—I don't know, somehow she made it seem possible. I suddenly realized what all that money could buy. I thought what a bang my ma would get to see me drive up in an Alfa Romeo and in a good suit—it sort of made all the things I've dreamed about jell.'

'Yeah, there was something about her,' Kitson said uneasily. 'I felt the same way.' He hadn't the courage to admit to Gypo that he had voted with the rest of them because he was afraid of the girl's contempt. He had no hope that this job would succeed. It was a bad one; too big for them; he was sure of that, and he felt a sudden surge of pity for Gypo because he was living out a dream: this was the one they wouldn't get away with.

'It's funny, isn't it?' Gypo said. 'She's only a kid, and yet there's that thing about her . . .' he broke off abruptly and lifted his head, his small black eyes suddenly alert.

Kitson stared at him.

'What is it?'

'I heard something,' Gypo said. He was motionless, listening. 'Something moved. It wouldn't be a snake, kid?'

'A snake? So what? A snake wouldn't come near us,' Kitson said irritably. He wanted to continue the conversation about the girl. She was the most important subject in the world to him.

'This could be snake country,' Gypo said. His fat squat body was rigid. 'I'll tell you something, kid. I've a horror of snakes. I thought I heard something move over there.'

Frowning, Kitson rolled over on his side and looked to where Gypo was pointing.

'Forget it,' he said, annoyed with Gypo for having broken the trend of the conversation. 'No snake is going to get anywhere near you unless you bother it.'

'My kid brother was killed by a snake,' Gypo said, his voice tense. 'He was lying just the way I am and this snake came from nowhere and bit him in the face. He died before I could get him home. He was around ten: imagine that: a lovely kid; fat like butter and as brown as a nut. This snake . . .'

'For the love of mike!' Kitson broke in. 'Why the hell should I want to hear about your brother? Okay, so he was bitten by a snake. It could happen to anyone. Let it lie, will you?'

Gypo lifted his head and looked at him reproachfully.

'You wouldn't talk like that if he had been your brother,' he said. 'It's something I'll never forget. It's given me a horror of snakes.'

'How the hell did we get talking about snakes?' Kitson said. 'We were talking about this girl, and then all of a sudden we have this crap about snakes and your brother.'

'I thought I heard something . . .'

'So okay, you heard something. So what? Get this snake crap out of your mind, will you?'

Gypo started to say something when he saw in the distance a cloud of dust. He put his hand on Kitson's arm and pointed. 'Think that's them?'

Kitson stared down the long, twisting road and he felt a sudden cold lump of fear form at the back of his throat.

Instinctively, he wedged his body closer into the ground, and he put out his hand, pressing Gypo down as he said in a whisper, 'Yes: here they come!'

Both men remained motionless, watching the approaching truck.

It came at a surprising speed, scattering dust as it approached the bottle-neck. Taking the bend, it was for a moment lost to sight, then it came around the bend, moving more slowly and more cautiously and Kitson glanced at his wrist watch, noting the time as the truck passed through the bottle-neck.

They had a brief but impressive view of the driver and the guard as the truck swept past.

Gypo sat up, his eyes taking in as much of the truck as his brain could memorize.

They watched the truck turn the next bend and disappear in a cloud of dust, and then both men relaxed, looking at each other uneasily.

'It looks tough,' Gypo said and started to scratch under his armpit. 'Did you see those two? Santa Maria! They look pretty tough too!'

Kitson had had a good view of both the driver and the guard as the truck had gone past. He knew these two men fairly intimately. He had warned Morgan about them, but now, seeing them sitting behind the windshield of the truck, he realized how formidable they were, and he had a cold clutch of fear when he thought that in a few days, he would be having a show-down with them.

'What are you worrying about?' he said as casually as he could. 'You don't have to tackle them. Okay, so they're tough. What do you think we are—powder puffs, like she said?'

Gypo shook his head, his face uneasy.

'Those two look mean to me. I'm glad I

61

don't have to tackle them.'

Kitson took out his notebook and wrote down the time the truck had passed through the bottle-neck.

'Who asked you to tackle them anyway?' he said curtly. 'Morgan and Bleck will take care of them.'

'And the girl,' Gypo said. 'She has the toughest end of it. A girl like that . . . I keep thinking what she said about if he grabbed her gun she would shoot him. Do you think she meant it?'

Kitson had been thinking about that too and he had wondered about it. He could see the sea-green eyes, her tense expression and he grimaced.

'I don't know.' He got up on to his knees and looked up and down the road. 'Let's get going. How do you feel about busting open that truck?'

'Frank says I can have three to four weeks to work on it,' Gypo said. 'That's a cinch. Give me the right tools and that amount of time and there's nothing ever made that I couldn't bust into. No matter how tough the job is, so long as you've got the time, you can fix it. Frank says three to four weeks. Okay, in that time, I'll fix it.'

'That's what Frank says,' Kitson said looking at Gypo, 'but suppose something goes wrong; suppose the pressure's on, how fast could you bust that truck, Gypo?'

Gypo's fat face showed sudden uneasiness.

'Why talk like that? Frank says three or four weeks. Okay, up to now Frank has been right, hasn't he? That's a tough truck. Even a guy like you with no experience of metal or locks can see that. It wants working at: slow, steady, with plenty of time. You couldn't bust that one open fast.'

'I'll get the car,' Kitson said. 'You wait here.'

Gypo watched him go, his fat face worried.

Then he thought of the girl with her cold assured sea-green eyes, her arrogant stare as she had faced Kitson, and he felt more confident.

Why make too much fuss about this job? he thought, feeling the hot sun beating down on him. Frank had said it was all right, and up to now, everything Frank had said was all right, had been all right. This girl had all the confidence in the world about the job. He wouldn't have the dangerous end of the job to handle. His job was to bust open the truck, and Frank had promised him he would have from three to four weeks to work at it. Anyone who worked in metal and knew locks could get into anything, no matter how tough, in that time.

The Welling Armoured truck drove on towards the Rocket Research station. Neither the driver nor the guard was aware that they had been timed and scrutinized.

They continued on their way, leaving a cloud of white dust behind them.

CHAPTER THREE

I

Morgan had called a meeting for eight o'clock and Bleck was a little early. He arrived at Lu Strieger's Poolroom at seven forty-five for no other reason except his watch was fast.

He moved through the crowded, smoke-hazed bar to where Strieger, a red-faced, enormously fat man, was watching a game of pool.

'Anyone gone up yet, Lu?' Bleck asked.

'No, but the door's unlocked. Help yourself,' Strieger said.

'I'll have a Scotch,' Bleck said, and when Strieger had served him, he wandered off into a corner of the room and sat down, pushing his hat to the back of his head and loosening his tie.

Bleck was feeling off-colour and moody that night. This café hold-up idea of Morgan's worried him.

Bleck had begun with many more advantages than the other three. His father had been a successful storekeeper who had given his son a good education. He had wanted him to become a doctor, but the drudgery of study had been too much for Bleck. After a couple of years at college he had suddenly quit

64

and had left home. He had become a car salesman and, at the same time, had discovered an insatiable appetite for women. He had spent more than he had earned, and when his debts had got out of hand, he had helped himself to the contents of the firm's safe which had amounted to nearly four thousand dollars. He had been under the mistaken impression that he had covered his tracks, and it came as a shock to him when two detectives closed in on him before he had had the chance of spending more than two hundred dollars of the loot. He went to prison for six months. This happened when he was twenty-two. Since then he had served two further sentences in prison: one of two years and one of four. He had now a horror of prison.

While serving his last sentence, he had met Morgan who was completing his fifteenth year: a sentence that had turned Bleck's blood cold. They came out together, and when Morgan suggested they should join forces, Bleck had agreed.

He had agreed because of Morgan's reputation. Those in the know had told him that Morgan was going to be Mr. Big one of these days. They said that sooner or later Morgan would pull the big one, and when he did, it would be a job to remember.

Bleck was thirty-five, and he knew his future would be bleak unless he was prepared to put everything into a gamble that offered the highest possible return. He had a feeling that Morgan was big enough to handle a job that would put him in the money for the rest of his life.

As he sat in the corner of the poolroom, sipping his whisky, Bleck's mind dwelt on his share of the money they would get from the truck. Two hundred thousand dollars! He would travel. He would try out the girls in every country in Europe. He would go to Monte Carlo and bust the bank there. He would . . .

Then he saw Ginny Gordon come in and his daydreams were abruptly interrupted. She came through the smoke haze, her chin tilted, her eyes hostile while the men in the poolroom stared at her, grinning at each other, winking and nudging. If it hadn't been that Lu Strieger didn't stand for mashing in his poolroom, she would have been besieged as she entered the bar.

Some dish, Bleck thought, eyeing her as she paused at the door that gave on to the steep staircase that led to the room Strieger rented to those who wanted some privacy.

Ginny was wearing a pair of black slacks, tight across her seat, and a bottle-green shirt, open at the neck.

But she's a toughie, Bleck thought, finishing his whisky. Where does she come from? She could be fun. Maybe I'll soften her up a little.

After the job, we might go places together for a week or so. She's got spirit, and with a body like that . . .

He got to his feet and crossed the room and followed the girl up the stairs. He overtook her as she reached the landing.

'Hi, Ginny,' he said. 'We're the first two. Those pants certainly suit your geography.'

She turned and looked at him. Her sea-green eyes were disconcertingly bleak.

'Think so?' she said, then she opened the door and entered the room, flicking on the light as she did so.

She went over to the table and sat down. Opening her bag, she took out a comb and a mirror and began to tidy her copper-coloured hair.

Bleck pulled out a chair and sat opposite her. He stared admiringly at her, watching the way her breasts lifted under the soft material of her shirt as she raised her arms.

'Well, it's fixed for tonight,' he said. 'Scared?'

She put the comb and mirror away and took out a pack of cigarettes.

'Scared? What's there to be scared about?' she asked, indifferently.

'You're pretty cool,' Bleck said, staring at her. 'I don't believe you are scared.'

He reached across the table, offering the flame of his cigarette lighter.

For a long moment she studied the flame

67

before leaning forward to dip the end of her cigarette into it. Her full, red lips curved into a smile that came and went so quickly Bleck wasn't sure if she had smiled.

'What's so funny?' he asked, his voice sharpening.

Again her eyes went to the flame of the lighter and he looked at it too. He saw it was far from steady, and he realized his hand was shaking. He snapped out the flame and sat back, forcing a grin.

'You're right. I'm scared, and I'll tell you why.' He folded his arms on the table and leaned on them. 'I'm scared we'll foul up this job tonight and sour the big one. I don't like this job. I tried to talk Frank out of it. It would be safer and easier to stick up that service station at Dukas, but he won't have it. With this café job, someone might turn brave. If that happens you have a shooting on your hands. If someone gets shot tonight, the heat'll be on so bad the big one could come unstuck.'

She let smoke drift down her nostrils as she stared at him.

'Then we must take care no one does turn brave.'

'Easier said than done.'

She lifted her eyebrows.

'Is it? If you show a vicious dog you're not scared of it, it'll behave. It's the same with brave people.'

Bleck frowned.

'I can't make you out. Have you worked for a mob before?'

Her eyes became cloudy.

'Then don't make me out,' she said curtly.

Bleck shrugged.

'Okay, if you want to play it mysterious, go ahead. But remember this: you have the toughest end of the job tonight. You have to collect the wallets. Some guy might make a grab at you. So watch it.'

Because he was so uneasy about the job himself, he hoped she too would become uneasy, but there was no change in her expression as she said, 'No one will make a grab at me.'

The door opened and Kitson and Gypo came in.

Kitson paused abruptly when he saw Ginny and Bleck alone together and his face flushed, his eyes becoming angry.

'Here comes the bridegroom,' Bleck said, and he began to sing Mendelssohn's Wedding March in a raucous voice.

Gypo chuckled, his small black eyes dancing with merriment.

He thought the joke harmless and a good one.

Kitson turned white.

'Shut up!' His voice shook. 'Cut it out!'

Bleck stopped singing and leaned back in his chair, a jeering grin on his face.

'So what? You and she . . .'

He waved towards Ginny who sat motionless, her eyes on Kitson. 'You two are the newly-weds, aren't you? Frank said you and she were renting the caravan for your honeymoon.'

'I said cut it out!' Kitson said.

'What's biting you, stupe? Don't you want to have a honeymoon with her?' Bleck said. 'You have the soft end of this job. What could be nicer than to have a baby like her all alone in a caravan: that is if you know what to do when you've got her alone . . .'

Kitson took two quick steps that brought him to the table. His fist flashed up and slammed against Bleck's jaw.

Bleck went over backwards, taking the chair with him and landed on the floor with a crash that shook the room. He sprawled there, staring up at Kitson, his eyes dazed.

'Get up, you louse!' Kitson said, 'and I'll shove your teeth through the back of your head!'

'Hey, kid!' Gypo cried, horrified.

He grabbed hold of Kitson's arm, but Kitson gave him a shove that sent him reeling across the room.

Bleck shook his head. His eyes became full of hate as he stared up at Kitson.

'I've always wanted to take you, you punch-drunk bum,' he said. 'Now I'll show you what fighting really means.'

As he got to his feet, Morgan came into the

room.

Gypo said breathlessly, 'Stop them, Frank! They're going to fight!'

Morgan took four quick sliding steps forward so he was between the two men, his back to Kitson while he faced Bleck.

'Gone out of your head?' Morgan asked with artificial politeness, his snake's eyes glittering.

Bleck hesitated, then he shrugged, pulled his coat into shape, ran his fingers through his hair, jerked out a chair and sat down. He stared down at the table, rubbing his aching jaw.

Morgan turned and looked at Kitson.

'You start trouble in this mob,' he said, 'and you'll be in plenty of trouble yourself. I'm not telling you a second time. Sit down!'

Kitson slouched to a chair away from Ginny and Bleck and sat down.

Still nervous, Gypo came over to the table and hesitated beside Ginny.

'Mind if I sit here?'

She shook her head.

'Why should I?'

Smirking with embarrassment, Gypo sat down.

Morgan began to prowl around the room, a cigarette hanging from his thin lips, his hat tilted over his eyes.

'Okay, fellows,' he said, 'pay attention. We do the job tonight at ten minutes past twelve.

That's when the place will be full, and the chances of anyone busting in on us small. Kitson handles the car.' He paused to stare at Kitson. 'You know the district. You remain with the car with the engine running. If it turns sour, you wait for us, then take the first on the left to cut out the traffic lights. I'll leave it to you to shake off whoever is following us. Okay?'

Still scowling, Kitson nodded.

'Ginny: you and Ed and me,' Morgan went on, continuing his prowling, 'will go inside. Lu's lending me a machine-gun. You, Ed, will have your gun. Ginny goes in after me, then Ed will take care of the door. As soon as we're in, Ed'll pull down the blind on the door. I'll get up on the bar so I can cover the whole room. The chopper should cool any hot-head. As soon as we have them where we want them, Ginny will go around and collect the wallets. We don't want anything but cash. If anyone comes in, it's your job to handle them, Ed. The whole job shouldn't take more than five minutes if we work fast. That depends on you, Ginny. Watch it no smart Alec makes a grab at you as you take his wallet. We don't want any shooting unless it really turns sour.'

Gypo's small black eyes rolled as he listened. He was glad he wasn't participating in this job.

Kitson rubbed his knuckles and stared down at the table. He too was thankful he had charge of the car. It needed a hell of a nerve to walk into that café and quell some forty to fifty people, and he wasn't sure if he would have had the nerve to do it.

Bleck was still seething with fury that Kitson had hit him, but Morgan's words shifted his mind away from Kitson and he experienced a cold, tight feeling in his stomach.

'Well, okay,' he said, 'if you're satisfied this is the way to do it, Frank, but I don't like it. We could take on something not so rugged.'

Morgan paused in his prowling.

'I know that, but we're doing this one because it's going to get us into the right shape for the big job. I know what I'm doing, Ed. This job will tell me if anyone of you is likely to sour the big one. That's why I've picked it.' He came over to the table and looked directly at Ginny. 'This is your test. You've talked a lot and it has sounded convincing. Now I want to see if it is all talk. That's why I've given you the tough end of the deal.'

The girl looked steadily at him.

'I'll handle it,' she said. 'It's not all that tough.'

Morgan smiled.

'We'll see. Well, okay, that's it. Let's break it up now. Kitson, you bring Gypo's car to the café at twelve-ten. Is your watch right? What do you make it now?'

'Eight-twenty,' Kitson said, consulting his strap watch.

73

'Eight twenty-three,' Morgan said, checking his watch. 'Lu will give you the machine-gun. Have it on the back seat. You come to the café on your own. Ed and me will come on foot. As I go in I'll pick the gun out of the car.' He looked over at Ginny. 'You come along Maddux Street. Be there at twelve-ten. We've all got to be dead on time. Have you got a watch?'

Ginny nodded.

'Okay,' Morgan said. 'Collect the gun as you go out, Kitson. You go with him, Gypo, and make sure that heap of yours doesn't let us down. See you at twelve-ten, huh?'

Kitson got to his feet. He paused, looking uneasily at Morgan, then his eyes moved to Ginny and away again. He turned and walked across the room to the door with Gypo following him.

When they had gone, Morgan sat down.

'Are you okay?' he asked.

She lifted her eyebrows.

'Why shouldn't I be?'

'Look, don't give me that stuff,' Morgan said sharply. 'I've done dozens of these jobs in the past, but I still get a little scared. Don't try to bluff me. I'm asking you—are you okay? Do you still want the tough end of this job?'

She held out her hand, a half-burned cigarette between her slim fingers. The smoke curled straight up. The cigarette was rock steady.

'Do I look scared?' she asked, then she pushed back her chair and stood up.

The two men stared at her while she looked directly at Morgan.

'Twelve-ten,' she said. 'Be seeing you.'

She turned and made for the door, her hips moving provocatively as she walked. She opened the door and went out, shutting the door behind her without looking back.

'A toughie,' Bleck said and grimaced.

'Maybe,' Morgan said soberly, 'but I've seen the tough ones crack at the wrong moment. We'll see.' He got to his feet. 'Okay: let's get out of here.'

II

At five minutes past midnight, Morgan and Bleck got off the street car at the corner of Maddux Street. They crossed the road and paused in a dark shop doorway, looking across at the Palace All-Night Café.

Lights showed through the curtained windows. They could see part of the bar through the glass door.

Morgan flicked his half-smoked cigarette into the street.

'There it is,' he said.

'I bet Gypo's thanking his stars he isn't on this caper,' Bleck said, aware that his heart was thumping sluggishly and his hands were moist.

'I'm thanking my stars he isn't on it either,' Morgan said. He too was aware that his heart was thumping and that his mouth was dry. 'As soon as Kitson drives up, we cross the street.'

'Yeah,' Bleck said, his hand going to his hip-pocket and resting on the cold butt of his .38. 'There she is,' he went on as he saw Ginny walking towards the café. She was still wearing her black slacks and the bottle-green shirt, but she had concealed her hair under a green scarf, and as she passed under a street light, Bleck realized how much the copper-coloured hair helped her kind of beauty. Now it was concealed she looked quite plain.

At that moment the dusty Lincoln came down the street and pulled up outside the café.

'Here we go,' Morgan said, and crossed the road with long, swift strides.

The street was deserted. They could hear the juke box grinding out a waltz from inside the café.

Morgan paused long enough to reach into the back of the Lincoln and snatch up the machine-gun.

'Take it easy,' he said to Kitson. 'When we go, we go fast.'

Kitson grunted; his hands tight on the steering-wheel.

Bleck had taken out his handkerchief and was tieing it across the lower part of his face. His hands were shaking so badly he had trouble in fixing the knot.

Ginny had already masked her face, and she was standing by the café door. Down by her side, she held a .38 Police Special.

Morgan didn't bother to mask his face. He was an old hand at this game, and he knew everyone got so scared they seldom were able to give the police any useful description.

'Let's go,' he said, drawing in a quick, deep breath. He moved up close to Ginny.

'You open the door, then get out of my way.'

'I know.'

Her voice was flat and steady, and he glanced at her, their eyes meeting.

Well, she's cool enough, he thought. I wouldn't have thought it possible . . . a kid like her.

She opened the door and leaned against it, giving him room to pass her. He stepped into the noisy, overheated café.

Bleck, sweat soaking the handkerchief tied across the lower part of his face, moved forward as Ginny followed Morgan. He closed the door and pulled down the blind.

There were two men at the bar who looked casually over their shoulders as they felt the sudden night air come through the open doorway. They stared at Morgan, and then at the machine-gun in his hands. Their unbelieving eyes moved to Ginny's masked face, and they stiffened, their faces turning white.

Morgan shouted: 'Get out of the way! Get

back!'

The buzz of conversation throughout the room suddenly began to peter out. Morgan's voice had cut the air the way a razor cuts through silk.

The two men nearly fell over themselves as they crowded back.

Morgan put one hand on the bar and vaulted up on to it. He kicked glasses and bottles out of his way and the sudden smashing of breaking glass brought people to their feet and the buzz of conversation to an abrupt silence.

'Take it easy!' Morgan bawled, sweeping the room with the muzzle of the machine-gun. 'This is a hold-up! Don't make a move and you won't get hurt! Sit down, all of you! Anyone who starts anything will get a gutful of lead! Just stay still and you'll be okay!'

Nearly blinded by sweat, his heart hammering so violently he could scarcely breathe, Bleck dragged down the handkerchief mask which was suffocating him. He held his .38 in a hand that was shaking, while he looked across the packed café, praying that some fool wouldn't start something.

A woman screamed. Two men started to get to their feet, but were immediately dragged back into their seats by the women with them. Everyone else in the café froze into statues.

'Okay,' Morgan said, pitching his voice high. 'We want cash. Put your wallets on the tables.

Come on! Get moving!'

Most of the men began fumbling in their hip pockets and this was Ginny's cue. She pulled the canvas sack that Morgan had given her from her pocket, then, holding the sack in her left hand and the .38 in her right, she started her lone walk down the aisle, stopping at each table to pick up the wallets that were lying on the table and dropping them into the sack.

Bleck, standing by the door, watched her. She moved slowly and cautiously like someone walking on brittle ice, but there was no hesitation. She paused at each table, collected the wallet that lay there, dropped it into the sack and moved on.

Morgan yelled: 'Come on! Come on! Get your wallets out! I've got an itchy finger, but I don't want to hurt anyone unless I have to! Get those wallets out!'

Bleck began to relax.

Morgan and the girl were swinging this, he thought. Talk about nerve! The snap in Morgan's voice was something to hear, and the way he stood, slightly crouching, his machine-gun pushed forward made him a blood chilling, menacing figure.

The girl suddenly stopped her mechanical movement forward. She had reached a table where a woman, wearing a mink stole, and a fat, hard-faced man were sitting. There was no wallet on the table.

She looked at the man, who stared at her,

his small grey eyes glittering.

'Come on, mister,' she said softly. 'Hand it over.'

'I've got nothing for you, you tramp,' the man said. 'I don't carry money.'

Bleck began to sweat. He smelt trouble. He looked anxiously at Morgan, who stood motionless, the machine-gun rigid. He was watching Ginny, his lips slightly off his teeth, his expression wolfish.

'Hand it over!' Ginny said, raising her voice.

'I've got nothing for you, you little bitch,' the man said, staring at her.

His companion suddenly went as white as a fresh fall of snow and shut her eyes. Her massive body began to sag against the man who shoved her off impatiently.

Ginny lifted her gun.

'Shed it, fatso,' she said, her voice suddenly strident, 'or you'll get a dose of lead poisoning!'

The man's face tightened, but he said, 'I've got nothing for you! Get out of here!'

Morgan shifted the muzzle of his gun around to cover the man, but he knew the movement was futile. He knew the man must realize he wouldn't shoot because Ginny was in the direct line of fire.

This was Ginny's show, and Morgan watched her anxiously, knowing this was the test. The cards were down and the pressure on. Would she crack?

He got his answer sooner than he expected it.

Ginny smiled at the man: a flickering smile that came and went beneath the mask, but showed for a brief flash in her eyes. Then she pistol-whipped the man across his face. Her movement was so quick he had no chance of protecting himself. The barrel of the .38 slashed him across his nose and cheek and blood spurted. He fell backwards, his hand going to his face, a grunting sound forcing itself out of his mouth.

She leaned across the table and hit him again, the barrel of the gun coming down hard on the top of his head, so he slumped forward, half unconscious.

The woman in the mink stole gave a shrill scream and slid out of her chair in a faint.

Morgan yelled, 'Hold it! Just one move out of anyone of you and you'll get it!'

His voice was so loaded with menace that even Bleck froze for a brief moment.

Ginny stepped close to the half-unconscious man, jerked him upright and pulled out his wallet from his inside pocket. She gave him a hard shove so he fell across the table as she dropped the wallet into the sack.

That was enough.

Wallets appeared on the tables as if by magic. All Ginny now had to do was to walk swiftly down the aisle, picking them up and dropping them into the sack.

Bleck was so fascinated that he had taken his attention off the door, and it came as a shock when the door jerked open and a big, broad-shouldered man came in.

Bleck stared stupidly at the man. The big man looked from Bleck to the gun Bleck was holding slackly in his hand. The big man moved swiftly. His hand came down in a chopping blow on Bleck's wrist. The gun flew out of Bleck's grip and slid across the floor to land near the bar.

As the big man set himself to throw a punch at Bleck, Morgan shifted the machine-gun in his direction and yelled at him: 'Hold it! Get your hands up! You hear me?'

The big man's eyes went to Morgan and the machine-gun and his courage sagged. He backed away from Bleck and put up his hands.

A thickset man with a pugnacious face who had shed his wallet and who was sitting at a table at which Ginny was standing, seeing Morgan's gun wasn't aiming in his direction, made a sudden grab at Ginny's .38 as she picked up his wallet.

His hand closed over the gun butt and her wrist and he tried to jerk the gun out of her grasp.

She held on to the gun and looked into his reckless, scared eyes. She squeezed the trigger. The gun went off with a crash that rattled the windows of the café. The man released his grip as if he had caught hold of something red hot.

The bullet cut through his sleeve, grazing his arm.

Ginny stepped back, threatening him with the gun while Morgan yelled and cursed at him.

'Get on! Get on!' Morgan shouted to Ginny. 'Hurry!'

As calm as a model at a dress show, Ginny moved on, picking up the wallets and dropping them into the sack. No one moved. They sat frozen, white-faced, their fear riveted on their faces.

Outside in the car, Kitson heard the crash of gunfire and he flinched. It needed a tremendous effort of self-control not to put the car into gear and drive away.

He sat motionless, his hands gripping the wheel, sweat on his face, holding on to himself, willing himself to stay where he was.

Then suddenly it was all over.

There was a sound of rushing of feet. He heard the rear door of the Lincoln jerk open and bodies spilt into the car. He felt a hot, sweating body thud against his as Bleck sprawled on to the front seat. Automatically, he started the car moving.

'Go on! Go on!' Morgan bawled in his ear from the rear seat. 'Get the hell out of here fast!'

Kitson, his breath whistling between his clenched teeth, sent the car surging forward. He swung left with a scream of tortured tires, cut down the narrow alley and out into the main street.

With the skill that was his natural talent, he skipped the car across the main street, and into another side street, slackening speed slightly, flicking on his headlights and flicking them off immediately as he drove across the intersections.

Morgan twisted around, was staring out of the rear window, intent on seeing if they were being followed. After a half a mile of such driving, he said abruptly, 'Okay, no one is on to us, let's get over to Gypo's place.'

There was a general relaxation of tension.

'Well, that was rugged!' Bleck said, wiping his face with the back of his hand. 'That could have turned pretty sour if we hadn't had the chopper with us. Phew! When that jerk tried to grab Ginny's gun . . .'

'What happened?' Kitson demanded, his voice shaking. 'What was the shooting? Did anyone get hurt?'

'No. Some guy tried to grab Ginny's gun and the gun went off. No one got hurt. It certainly put the fear of the devil into that punk. Then a guy took me by surprise and knocked the gun out of my hand. That was pretty rugged too.'

Ginny was sitting next to Morgan, and he could feel her body was trembling. He looked sideways at her, and as they passed under a street lamp, he saw she was looking bad, her skin a bluish white.

He patted her knee.

'You did fine, kid,' he said. 'You really did fine. The way you handled that fat jerk! I've never seen anything like it for nerve.'

She moved her knee away.

'Oh, stop it!' she said, and to his surprise, she turned her head away and began to cry.

Neither Kitson nor Bleck, sitting in front, knew what was happening, and Morgan shifted away from the girl, leaving her alone.

'What's the loot like?' Kitson asked, driving carefully now as he headed for Gypo's workshop.

'Should be okay. At least fifty wallets and the till was loaded,' Morgan said. He lit a cigarette, noticing with a sense of pride how steady his hands were.

He could still hear Bleck's laboured breathing. He had watched Bleck while they were in the café, and he had an idea he might crack. This bothered him. He had been under the impression that Bleck's nerve was reliable, but the way he had acted and the way he had let that big jerk knock his gun out of his hand warned Morgan that from now on Bleck would have to be watched.

Kitson too had been in a pretty bad way when they had scrambled into the car. He hadn't got going as he should have done. If Morgan hadn't yelled at him, he would have driven away so slowly someone from the café could have got a description of the car.

Before the big one, there would have to be some tightening up. At least he was now sure of the girl. She had handled herself magnificently. She was the best of the whole bunch.

He glanced at her again. She had stopped crying, and was sitting up, her white face wooden, her eyes a little glassy, and she was staring out of the window.

Morgan pushed his cigarette towards her.

'Here, take it,' he said curtly.

She took the cigarette and put it between her lips, not saying anything.

As Morgan lit another cigarette for himself, Kitson drove up the rough road that led to Gypo's workshop.

The workshop consisted of a big shed and a wooden shack in which Gypo lived. It was in the shed that he did occasional welding work, made wrought iron gates when anyone wanted gates, which was seldom, or cut a key or fixed a lock for the hardware stores in town.

The workshop gave Gypo a legitimate excuse to keep a few cylinders of acetylene as well as a few cylinders of undiluted hydrogen which were useful when he had to cut into a safe. He scarcely made enough profit from the workshop to pay for the rent of the shed.

They found him waiting anxiously for them, and as the headlights of the Lincoln lit up the double doors, he appeared, shoving open the doors with the frantic clumsiness of a frightened man.

Kitson drove the Lincoln into the shed, and they all got out.

'Well?' Gypo asked as soon as he had closed the doors. 'What happened?'

'It's okay,' Morgan said. 'We could all do with a drink. Here, Kitson, get those number plates off and drain out the water from the radiator and fill it up with cold. You never know: the cops may give this joint a rumble. Snap it up. Gypo, get us a drink.' He looked over at Bleck who was lighting a cigarette with a shaking hand. 'Give Kitson a hand.'

Having got some action, he crossed over to Ginny and smiled at her.

'Okay?'

Her mouth tightened. She was still looking pretty bad and her skin still had the bluish tinge.

'I'm all right.'

'You handle the big one the way you handled this one,' Morgan said, 'and you'll do.'

'Oh, stop talking to me as if I were a child,' the girl said irritably and turned away, moving over to the work bench were she began to finger the tools aimlessly.

Morgan shrugged, then when Gypo came hurrying up with a bottle of whisky and glasses, he made five drinks and carried two glasses over to Ginny. He offered her one.

'If you need this the way I need it, you need

it,' he said.

She took the whisky and swallowed a little, grimacing, then the blueness went out of her face.

'It was tougher than I imagined,' she said. 'I nearly cracked.'

'But you didn't.' Morgan paused to drink half his whisky, then went on, 'you were fine. Let's get over there and see what the haul is.'

While Gypo, Kitson and Bleck worked feverishly on the car, Morgan emptied the contents of the sack on to the work bench and began to strip out the wallets. Ginny worked with him.

This is his,' the girl said, picking up a pigskin wallet. 'The one I hit.'

'Let's see what he was trying to protect,' Morgan said. 'How much?'

She hooked out ten one hundred dollar bills and laid them on the bench.

'No wonder he acted tough.'

The other three, having fixed the car, came over and stood watching. After a few minutes, Morgan and the girl finished stripping out the wallets, then Morgan sat down on a box and began counting the money.

The four watched him.

Morgan looked up as he laid the last five dollar bill down on the bench.

'Two thousand, nine hundred and seventy-five bucks,' he said. 'Well, here's our working capital. Now we can go straight ahead.'

'Is that right she had to hit a guy?' Gypo asked, his eyes as round as marbles.

'She hit him,' Morgan said, carefully stacking the money. 'He asked for it and he got it. She handled him better than I could . . . better than any of you could.'

Ginny turned away and walked over to the car.

The four men looked at her and exchanged glances.

'She'll do,' Morgan said quietly. 'If you boys do as well, the big one is in the bag.'

He looked directly at Bleck who tried to meet his eyes, but couldn't make it. He took out a cigarette and went through an elaborate search for a match, aware that Morgan's glittering eyes were still probing at him.

'Hear me, Ed?'

Bleck lit his cigarette.

'Sure.'

Sensitive to the atmosphere, Gypo asked, 'Something go wrong, Frank?'

'Ed let a guy knock his gun out of his hand,' Morgan said. 'That could have soured the whole caper.'

Bleck moved his powerful shoulders under his coat, scowling. 'He caught me on the wrong foot. It could have happened to anyone.'

'Yeah,' Morgan said, 'but don't let it happen again.' Turning to Kitson, he went on, 'And you: you were too slow off the mark. You should have got the car away a lot faster.'

Kitson knew Morgan was right. The sound of the gun going off had paralysed him. He had imagined someone in the café had been killed and this job had turned into a murder rap.

'Ginny . . .'

The girl turned at the sound of Morgan's voice and came over to where the four men were standing.

'We can go ahead with the big one now,' Morgan said. 'You and Kitson go into Marlow tomorrow and get the caravan. Gypo will give you the measurements.' Morgan sat on the bench, his cigarette sending a thin spiral of smoke past his nose. 'Keep the price as low as you can. We'll need every cent of this dough. I don't have to tell you that.' He looked over at Kitson. 'You know the setup: you and she have just got married and want this caravan for your honeymoon. Most young people buy caravans for that reason, and we've got to make sure the guy who sells you the caravan doesn't remember either of you.'

Kitson glanced suspiciously at Bleck, but Bleck was feeling pretty sick with himself, knowing that he hadn't made much of a showing at the hold-up, and he wasn't in the mood to jeer.

'Try to stop looking like a block of wood, will you?' Morgan went on. 'Act like you're in love with the girl or this guy will wonder what kind of honeymoon you're on.'

Gypo chuckled.

'Maybe I should handle the job,' he said. 'I am affectionate by nature. Me and Ginny would make a very pretty couple.'

Even Ginny joined in the laughter.

'You're too fat and old, Gypo,' Morgan said. 'The guy might remember you. It's got to be Kitson.'

He counted out two thousand dollars and handed the bills to Kitson.

'Try and get it cheaper. I'll bring the Buick with the towing tackle to your place at eleven tomorrow.' He looked over at Gypo. 'You follow me to Kitson's place in the Lincoln. I'll need transport back.'

'Sure,' Gypo said.

'Okay, let's break it up now,' Morgan said. 'I've got to take the chopper back to Lu. You come with me, Ed.' He looked at Ginny and Kitson. 'You two take the bus. It'll be safer if we four aren't seen together.'

He put the rest of the money in his hip pocket.

'You two arrange where you meet,' he said to Ginny. 'I want you both back here with the caravan by tomorrow afternoon.' He jerked his head at Bleck. 'Let's go.'

When they had gone, Ginny took off the green scarf and shook her copper-coloured hair free.

Looking at her uneasily, Kitson thought she was beautiful. He stood against the work bench, rubbing his knuckles, awkward and ill at ease.

'Another drink?' Gypo asked.

The girl shook her head.

'No, thanks.' She took out her pack of cigarettes and, putting a cigarette between her lips, she looked at Kitson.

Kitson fumbled for matches, lit one with a hand that was far from steady and held the flame so she could light the cigarette. She put her cool fingers on his hand to steady the flame and the touch of her flesh on his sent a surge of hot blood through his veins.

She moved away over to the double doors.

'Well, so long,' she said to Gypo.

'So long,' he said, winking at Kitson, who ignored him and followed the girl out into the hot night air.

They walked side by side down the road and on to the highway.

'Where do you live?' Ginny asked as they paused at the bus stop.

'Lennox Street,' Kitson said.

'Then I'll be waiting at the corner tomorrow at eleven.'

'I can pick you up at your place if you like.'

'It's not necessary.'

There was a pause while Kitson kept eying her as she stood at his side.

'The other night . . .' he said abruptly. 'I wouldn't have hit you. I—I guess I lost my temper. I'm sorry.'

She smiled.

'I thought you were going to. You scared me.'

Kitson flushed.

'I wouldn't have done it. I don't hit anyone smaller than myself. I wouldn't have done it.'

'If you had, it would have served me right. I was asking for it.' She flicked her cigarette away. 'Was it such a good idea to hit Bleck?'

Kitson scowled.

'It's time someone took a poke at that punk,' he said. 'He had it coming.'

'Yes, but it wasn't such a good idea. You'll have to watch him. He's not the type to forget.'

Kitson shrugged.

'I can handle him.'

'I think you can. I saw you in the ring about a year ago. When you beat Jackie Lazards. That was quite a scrap.'

Kitson looked at her, his face lighting up. That had been quite a scrap. He had been lucky to have beaten Lazards. They had fought nine slugging rounds, and it had been anyone's fight.

'He was a good fighter.'

'You weren't so bad yourself. Why did you quit the ring?'

This was an embarrassing question and Kitson hastily improvised.

'After my last fight I got double vision,' he said, running his fingers through his curly hair. 'That scared me. I was doing all right, but this double vision . . . The Doc said I should quit, and he was pretty serious about it. I didn't want to. I had a good chance for the title, but when the Doc said I should quit, I quit.'

This was his version of the story. His manager would have told her something completely different.

He looked anxiously at her to see if she accepted the explanation, but her expressionless face told him nothing.

'What made you pick on Frank?' he asked after a long pause.

'Who else is there in this town to pick on?' she said. 'Here comes the bus.'

They boarded the bus. She let him buy the tickets, and they sat side by side, their faces reflected in the glass of the window. The bus was full. Except for a moment's interest when the men in the bus stared at her as she went to her seat, no one paid any attention to them.

They rode back to town in silence.

At the railroad station, she said, 'This is where I get off. See you tomorrow at eleven.'

He got up to let her pass and he felt a surge of blood move through him as her body brushed against his.

As the bus moved off, he pressed his face against the window, looking out into the darkness, trying to get a last glimpse of her.

CHAPTER FOUR

I

At eleven o'clock the following morning, Kitson drove Morgan's Buick out of town and headed towards Marlow, a sixty mile drive on Highway 10.

By his side sat Ginny, whom he scarcely recognised. She looked what she was supposed to look: a young girl who had just got married and was about to experience the excitement and the fun of a honeymoon. The simple summer frock she wore gave her youthful charm. Her expression had softened and she was surprisingly talkative.

Kitson was a little stunned by this transformation. He had taken pains with his appearance, and he now gave the impression of being a fairly prosperous young man, just married and embarrassed that anyone should know he was off on his honeymoon.

Morgan had brought the Buick, towing tackle now in position, to Kitson's place. Gypo had followed him in the Lincoln and he had become sentimental as he watched Kitson and Ginny drive away.

'They look made for each other, don't they?' he said to Morgan as he stared after the swiftly moving Buick. 'She's not as hard as she

95

makes out. A girl with a body like that is made for love. They look like a honeymoon couple. They could have beautiful children.'

'Stop flapping with your mouth!' Morgan said. 'What's the matter with you? You're talking like an old woman!'

Gypo spread his hands and lifted his shoulders.

'Okay, so I flap with my mouth. So I shut up, but without a little love in this world, where is the happiness?'

'Come on. We've got work to do. Take me over to Ed's place,' Morgan said, scowling.

This sort of sloppy talk was bad, he thought. They had a dangerous job ahead of them. This was no time for sentiment.

Bleck had a two-room apartment in a brown stone building that overlooked the river.

Morgan took the elevator to the fourth floor, walked along the passage and dug his thumb into Bleck's bell push. There was a delay, then Bleck opened the door.

He was wearing a pair of black pyjamas with white piping and his initials in white on the pocket. His hair was tousled and his eyes heavy and a little bleary.

'For the love of mike!' he said, staring at Morgan. 'What's the time then?'

Morgan moved forward and rode Bleck back into the small sitting-room, comfortably furnished, but untidy, with a number of empty gin and whisky bottles lined up on the window seat.

There was a stale smell of cigarette smoke and perfume that made Morgan wrinkle his nose.

'It smells like a cat house in here,' he said. 'Can't you open a window?'

'Why, sure.' Bleck went to the window and threw it open. He looked at the clock on the overmantel and saw it was twenty minutes after eleven. 'You're early, aren't you? Kitson gone?'

'They've gone,' Morgan said. He looked across the room to the bedroom door. 'You got someone in there?'

Bleck grinned sheepishly.

'She's asleep. You don't have to worry about her.'

Morgan reached forward and hooked his finger into Bleck's pyjama pocket, pulling him close to him.

'Listen, Ed, this is the big one. Your showing last night wasn't so hot. You'll have to do a damn sight better than that or you're not going to be much help. Until we've done this job, cut out the women and the booze. You look like something a cat has sicked up.'

Bleck jerked away, his face tightening.

'You don't talk that way to me, Frank . . .'

'I do, pal. If you want it the hard way, say so. I can handle you any time and don't forget it. You do what I say or you're out of this job.'

The expression in the flat, black eyes chilled

Bleck.

'Okay, okay,' he said hurriedly. 'I'll watch it.'

'You'd better watch it,' Morgan said.

Bleck moved away.

'Anything in the papers about last night?'

'The usual junk. Everyone was so scared they couldn't give the cops any kind of description. I guess we're going to get away with that one. I want you to get down to Gypo's place right away. He is getting the long bolts for the steel work now, but he'll need help with the job. Get down there, will you?'

'Okay,' Bleck said grudgingly. He didn't feel like working this morning.

'And snap it up!' Morgan barked. 'I'm going over to Dukas to get an automatic rifle. Ernie has one and he's willing to sell it.'

'Sure,' Bleck said. 'I'll get down there right away.'

When Morgan had gone, Bleck cursed under his breath and walked into the bedroom, crossing the half-dark room and pulling up the blind, letting a stream of strong sunlight fall directly across the face of the girl, lying in his bed.

'For heaven's sake, Eddy,' the girl protested, sitting up and blinking at him. She was dark, her black hair cut across her forehead in a fringe. Her eyes were big and blue and her features were small. She had on a pair of yellow pyjamas that set off her well-made body.

'On your way, baby,' Bleck said as he struggled into his shirt. 'I've got business. Come on! Make the legs walk!'

'But, Ed . . . I'm dead beat. If you have to go out, I can stay, can't I?'

'No! I'm not leaving you here on your own. Come on! Get moving!'

The girl—her name was Glorie Dawson—groaned, threw off the sheet and staggered out of bed. She stretched her arms, yawned and walked unsteadily into the bathroom.

'But what's the panic, honey?' she asked, running her fingers through her dark hair. 'Who was your boy friend?'

Bleck began to mow his beard with an electric razor.

'Come on! Dress the body and beat it!' he said. 'I'm in a hurry.'

She stripped off her pyjamas and got under the shower.

'Sometimes I think I must have a hole in my head,' she said, raising her voice above the noise of the running water. 'It's always the same. It starts right: soft music, soft lights and soft words, then all of a sudden it's: dress the body and beat it. What a way to talk to a girl! My dream man! My Prince Charming!'

'Cut it out and snap it up!' Bleck said irritably.

He disconnected the razor and then went into the kitchen to heat up some coffee.

His head was aching and his mouth felt as if

it were lined with felt. He wished he hadn't drunk so much the previous night, but his nerves had been shot. He wished too he hadn't invited Glorie to share his bed. He realized that this must have made a bad impression on Morgan.

He poured a cup of coffee, found a pack of Aspro and took three tablets, noting with a sense of uneasiness that his hand was shaking badly. By the time he had finished his coffee, Glorie came into the kitchen, dressed.

'Hmmmm—coffee. Pour me a cup, honey.'

'No time. Come on, let's get out of here. You can get yourself some coffee across the way.'

'Wait a moment, Eddy.' There was a sudden sharpness in her voice that made Bleck look quickly at her. 'That was Morgan who was here just now, wasn't it? What was he talking about—the big one? What does that mean?'

Bleck was startled. For a moment he stared uneasily at Glorie.

'You keep your snout out of my business,' he snarled. 'Hear me? This is nothing to do with you.'

'Eddy, please listen to me,' she said, putting her hand on his arm. 'Morgan's no good. I've heard things about him. He's been in bad trouble all his life. He's done everything except a killing, and the way he's shaping, that'll come. Please, Eddy, don't get mixed up with him. You'll only get yourself into trouble.'

Bleck had been sleeping with Glorie now regularly for three months or so, and he liked her. She was the first person he had ever met who was interested in him for himself and for nothing else, but that didn't mean he was going to let her dictate what he was to do and whom he should associate with.

'Skip it, will you?' he growled. 'You mind your own business, and I'll mind mine. Now, come on.'

She shrugged helplessly.

'Well, all right, darling, but remember what I said. I can't do more, Eddy. Morgan's bad trouble. You shouldn't mix with him.'

'Okay, okay, so he's bad trouble,' Bleck said impatiently. 'Come on, for Pete's sake! I'm in a hurry!'

'Will I see you tonight?'

'No. I'm busy. I'll call you. Maybe next week, but not before.'

She looked at him, her expression worried.

'So you're planning something with him. Oh, Eddy, please . . .'

He took her by her arm and hustled her out of the apartment, locking the door behind him. As he was turning the key, he said, 'Will you pipe down? I'm not going to tell you again. There are plenty of other fish in the sea. Remember that, will you?'

'All right, Eddy. The least I can do is to warn you, but if that's the way you feel about it . . .'

'That's just the way I do feel about it,' he said, hurrying down the stairs. 'Just pipe down, will you?'

As they reached the front door, she said, 'I'll be waiting for you. Don't be too long.'

'Sure, sure,' Bleck said indifferently and waving his hand, he set off at a rapid walk towards the distant bus stop.

Sitting in the bus, feeling the hot sunshine on his face, his mind drifted to Ginny.

Now, there was a girl! What a difference between her and Glorie. What a nerve she had! In smart clothes, she could be class whereas anyone could see Glorie was just a tramp.

He scowled to think Kitson was with her on his own now, acting the part of a newly-wed. Not that anyone in his right mind would regard that punch-drunk bum as a likely rival.

Bleck rubbed his sore jaw, his eyes suddenly vicious as he thought how Kitson had hit him. That was something he wasn't going to forget. A time would come when he would get even, and Kitson would be sorry he had hit him.

He was still thinking about Ginny as the bus pulled up at the stop near Gypo's workshop, and as he walked up the rough road leading to the workshop, he wondered what Kitson was finding to say to her.

Kitson was finding very little to say to Ginny, and he thought of the stretch of sixty miles he had to drive with her with a feeling of dismay.

He had always been talkative enough with the girls he usually went around with, but Ginny did something to him. She gave him a feeling of inferiority and made him tongue-tied, and yet she excited him as no other girl had ever excited him.

To his surprise, she was talkative, but only in spasmodic bursts, asking him abrupt questions about his fighting days, if he remembered so-and-so and such-and-such who at one time had had big reputations in the ring and what did he think of them. Kitson would reply hesitantly, his face tight with concentration as he tried to make intelligent replies. Then they would drive for three or four miles in silence, and then she would start asking questions again.

Suddenly she asked, 'What are you going to do with the money when you get it?'

As she looked at him, she crossed one slim leg over the other, showing her knees for a brief moment before she adjusted her skirt with a movement so prim that it caught Kitson's attention, and he had to swing the wheel to put the car back on course.

'I haven't got it yet,' he said. 'I don't make plans so far in advance.'

'You don't really believe you are going to get it, do you?'

He hesitated, then slowly, his eyes fixed on the road, he said, 'We'll be lucky if we do get it. I know that. I've worked with those two. They're not quitters.'

'That depends on us,' she said quietly. 'They'll quit if they're sure we mean business. Anyway, they don't matter. We can handle them. We're going to get this money. I am sure of it.'

'We'll be lucky if we do,' Kitson repeated. 'The plan is pretty good. I know that. Hiding the truck inside a caravan is a smart idea, but that doesn't mean we'll be able to open the truck. Suppose we have some luck and do open it, what are we going to do with the money? Two hundred grand is a heap of jack. You can't put it in a bank. The cops will be watching for just that move. What can you do with all that money in cash?'

'You put it in a safe deposit vault,' Ginny said. 'That's not so hard, is it?'

'Would that be so smart? Someone knocked a bank off last year and stuck the money in a safe deposit vault. The cops opened every vault in town and they found it,' Kitson said, his big hands gripping the steering wheel until his knuckles turned white.

'So you don't put it in a vault in town. You take it to New York or Frisco or even some little town miles away from here. They can't open every vault in the country, can they?'

'But you've got to get it there,' Kitson said. 'Imagine all that money! It'll fill a suitcase! Imagine getting on a train with a suitcase full of hot money, not knowing if the cops are going to search the train. When we pull this job, the heat will be fierce. The cops won't stop at a thing to get the money back.'

'You certainly look for trouble, don't you?' Ginny said, and he was surprised there was a sympathetic note in her voice. 'If you feel that way about it, why did you vote to do the job?'

That was something he didn't intend telling her.

'Forget it,' he said. 'I guess I'm flapping with my mouth as Frank says. I guess it'll work out all right. What are you going to do with your share?'

She leaned back, resting her head on the back of the seat so her chin was tilted upwards. He could see her reflection in the windshield and he thought how beautiful she was.

'Oh, I have plans, but they wouldn't interest you,' she said. 'There are so many things one can do when one has money. My father died last year. If he had had some money, he might have been alive now. At the time I was working as an usherette in a movie house. I couldn't help him. I made up my mind when he died that I'd never be in his position. That's why I dreamed up this plan to hijack the truck.'

This unexpected, unasked for revelation intrigued Kitson. That she should make up her mind to do this thing impressed him enormously.

'But how did you know about the truck and the pay roll?' he asked.

She started to say something then abruptly stopped.

There was a pause, and when Kitson glanced at her, his heart sank when he saw the wooden, cold expression back on her face.

'Don't think I'm prying,' he said hurriedly. 'I was just curious. But forget it. I don't want to know.'

She looked at him, her sea-green eyes impersonal, then she leaned forward and turned on the radio. After fiddling with the station control, she tuned into a dance band and, turning the volume up, she leaned back, tapping her foot in time with the music.

This, Kitson realized, was a broad hint that she didn't intend to talk any more, and sick with himself, he increased the speed of the car.

Twenty minutes later, he pulled up outside the Caravan Mart.

The Quality Car and Caravan Centre was situated on the main highway, half a mile from the centre of Marlow. It consisted of a waste lot full of second-hand cars and a number of caravans and a neat wooden hut, painted white and green, that served as an office.

Kitson had scarcely brought the Buick to a standstill before a young man came hurriedly out of the wooden hut. He was the type that Kitson loathed more than most. He was handsome, bronzed and fair with a deep crimp in his hair. He wore a white tropical suit, a cream-coloured shirt and a flame-red tie. On his thin, bronze wrist was a gold expanding bracelet that held a gold Omega watch in position.

He came down the drive towards them like an ambitious bee who sees an exotic flower that must be milked for honey.

Moving fast, he went around to the off-side door of the Buick and opened it to let Ginny out. He gave her a wide, friendly smile that made Kitson itch to hit him.

'Welcome to Caravan Centre,' the man said as he helped Ginny alight. 'How wise of you to come to us! You're looking for a caravan, aren't you? You couldn't have come to better people!'

Kitson, who had got out of the car, grunted. This buzzing, handsome wasp of a man badly bothered him.

'Let me introduce myself,' the man went on, moving quickly around the Buick and grasping Kitson's flaccid hand and shaking it.

'You're right,' Ginny said, suddenly very young and gay. 'We are looking for a caravan, aren't we, Alex?'

'The best place,' the man said, beaming. 'I'm Harry Carter. This is an important moment for you, but I assure you, you can relax. We have never sold a thing to anyone unless we are sure they are satisfied. We have all kinds of caravans. Just what had you in mind?'

Freeing his hand, Kitson growled, 'Something cheap.'

'We have them at all prices,' Carter said, his eyes on Ginny's long, slim legs. 'Suppose we walk around? You can then see what we have to offer, and I can tell you the price of anything that catches your eye.'

They followed him down the path made between the weeds to where the caravans were drawn up in two long lines.

It took some time to find the one Kitson was looking for. It had to be at least sixteen feet long and not elaborately equipped. He found it in the middle of the second row and he paused to examine it.

It was a white trailer caravan with a blue roof with two side windows and two windows at the rear and in the front.

'This might do,' he said, looking at Ginny, who gave him a quick nod. 'What are the exact measurements?'

'This one?' Carter seemed surprised. 'I don't think you'd be comfortable in this one.' He looked at Kitson. 'I didn't get your name.'

'Harrison,' Kitson said. 'What are the measurements?'

'Sixteen and a half by nine. Frankly, Mr. Harrison, the trouble with this one is it's been designed for a hunting trip and it's pretty rugged. There are no conveniences. Not the kind of thing your wife would like to live in,'

Carter said, his eyes again straying to Ginny's legs. 'But if you like the layout I have another that's fully equipped. Let me show it to you.'

Kitson didn't move. He eyed the blue and white caravan, looking at the wheels, noting their strength, and the automatic brakes which he had been told by Gypo were important.

'My husband is clever with his hands,' Ginny said. 'We plan to make the caravan we buy comfortable ourselves. Could we see inside this one?'

'Why, sure. See this one, and then take a look at the other. You'll see what I mean then. This one is really just a shell.'

He opened the door and Ginny and Kitson peered inside.

Kitson saw at once this was the one they were looking for. The fitments were flimsy and could easily be removed. The floor looked strong and, when he stepped inside, he found he could move around upright with a few inches to spare.

They went to look at the other caravan which was the same shape and size, but much more elaborately fitted, and Kitson only had to take a quick look inside to satisfy himself that it wasn't the one to buy.

'I guess the other one is what we're looking for,' he said, and as he walked back to the blue and white caravan, he asked, 'How much is it?'

Pausing beside the caravan, Carter eyed him over. His eyes seemed to be calculating what

Kitson might be worth.

'Well, it's a strong, well-built job, Mr. Harrison. It's not flimsy, and it'll give you years of good service. The list price is three thousand, eight hundred dollars. That is what you would have to pay for it new. This one is second-hand, but as you see, there's not a scratch on it. Two fellows bought it off me for a hunting trip. They weren't away more than six weeks so you could say it's practically new. Since you're struck on it, and since you're on your honeymoon, I'll make a special price. Suppose we say two thousand, five hundred. That's practically a give-away price.'

'Oh, no, we couldn't possibly afford that,' Ginny said quickly, cutting off Kitson's growling protest. 'If that's the best you can do, Mr. Carter, then I'm afraid we must look elsewhere.'

Carter smiled at her.

'It's a reasonable price, Mrs. Harrison, and you won't find caravans lining the road in this district. If you went to St. Lawrence you'll find caravans, but you'll also find the prices are a lot sharper than ours. Maybe if this comes a little too high, I can fix you with something smaller. I have a caravan over there that comes out at fifteen hundred, but it's small, and it's not over-strong.'

'I'll give you eighteen hundred dollars for this,' Kitson said in a flat take-it-or-leave-it voice. 'That's the best I can do.'

Carter's insincere smile widened.

'There's nothing I would like better, Mr. Harrison, than to do business with you, but not on those terms. Eighteen hundred for a job like this would put me right in the red. But since you are really interested in this job, suppose we say two thousand, three hundred and fifty? That's the very lowest I can quote.'

Kitson felt his temper rising. He resisted the impulse to take Carter by his shirt front and shake him.

The smooth talk, the easy manner, the shrewd calculating eyes goaded him. This man was something that Kitson would have liked to be in his immaculate clothes and his air of superiority.

'But we can't afford so much, Mr. Carter,' Ginny said, and Kitson felt a spurt of anger run through him as he saw the way she was looking at Carter, her eyes large and appealing. Somehow she managed to convey a sex appeal that infuriated Kitson. She had never looked like this at him. 'Couldn't you possibly make it two thousand? Frankly, that is all we have.'

Carter ran his thumb nail along his pencil-lined moustache. As he appeared to hesitate, his eyes moved over Ginny's body with an intent interest, then he lifted his shoulders in a mock-helpless gesture.

'I can't resist that appeal. For you, Mrs. Harrison, and for no one else, it's a sale. I don't mind telling you I lose a hundred bucks on the deal, but what is money? You are on your honeymoon. Well, okay, consider this a wedding present. If you really want it, it's a sale at two thousand bucks.'

Kitson's face went a deep red and his hands closed into fists.

'Now, look, fella . . .' he began, but Ginny's restraining hand stopped him.

'Thanks, Mr. Carter,' she said, her smile suggestive and charming. 'Then it's a sale, and we're both very obliged to you.'

'You certainly have a bargain,' Carter said. 'Make no mistake about that. I'll get my boys to couple it up with your car while we go to the office and complete the sale.' He looked at Kitson, his smile now a little patronizing. 'My congratulations, Mr. Harrison. You've certainly found a wife who can make a very sharp deal.'

Back in the little office and the sale completed, Carter seemed inclined to dally. Holding the receipt between his fingers, he looked at Ginny, unconcealed admiration in his eyes.

'And where do you plan to go, Mrs. Harrison?' he asked. 'Where's the honeymoon ground going to be?'

'We're going up into the mountains,' Ginny said. 'My husband is fond of fishing. We're looking forward to it. It should be a lot of fun.'

Kitson reached forward and took the receipt

from Carter's hand. The way Carter was looking at Ginny was more than he could bear.

'We'll have to get going,' he said. 'We have a lot to do.'

Carter again gave him the same patronizing smile as he got to his feet.

'I can imagine,' he said. 'Well, happy journey to you both. Anytime you want to trade this job in for something better, come and see me.' He shook hands with Ginny, holding her hand a little longer than necessary.

Kitson, determined not to shake hands with him, pushed his hand deep into his trousers pocket and slouched to the door.

The caravan was now coupled to the Buick and they went down the path with Carter still talking to Ginny.

It inflamed Kitson's anger at the way Carter handed Ginny into the car, and he could scarcely contain himself as Carter gave him a patronizing pat on his back and wished him luck.

'This is just what we want,' Ginny said as they drove away from the Caravan Mart. 'Morgan will be pleased.'

Kitson said in a low, furious voice, 'The way that jerk was looking at you . . . I should have taken a poke at him.'

Ginny turned her head sharply, staring at him, her sea-green eyes suddenly hostile.

'What do you mean?'

'What I say!' Kitson said, beside himself.

'The way he looked at you! The jerk! I should have hit him!'

'What does it matter to you how any man looks at me?' she asked, her voice ice cold. 'You're not married to me, are you? What are you getting so heated about?'

Kitson's big hands gripped the wheel, his face flushing.

He maintained a sulky silence all the way back to Gypo's workshop.

II

It took little less than two weeks to make the caravan ready for the task for which it was needed.

During those eleven days, Bleck took up quarters with Gypo, bunking with him in his rather sordid shed. He had done this deliberately because he realized he had lost considerable ground with Morgan, and he was anxious to show Morgan he now meant business.

Sharing the same sleeping quarters with Gypo had been a trial. Gypo was an Italian peasant. His personal habits grated on Bleck's nerves, his sublime indifference to dirt and discomfort was something that Bleck failed to understand.

Each morning, Kitson had come to the workshop around eight o'clock in the morning and had left just after midnight. The three men had slaved on the caravan to get it ready to take the weight of the truck.

It was during this time that both Bleck and Kitson were forced to realize Gypo's worth as a technical man. Without his skill and his ingenuity, they would have got nowhere.

Bleck, who had always despised Gypo, was startled to find him so much superior to himself when it came to a technical job. It irked him to realize that, without Gypo's sound craftsmanship, the job they were working on just could not have been done.

On the other hand, Kitson, who liked Gypo, was quick to admire the Italian's ability, and he looked forward to the work each day, feeling that, for the first time in his life, he was learning something useful.

The work was completed on Tuesday night, and on this night, Morgan had called a meeting to be held in Gypo's workshop.

None of them had seen Ginny during these eleven days. She had given Morgan a telephone number at which she could be contacted in the case of a change of plan, but neither he nor the other three had any idea where she was living or what she did with herself during this time.

While Kitson worked on the caravan, he thought continually about her. He was now in love with her, entirely against his will, feeling sure that nothing would come of it as he felt sure that nothing but disaster would come of this job they were planning to do.

But his feelings for Ginny were too strong for him to struggle against. The girl was in his blood like a virus, and he had to accept the fact.

While the others had been working on the caravan, Morgan had been spending a lot of time on the route between the Truck Agency and the Rocket Research Station. He had been investigating every by-road, seeking the best means of escape, timing every move, checking, rechecking and making maps.

There was nothing haphazard in Morgan's methods. Once the truck had been captured, he knew everything depended on making a quick get-away. It was essential to put as many miles between the place of the ambush and themselves as possible before the heat was turned on.

This called for the most careful planning and the familiarizing of the district.

He was feeling optimistic as he drove up to Gypo's workshop around eight o'clock for the meeting.

For the first time during the month, there was rain which fell steadily on the parched ground, releasing a smell of dampness that pleased Morgan.

There was no light showing from the carefully screened windows of the workshop and the big shed had a deserted appearance.

116

As he got out of the Buick, and just before turning out the headlights, he heard quick, light footfalls coming towards him. He looked searchingly into the darkness, his hand automatically closing on the butt of his .38.

Ginny came out of the darkness and into the beam of the car's headlights. She was wearing a blue plastic mac that glistened in the rain. Her copper-coloured hair was protected by a plastic hood.

'First wet night for weeks,' Morgan said. 'I'd have picked you up if I knew where you lived.'

'It doesn't matter,' she said, her voice curt.

Morgan moved between her and the workshop, hunching his shoulders against the rain.

'Just where do you live, Ginny?'

She paused, the rain beating down on her and she looked at him.

'That's my business.'

He put his hand on her arm, pulling her to him.

'That's no way to talk to me, kid,' he said. 'You're playing it a shade too mysterious. I don't know who you are, where you come from, how you dreamed up this idea or even where you live. You could fade away if anything goes wrong and you might never have existed.'

She jerked free.

'Would that be such a bad idea?' she said and moving quickly around him, she walked up to the workshop door and knocked on it.

For a moment or so, Morgan remained motionless, his flat, black eyes narrowed, then as Kitson opened the door, he joined the girl and entered the workshop.

'Hello there,' he said, shaking the rain off his coat. 'How's it going?'

'It's finished,' Kitson said, his eyes on Ginny as she stripped off her wet mac and tossed it on to the work bench. She was wearing a grey coat and skirt with a green blouse that set off the colour of her hair. Kitson felt a little pang in his heart to see how beautiful she looked. He stared searchingly at her.

But for one brief glance at him, she paid him no attention. Picking up a brown-paper parcel she had brought with her and which she had put on the bench while she had taken off her mac, she walked over to where Gypo was standing by the caravan and gave it to him.

'Here are the curtains,' she said.

Morgan came over.

'Well?' he asked, looking at Gypo, who beamed at him, his fat face full of pride.

'It's finished, and it's a good job, Frank,' Gypo said, stripping off the paper from the curtains. 'Just let me get these up and then you can see the sonofabitch.'

Bleck came out of the shadows, cleaning his hands on a lump of cotton waste. He saw Kitson was staring at Ginny and he looked at her intently himself.

118

He had been cut off from the society of women now for eleven days and he found Ginny irresistibly desirable. It amused him to see the way Kitson was staring at her. What did the punch-drunk bum imagine? Did he seriously think he could get to first base with a girl like her? He must be out of his head if he did!

'Hello there,' he said moving up to Ginny. 'Long time no see. Where have you been hiding yourself?'

The girl smiled at him and this was unexpected. Bleck had imagined he would have had to work hard to get even a smile from her.

'Oh, I've been around,' she said casually. 'Here and there, but I haven't been hiding.'

'Why didn't you come down once in a while?' Bleck asked, offering her his cigarette case. 'We all could have done with a little female diversion.'

She took the cigarette and accepted the light he offered her.

'I admit to being a female, but I don't pretend to divert,' she said.

Watching and listening, Kitson felt a sharp pang at his heart. The easy, silly conversation grated. He knew he could never make that sort of conversation with her and it hurt him to see that she seemed to like it.

'Well, at least you should have come down and said hello,' Bleck said. 'I've been lonely.

Imagine! For ten nights I've been sleeping with Gypo!'

She laughed.

'That must have been quite a change for you,' she said and, turning, she moved over to the caravan around which Morgan was prowling, staring at it from every angle.

Hot and sweating, Gypo came out of the caravan, having put the curtains in place.

'Go ahead and take a look,' he invited. 'It's finished.'

Morgan continued to stare at the caravan.

'How about the door, Gypo?'

Gypo beamed. This was his triumph: his masterpiece!

'The door works. Hey, kid,' he went on to Kitson, 'show him how we've fixed it.'

Kitson went to the front of the caravan while Gypo and Morgan stood at the back.

Morgan examined the back. It appeared solid, part of the caravan's bodywork.

'Looks okay, huh?' Gypo said, shuffling his feet with excitement.

'It looks fine,' Morgan said.

'Open up, kid,' Gypo said.

Kitson pulled down a lever and the back of the caravan swung upwards like the lid of a box, and at the same time part of the floor lifted and came down forming a ramp.

'Pretty good, huh?' Gypo said, rubbing his hands. 'I had plenty of trouble getting the back and the floor to work together, but it's done and it's fast and smooth. The ramp will take the weight of the truck. As you see, I've bound it with steel.'

As Bleck and Ginny drew closer, Morgan nodded approvingly.

'That's what I call a real job of work, Gypo,' he said. 'Let's see it work several times.'

Before he was entirely satisfied, Kitson had to open the back of the caravan and shut it a dozen times.

'Yeah,' Morgan said. 'That's fine. Good work, Gypo.'

He walked up the ramp and into the caravan.

As proud as any housewife showing off her new home, Gypo stood on the ramp and pointed out the alterations he had made.

'Those brackets up in the ceiling are for the acetylene and hydrogen cylinders,' he said. 'That cupboard there is to take the tools. The two bunks along the sides are for the stuff we take with us. The floor has been strengthened. We've put two steel girders across the chassis. There's no chance now of the bottom falling out if we hit a bump.'

Morgan took time to examine everything, concentrating in particular on the floor of the caravan. He lay on his back under the caravan with an inspection lamp and checked the steel girders that had been bolted into position.

Gypo watched anxiously.

Finally Morgan stood away, his hands in his

trousers pockets, his eyes glittering with excitement.

'This is the job, Gypo,' he said. 'Just the way I wanted it. It's going to be a hell of a weight when loaded, isn't it?'

'It'll be heavy,' Gypo said, 'but the Buick should pull it. You said we don't have any bad hills to climb.'

'Well, no, we haven't if we keep out of the mountains,' Morgan said, scratching his jaw. 'A lot depends, Gypo, on how fast you can bust into the truck. If it takes long, then maybe we'll have to get into the mountains. That's the one place where we can lose ourselves, but I don't want to do it. The road up there is tricky and steep and I'm not sure if the Buick would get up there with this load.'

Gypo immediately became uneasy.

'But you said I could have all the time in the world, Frank,' he said, wiping his sweating hands on the seat of his trousers. 'We're not going to bust into that truck in five minutes.'

'Okay, okay, take it easy,' Morgan said soothingly while Ginny and the other two looked sharply at Gypo. 'I don't expect you to bust into it in five minutes. You've got two or three weeks, but after that, we may have to get into the mountains.'

Gypo shifted his weight from one foot to the other, his small eyes growing round.

'But wait a minute, Frank, you said I could have a month's uninterrupted work on the truck, now you're talking about two or three weeks. This truck is tough. I've seen it. You can't rush a thing like that.'

Morgan thought of the hundreds of men who would be thrown into the hunt as soon as the truck vanished. He thought of the aircraft checking every road and the motor-cycle cops checking every car. If they were going to get away with this job, Gypo would have to rush it a little. He knew how excitable Gypo was and realized there was no point in getting him worked up before the truck was in their hands. It would be time enough then to put on the pressure.

'Yeah, I guess you're right,' he said. 'Well, maybe if we're lucky, you'll have a month to work on it. Who knows? You might even bust it first try.'

'That's a tough truck,' Gypo said scowling. 'It's going to take time.'

Morgan lit a cigarette.

'I guess we're about ready to take it,' he said.

The three men facing him stiffened.

Ginny rested her hips on the fender of the caravan; her eyes suddenly alert.

'Today's Tuesday. That gives us three clear days to make the final preparations,' Morgan said. 'Anyone see any reason why we don't take the truck on Friday?'

Kitson felt a sudden constriction in his throat. For the past eleven days he had been absorbed in working on the caravan, and he had put from his mind just why he was working on it. It had been a job that had interested him, the first job of construction he had ever done.

But now he was sharply jolted back to earth and he felt frightened.

Bleck felt a creepy sensation crawl up his spine, but it wasn't fear. If he had any luck, in a couple of weeks, he would be a rich man. He would be worth two hundred thousand dollars! The thought quickened his heart beat.

Gypo was very uneasy. He didn't like this veiled hint that he might have to open the truck fast. He wasn't scared of taking the truck because he knew he wasn't going to play an active part in the operation, but he didn't want Frank to imagine he could open the truck quickly. He didn't want Frank to be under any false impression.

'Let's make it Friday,' Bleck said, anxious that Morgan should know how keen he was.

'Yes,' Ginny said.

Morgan looked at Kitson and Gypo.

Both of them hesitated, then aware that Ginny was staring at him, Kitson said huskily, 'Sure, why not?'

Gypo lifted his fat shoulders.

'That's okay with me,' he said.

CHAPTER FIVE

I

Morgan walked over to the work bench and sat on it.

'If that's the unanimous verdict,' he said, looking around at the other four, 'then let's fix the rest of the things still to be done.'

The others found seats on the assortment of cases that cluttered up Gypo's workshop, the atmosphere suddenly becoming tense.

'We've got to get a car for Ginny,' Morgan said. 'We need a two-seater open sports job. Ed and Kitson will handle that.' He looked over at the two men. 'When you've found one, bring it here and Gypo will spray it and change the number plates. It'll have to be overturned at the bottle-neck. On this side of the bottle-neck there's a ditch running along the road. We'll want two ten-foot crowbars for the job. With them we can easily tip the car over into the ditch. You get those crow-bars, Gypo.'

'Sure,' Gypo said. 'And I've got those road signs ready.'

'Let's have a look at them.'

Gypo produced two signs mounted on poles. Morgan nodded his approval.

'Right; now let's run through the whole plan,' he said. 'How would it be for someone to make notes? I want everyone to be absolutely clear about what he has to do. Ginny, will you take notes?'

'Yes,' the girl said. 'If you'll get me paper and a pencil.'

There was a delay while Gypo went over to his hut to get a writing pad and a pencil.

As soon as he had left the shed, Bleck said, 'He seems jumpy, Frank. He worries me.'

Morgan's face hardened.

'We'll handle him. We've got to jolly him along until we have the truck. Then if he starts flipping his lid, we'll get tough with him. He'll be all right.'

'I hope you're right,' Bleck said.

Morgan looked over at Kitson.

'Well, kid, how are you feeling? Have you started to plan how you're going to spend that dough?'

'I haven't got it yet,' Kitson said, his voice sullen. 'Time enough to make plans when I have got it.'

Morgan regarded him thoughtfully, then he glanced at Ginny.

'Okay, Ginny?'

Her sea-green eyes were expressionless as she said, 'Why shouldn't I be?'

Gypo returned with a pad and pencil which he gave her.

'I'll run through the whole plan,' Morgan said. 'If any of you don't follow what you've got to do, stop me. This is important.

Everyone has got to know what his job is, so don't be scared to ask questions.' Morgan paused to light a cigarette, then went on, 'We meet here at eight o'clock a.m. on Friday. Ginny and Kitson will wear the kind of clothes you'd expect anyone to wear on a vacation. Kitson drives the Buick. Ginny drives the sports car. The rest of us travel in the caravan out of sight. Ginny drives to the trucking agency and parks there and waits for the truck to come out. Kitson drives the Buick, hauling the caravan to the start of the dirt road. Here we let Gypo out with one of the signs.' He pointed his finger at Ginny. 'Make a note we'll need two club hammers to drive the signs into place.' He looked over at Gypo. 'We leave you at the bottom of the road. There's plenty of cover for you, and you can keep out of sight without trouble. Your job is to wait for the truck to pass. As soon as it has passed, you put up the sign, diverting all traffic to the other road, then you start walking back so we can pick you up. Get that?'

His eyes round, his expression tense, Gypo nodded.

'Kitson drives to the bottle-neck and stops. Here, Ed and me leave the car and get under cover by the side of the road. Kitson drives on.' Looking at Kitson, Morgan went on, 'You'll leave the caravan in the wood and uncouple it. You'll drive fast to the end of the road and put up the second diversion sign. Then you'll come

127

back, couple up the caravan and turn the car to face back the way you've come. The ground each side of the road is hard enough for you to make a circular sweep, and you have the same kind of ground when you get back to the bottle-neck so you can again turn the car and the caravan so the back of the caravan will be facing the front of the truck. What you have to remember is when you get the signal, you have to move fast—and when I say fast, I damn well mean fast!'

Kitson said, 'What's the signal to be? How do I know when you'll be ready for me?'

Morgan took his cigarette from between his lips and stared at the glowing end, frowning.

'Well, I guess you'll hear some shooting, but if there isn't any, I'll have a whistle with me. Act on the whistle. One long blast and you come fast.'

Kitson's face tightened.

'You think there'll be shooting?'

Morgan shrugged.

'I don't know. I don't think so, but there could be.'

He looked over at Bleck and then back to Kitson. 'Anyway, come when I whistle.' He turned to Gypo. 'You've got it soft, but your end could be the toughest before we're through: remember that.'

Gypo nodded uneasily. It gave him a feeling of relief to know that he wasn't going to be mixed up in any violence. He was a technical man. His job was to bust into the truck. He felt it was only fair and right that he shouldn't be expected to have anything to do with the capturing of the truck.

'You understand what you've got to do now?' Morgan asked, turning his attention to Kitson.

'Yes,' Kitson said.

He, too, was relieved that he had this end of the job to do. At least he wouldn't be mixed up in the shooting if there was to be any shooting.

'You, Ginny,' Morgan said, swinging around to look at the girl who was listening, her face expressionless. 'You wait in the sports car outside the Agency until the truck comes out. You follow it, keeping well behind it. The driver mustn't see you. In the little car you'll be driving, it shouldn't be hard to keep out of sight. When the truck gets on to the secondary road, crowd up behind it. Start blasting with your horn. The driver will pull to one side to let you through. You've got to attract his attention: make him remember you. So blast with the horn while you are passing him, and pass him as fast as you can. We want him to think you're in a hurry and you're taking chances. Wave as you go by, and then drive flat out. If you time it right, you'll have a mile stretch of straight road. The car we'll get you will be capable of doing over a hundred, and I want you to push it so these two will tell each other driving that fast is asking to get killed. At

129

the bend, they'll lose sight of you, but keep coming as fast as you can without getting into trouble. You needn't worry about any on-coming traffic. Kitson will have fixed the sign and have diverted the traffic, so you can risk driving fast, but for Pete's sake, don't have a smash. We'll be waiting for you at the bottle-neck with the crowbars. Ed and I will turn the car over into the ditch. We should have about a quarter of an hour to set the scene before the truck arrives, depending on how fast you drive. To make it look convincing, we'll set fire to the car. We'll need a long strip of rag to touch off the gas tank. Make a note of that.' He looked at Kitson. 'You go to the slaughter house at Dukas and get a couple of pints of pigs' blood. Tell them you want it to use in your garden. You'll have to have another dress with you, Ginny. The one you'll be wearing will be messed up with blood. We've got to startle these guys into thinking you're bleeding to death when they see you lying in the road.' He paused to ask, 'Any questions?'

Ginny shook her head.

'It's all right so far.'

'Okay; you're lying in the road in a pool of blood; the car's burning in the ditch. Ed and me are under cover. Ed has the automatic rifle. The truck turns up and stops.' Morgan crushed out his cigarette. 'Here we have to start guessing and we may have to improvise as we go along. It's impossible to forecast exactly

130

what the driver and the guard will do when they see Ginny lying in the road. One thing we can count on: they won't run over her, so they will stop. Maybe both the driver and the guard will get out, but I don't think so. I reckon the guard will go to Ginny, leaving the driver in the truck. When he is within a few feet of Ginny, I'll come out behind the truck. Ed will be covering the guard with his rifle. As the guard bends over Ginny, I'll step up to the truck window on the driver's side and stick my gun in his face. Ginny sticks her gun into the guard's face.'

There was a pause while the four looked at Morgan.

'Your guess is as good as mine what will happen next,' Morgan went on. 'They may quit or they may start something. We've got to be ready for trouble. If the guard starts something, Ed will wing him. I'll do the same with the driver. This is something that'll have to work itself out. We can't make a forecast. Whatever happens I've got to stop the driver from pressing his buttons. It shouldn't be difficult if everyone keeps his head.' He looked at Bleck. 'You'll be shooting at twenty feet, if you have to shoot. You'll have a rifle, and this guy is as big as a house. Make sure to shoot fast and straight.'

'I'll do that,' Bleck said, but he looked anywhere but at Morgan.

'Okay,' Morgan said. 'The guard and the

driver out of action, I'll blow the whistle for Kitson. You'll be about five hundred yards down the road.' He turned his head to look at Kitson. 'Listen hard for the whistle, and when you hear it, come fast.'

Kitson nodded. He was beginning to breathe hard, snorting a little through his broken nose.

'From then on, we'll have to work fast,' Morgan said. 'The Buick arrives and turns, so the back of the caravan faces the front of the truck. I'll drive the truck up the ramp and into the caravan. You, Ginny, will have to change your dress. Ed will collect the crowbars and the rifle and put them in the caravan, then he joins me in the truck. Ginny and Kitson get into the Buick; Kitson turns the car and the caravan and we go down the road fast for Gypo, who has started to walk back to meet us. He gets into the truck too. So we have Ginny and Kitson in the Buick, and the truck inside the caravan with we three in the cab of the truck, out of sight. We have to get to the highway as fast as we can, but that doesn't mean Kitson takes any risks. If we're in luck, we should get on to the highway in around fifteen minutes. By that time the Agency will have realized the truck has gone off the air. Maybe they will think the radio has broken down and they'll check with the Research Station. I reckon we have half an hour before the nickel drops and the balloon goes up.

Once on the highway, Kitson is not to drive faster than thirty miles an hour. By then there'll be a lot of traffic on the road and no one will think anything of a caravan being hauled by two young people obviously on vacation. Any questions so far?'

Kitson screwed his fist into the palm of his hand as he said, 'How about the driver and the guard? Do we leave them at the bottle-neck or what do we do with them?'

Irritably, Morgan ran his fingers through his hair.

'Don't worry your brains about them. Ed and me will take care of them.'

Kitson began to sweat. He was sure now the guard and the driver were going to be murdered.

'They'll see the caravan,' he said huskily. 'They'll be able to describe it and us as well.'

'That's okay,' Morgan said, his voice suddenly bored. 'That's something we'll have to take care of, won't we? You don't have to work yourself into a lather about it. Ed and me will fix it.'

Kitson looked over at Ginny. Her wooden expression gave him no comfort. Something inside him began to urge him to quit. This was going to be a murder rap . . . A blind man could see it. They wouldn't dare leave the driver and the guard alive.

Morgan was saying, 'Well, if there're no more questions, I'll get on.'

133

Gypo said nervously, 'Look, Frank, this worries me. I want to get it straight. How are you going to fix the guard and the driver? How are you going to make sure they don't give a description of us to the cops?'

Morgan's eyes turned suddenly bleak and his face hardened.

'Do you want me to draw you a goddamn map?' he snarled. 'How do you imagine we're going to fix them? Now listen: you two voted on the job. I warned you if we slip up we'll find ourselves on the hot squat. I told you to think it over before you voted. Well, you both voted. Don't give me this crap about how are we going to stop them shooting their mouths off! You know as well as I do how we'll do it! I'm not asking you to do it. Ed and me will handle it, but if you think you can back out now, you've made a mistake! We're all in this together. I'm not going to have the skids put on this set-up because you two are suddenly feeling righteous! Do you understand?'

Gypo gulped. The ruthless light in Morgan's eyes chilled him. Right then he had an idea that Morgan wouldn't hesitate to put a bullet in him if he protested further.

'Okay,' Gypo said in a small voice. 'You're the boss, Frank.'

'You bet I'm the boss,' Morgan said, then he swung around to stare fixedly at Kitson. 'What do you say?'

Morgan didn't scare Kitson, but Ginny did.

If she had the nerve to go through with this, he knew he had to, too.

'I just asked the question,' he said, staring back at Morgan. 'What's wrong with that?'

'Okay,' Morgan said, relaxing a little. 'You've got your answer. Now I can get on or do you two want to waste some more time?'

'Go ahead,' Kitson said, his face flushing.

'Once on the highway,' Morgan said, 'we head for Fawn Lake. There's a big caravan camp there, and that's where we're going to plant the caravan, slap bang in the middle of two hundred other caravans. We should get to Fawn Lake by midday. There are cabins around the lake and Kitson will hire one.' Morgan's voice was harsh now, his temper still edgy. He looked at Kitson. 'You'll park the caravan close to the cabin. You and Ginny will act like honeymooners. You'll fish, swim and enjoy yourselves. You'll let people know you are on your honeymoon and you want to keep to yourselves. While you are creating this atmosphere, Gypo, Ed and me will be working on the truck.'

'For Pete's sake!' Bleck exclaimed, an exasperated note in his voice. 'This bum certainly has picked himself the soft end of the job!'

Kitson started to his feet, his fists clenched, his face red with anger.

Morgan snapped, 'Pipe down, will you?' The snap in his voice made Kitson pause.

'Look, Ed, just listen to me. We are a team. Kitson gets the honeymoon end of the job because he can handle a car better than any of us can. You cut out picking on him or you and me will have trouble. I'm getting sick of the way you lot are beefing. The only one who keeps her mouth shut is Ginny. If this job is going to be pulled, we've got to work as a team. Remember that and shut up!'

Bleck shrugged.

'Okay, okay. Can't I make a remark?'

Morgan stared at him for a long moment, then when Bleck's eyes shifted, he said, 'As soon as the caravan is parked, Gypo starts to work on the truck. It won't be easy. There isn't much room to work in, and it'll be hot in the caravan, but that's something you'll have to put up with, Gypo. Ed and me will remain in the cab of the truck out of your way. If you want any help, we're right there to give it to you. We three have the rugged end of it because we'll have to stay in the caravan until it is dark. When it is dark, we'll move into the cabin for the night, but we've got to be back in the caravan as soon as it is light. We can't take the risk of being seen by anyone. We'll have to he careful. We may have to move on if Gypo finds the job is going to take some time. If we have to, we'll go up into the mountains, but I don't want to go up there. I'm worried the Buick won't haul the load and we'd look damned cockeyed if we got stuck.' He looked over at Gypo. 'Any questions?'

'You mean you want me to work on the truck while it's still in the caravan?' Gypo asked. 'I couldn't use the flame in there, Frank. It'd be seen through the curtains, and besides, it would be dangerous. The caravan could catch fire.'

'Maybe you won't have to use the flame,' Morgan said. 'The time-lock will have operated by then. Maybe you'll be able to find the combination.'

Gypo nodded, his face clearing.

Morgan slid off the work bench and stretched.

'Well, that's the plan. It's pretty comprehensive, but it's not perfect: no plan is. I'm pretty certain we'll be able to keep the truck hidden. No one'll think of looking for it inside a caravan among hundreds of caravans. That's the brightest part of the plan.' He looked over at Ginny. 'That was smart, kid: really smart.'

'It'll work,' she said. 'Just so long as you all do what you have got to do.'

The cold, determined expression in her eyes bothered Kitson. He remembered what Gypo had said about a girl like her with a body like hers was made for love. Now watching the cold, set face and the hard eyes he decided Gypo had been romancing.

'Well, I guess that's it,' Morgan said, looking at his watch. 'Ed, you and Kitson, take Gypo's car and take a ride around the car parks. I want a sports car tonight. When you've found it, bring it here and Gypo will do a spray job on it. You two get off now.'

Scowling, because he didn't fancy spending the evening in Bleck's company, Kitson got to his feet and slouched over to the door.

Bleck followed him, whistling under his breath, winking at Ginny as he passed her. Ginny stared blankly back at him, but Bleck continued to grin, and he paused at the door to wink again.

A few moments later they heard the Lincoln start up and drive away.

'All I want you to do, Ginny,' Morgan said, 'is to organize the food. Get a couple of baskets and buy canned food.' He took some money from his pocket and gave it to her. 'Get stuff that will keep and put a couple of bottles of Scotch in the basket. There's nothing else for you to do. We'll see you here on Friday morning at eight. Okay?'

'Yes.'

From the writing pad, she tore out two pages of notes she had made and gave them to him.

'Can I drop you anywhere?' he asked, knowing what the answer would be. 'It's still raining.'

She put on her plastic mac, shaking her head.

'No, thanks. I'll take the bus.' She looked at

him. 'You think this is going to work out all right, don't you?'

'Yeah,' he said. 'You think so too, don't you?'

'Yes.' She hesitated, then nodded. 'Well, so long.' She nodded to Gypo and then went quickly out into the rain.

Gypo was feeling pretty shaky. Only the thought of laying his hands on two hundred thousand dollars and the silent threat from Morgan kept him together. He was scared of this job now. If something went wrong! If the cops caught him! Santa Maria! What would his mother think?

Morgan patted him on the shoulder.

'Relax,' he said. 'This time next week, you're going to have the world in your pocket. That's worth taking a risk for, isn't it? I'll be down tomorrow morning. You've done a swell job on the caravan, Gypo. Be seeing you,' and giving Gypo a gentle punch on his chest, Morgan left him.

II

As Kitson drove towards the big parking lot at the back of the Gaumont Cinema, his mind was in a state of confusion. He had no hope that this job would succeed. He had now committed himself to a murder rap. This would have frightened him had it not been for

139

what Morgan had said. He and Ginny were to act as honeymooners. They were to swim and dance and have a good time together, and knowing by now how thorough Ginny was in everything she did, Kitson had no doubt that she would act out her part as if it were the real thing.

The thought of having two or three days in such close intimacy with her more than counter-balanced the fear of failure and eventual arrest.

Bleck, lounging beside him in the Lincoln, watched him out of the corners of his eyes.

'Hey, kid,' he said abruptly, 'maybe I should tip you off. I wouldn't want you to get any ideas about Ginny. She and I have an understanding. When this job's over, we're joining up. I promised her I'd show her Paris and London. I thought I'd mention it in case you were getting ideas of your own.'

Kitson nearly drove into the back of a truck that had slowed down before stopping at the traffic-lights as the red came up.

He felt as if someone had given him a hard blow under his heart.

He managed to pull up and he turned to glare at Bleck.

'You're lying!' he said furiously. 'She wouldn't go any place with you, you jerk! You're lying!'

Bleck was pleased to see how Kitson had immediately risen to the bait, looking like an infuriated bull.

'Yeah?' He laughed. 'That's where you're wrong, stupe. She's more likely to go around with a guy like me than you. After all I've had education. You—well, you'd look pretty silly trying to order a meal in Paris, taking her any place with class with that squashed snout of yours. You can't even read, can you?'

'You shut up!' Kitson said, 'or I'll take a poke at you.'

'I wouldn't,' Bleck said, with a sudden rasp in his voice. 'Last time you took me by surprise, but don't try it again, bum. You'll think the bomb has hit you.'

Kitson half turned, ready to swing a punch, when a horn blasted behind him, bringing him to his senses.

He saw the traffic light had changed to green and the cars ahead of him were almost out of sight.

Breathing heavily and muttering under his breath, he sent the car forward.

'Yeah,' Bleck went on, delighting in needling Kitson. 'I had a talk with her the other day and we got around to Paris. I was over there a couple of years ago and I got to know the place. She said she always wanted . . .'

'Will you shut up!' Kitson exclaimed, 'or I'll stop the car and I'll shut you up!'

'Okay, okay,' Bleck said patronizingly. 'I just wanted to warn you when you are playing the

141

love-sick groom to remember I've got the first claim. If you don't remember, then you and me will have trouble.'

They reached the parking lot before Kitson could think of a suitable rejoinder. He was suddenly depressed. A girl like Ginny could fall for a smooth operator like Bleck: a guy who knew his way around, who had education and who probably did know Paris like he said. That was opposition that overwhelmed Kitson.

He wasn't sure either if he could take Bleck in a fight. Bleck was fourteen pounds heavier than Kitson, and he was in good condition. Kitson had seen him fight once in a saloon brawl and he had been impressed by the weight of Bleck's punching. He was a savage, ruthless fighter with every dirty trick for disabling a man up his sleeve.

When they arrived at the parking lot they found there was no attendant to look after the cars parked in two long rows.

As the two men got out, Bleck said, 'You take the top row. I'll take the other. If you find anything, whistle.'

The two men separated, and Kitson walked fast along the long line of cars, his mind seething.

He kept trying to assure himself that Bleck had been lying about Ginny and he joining up together, but it worried him. At least, he told himself, he would have a couple of days— three with luck—with her alone, and he decided this would be his one chance to win her if she was to be won, which he felt doubtful about. There were moments when she looked so hard and wooden, Kitson wondered if any man could possibly win her.

He paused abruptly as he came upon an M.G. two-seater sports car, parked between a Cadillac and a Jaguar.

This would do, he told himself, and, looking quickly to right and left to make sure no one was in sight, he went to the car and examined it.

He had a small flashlight with him, and with the aid of its beam he checked the car over. In the glove compartment he found the ignition key.

He whistled to Bleck, who he could see walking along the lower row of cars.

Bleck joined him.

'This looks okay,' Kitson said, 'and the ignition key's here.'

Bleck studied the car and nodded.

'Yeah. You're getting smart, plough boy.' He looked at Kitson with a jeering smile. 'Well, you drive it to Gypo. Since you've been elected as the bright boy driver and since you've got the soft end of the job, you may as well take a little risk now before you start making sheep's eyes at Ginny.'

This was more than Kitson could stomach. Without thinking, he slammed his fist at Bleck's head.

Bleck was hoping he would do exactly that and he was ready for him. He shifted his head a fraction to the left so Kitson's fist sailed over his shoulder, then as Kitson lurched forward, off balance, Bleck hit him in the pit of his stomach, solidly, all his weight and strength gathered into a punch that didn't travel more than a few inches.

Kitson had been out of training now for months, and his muscles had softened. The blow paralysed him. He fell on his knees, gagging, a white flame of pain engulfing him.

Bleck stepped back, a cruel grin on his face.

'That makes us even, bum,' he said. 'Don't swing another punch at me again or I'll make you even more sorry. Get that car to Gypo and snap it up.'

He walked away to the Lincoln leaving Kitson still on his knees, his head hanging, while he struggled to get his breath back into his tortured lungs.

It took him some minutes to recover from the impact of the punch. Finally, he got to his feet, then, moving painfully, his mind on fire with the humiliation of his defeat, he got into the M.G., started the engine and drove out of the parking lot.

He had asked for it, he told himself savagely, as keeping to the back streets, he headed for Gypo's workshop, but the next time would be different.

He felt sure that there would have to be a

144

final clash between Bleck and himself. For months now Bleck had been picking on him, and if Bleck thought he was going to steal Ginny from him, he had another think coming. When the clash did come, he was forewarned. Bleck could punch and he would have to keep away from that devastating right hand. Both of them had surprised each other with a sucker punch. Both of them wouldn't be taken by surprise again.

While Kitson continued on his way to Gypo's workshop, Morgan was driving back to his room off the town's main street.

Morgan's mind was occupied with the coming job. He had gone over the plan time and again, taking the job much more seriously than any of the other three. This would be the last job he would do, he told himself as he steered the car through the heavy traffic. The rain had now ceased, but the roads were slippery and glistened in his headlights, and he drove carefully.

As soon as they had the money, he thought, the mob would split up. He had already made arrangements for his own get-away. In his wallet he had an air ticket for a Mexican-Californian border town; a priority ticket, undated, but that gave him the right to board any plane out at any time. He had rented a safe deposit in the town in which he intended to lodge his share of the loot. He would then cross the border into Mexico and wait. When he felt it safe enough, he would begin to buy bearer bonds, and once he had turned the whole two hundred thousand dollars into bonds, he felt he not only had the world in his pocket, but also at his feet.

He wasn't kidding himself about this job. He had a fifty-fifty chance of survival. The opposition would be fierce. The police and the Army would throw in every man and every trick they knew to get the money back. He didn't trust Bleck nor Kitson nor Gypo. So long as he directed them they would be all right, but once his hand was off the helm, once they were on their own, their chances of escape were small. It irked him to think that he had organized a steal as big as a million dollars, only to get a fifth share for himself. He felt sure that the rest of the money would eventually be grabbed by the police with the possible exception of Ginny's share.

Ginny intrigued him, but she also worried him.

Her plan to capture the truck had been complete and brilliant. He couldn't believe she had thought the plan out herself. Then who was behind her? Had she double-crossed someone?

He supposed it wasn't his business. She had given him the plan and he was going to profit by it. She had accepted the hardest and most dangerous part of the job.

He shrugged his shoulders, frowning. Then,

putting Ginny out of his mind, he concentrated once more on the plan.

CHAPTER SIX

I

Six o'clock a.m. on Friday morning, after a restless night, Gypo got out of his bunk and walked over to the open window to look at the sun as it came up from behind the mountains.

In two hours time the job that had been discussed and discussed until his brain was dizzy would begin. He would be pitting his training, his skill and his cunning against one of the most difficult locks devised, and he felt uneasy. Suppose it defeated him? He flinched at the thought of Morgan's anger.

Making an effort to control his nerves, he went over to a tin bowl, filled it with cold water and washed his face. He shaved, knicking himself in several places, noticing with a feeling of dismay that his hand was far from steady. To feel the fall of the tumblers of the lock, to catch them at the right moment meant moving the dial a hair's breadth at a time, and this called for a rock-steady hand.

Looking at his trembling hands, Gypo drew in a long, deep breath. He must control his excitement and anxiety, he told himself.

147

Always he had prided himself on the sensitiveness of his fingers and the steadiness of his hands. If he allowed himself to get nervous the lock was certain to defeat him.

He looked across the room to where an ornate wooden crucifix, which his mother had given him, hung on the wall. Perhaps this was the time to pray, he thought: something he hadn't done for years.

But when he knelt down before the crucifix, crossing himself as he had been taught, he discovered that he had forgotten how to pray. He realized that he couldn't ask for help when he was going to do something he knew to be wrong, and he could only mumble incoherently, repeating over and over again, the words: 'Forgive me . . .'

In a room on the outskirts of the town, Kitson was heating coffee, having just got out of bed. He was aware of a cold clutch of fear gripping him.

He had spent a bad night, worrying and tossing on the bed. Everything was now ready. At eight o'clock, it would begin, and there would be no turning back. It was only the thought that he would have Ginny to himself for two days that kept him from throwing his few belongings into a bag and getting out of town and as far away from Morgan as a train could take him.

He felt in his bones that this job was doomed to fail, but Ginny's attraction and his feverish, immature love for her urged him on.

When the coffee was ready, he found he couldn't drink it. The smell of it made him feel sick, and he hurriedly emptied the contents of the cup into the sink.

In another room, in another street, not far from Kitson's home, Morgan sat at the window, looking across the roofs of the buildings, watching the sunrise, a cigarette between his thin lips, his mind going over the final preparations that he had checked the previous night.

He was like a general before the battle, checking over in his mind each move that he had planned, satisfied that he had done his job well. He was now prepared to accept the consequences of either victory or defeat, knowing that there was nothing more he could do to make his plan better or safer.

Everything now depended on the individuals concerned. If Ginny lost her nerve; if Ed failed to shoot straight; if Kitson failed to handle the car and the caravan on his own; if Gypo went haywire and couldn't bust into the truck . . . innumerable 'ifs', but nothing he could do about it. Not once did Morgan question his own ability. He was completely sure of himself, and he looked down at his rock-steady hands, satisfied that his nerves were tough and he wouldn't crack.

In another part of the town, in his two-room apartment, Bleck was still in bed. He lay on his back, watching the sunlight creep up the wall, knowing that when it reached the right-hand corner of the ceiling, it would be time to get up.

Bleck had been tempted to call up Glorie the previous night and get her to spend the night with him, but he knew the danger of this. His bags were packed and his personal belongings had been put into store. Glorie would know immediately that he planned to leave town and she would ask questions. She might even make a scene, so on this night before the big job, Bleck had to sleep alone: something he hadn't done in years, and he found the night long and lonely.

Now, as he watched the sunlight edge slowly into the room, he wondered how he would feel after he had killed the guard. This would be the final step in his criminal career. Never before had he planned to kill anyone, being always careful to arrange his petty robberies so that no one got hurt.

He had no compunction about killing the guard. It was part of the job, and he accepted the fact. The man had to die, otherwise the plan would fail, but in spite of accepting the fact, Bleck couldn't help wondering how he would feel when he came out from behind his cover and walked over to the dead man and looked at him. He had talked to killers while he had been in prison, and he had seen a shifty, uneasy, scared expression in their eyes as they had boasted of what they had done. He knew they felt themselves to be people apart. The expression in their eyes was something he had never seen in the eyes of any other man no matter how badly they had lived. He wondered if he too would look like that after he had killed the guard and the thought bothered him.

When he squeezed the trigger of the rifle, he would not only be killing a man, he would also be offering his own life as a hostage to fortune. From the moment the bullet sped on its way, his own life would no longer be safe until he was dead.

It would mean he would no longer trust anyone, that he would always stiffen at a knock on the door, that his hands would turn moist at the sight of a policeman and his sleep would be haunted by dreams. He would become one of the men apart.

The sunlight had by now reached the right-hand corner of the ceiling and he threw off the sheet and got out of bed.

He crossed the room, picked up a half-empty bottle of Scotch and poured a stiff drink into a glass. He grimaced as the liquor filled his mouth, then with an effort, he swallowed it.

For a few moments he stood motionless, then when he began to feel the effects of the liquor, he went into the bathroom and turned on the shower.

In a shabby little room on the top floor of a rooming house on the outskirts of the town,

Ginny was closing the lid of a suitcase that contained all her worldly belongings.

She looked at her wrist watch and saw the time was twenty minutes to seven.

There was no need for her to leave for Gypo's workshop for another half an hour, she told herself and she went over to the window and looked down into the narrow, dirty street, lined on either side by refuse cans.

If they were lucky, she thought, in a few days or a few weeks, this sordid, dreary life she had been living would be a thing of the past. She would have money. She could go to New York, buy clothes, perhaps rent a pent-house apartment and live the life she had dreamed of living for years.

If they were lucky . . .

She had faith in Morgan. He thought the way she did. She had liked the phrase he had coined: *the world in your pocket.* The phrase exactly represented the life she wanted to live, and there was no other way of getting what she wanted except with a large sum of money.

If anyone could capture the truck and get at the money, it was Morgan.

As for the others . . .

She made a little face.

So much depended on Gypo. His excitability made her nervous. She only hoped Morgan would handle him.

Bleck might be troublesome. She had seen the way he kept looking at her. She would have to be careful when they were at the caravan camp never to be left alone with him.

She frowned when she thought of Kitson. He was so obviously in love with her. Her cold, calculating mind warmed a little as she remembered the expression in his eyes and his desperate anxiety to please during the drive to Marlow.

When she had the money, the wolves would move in, trying to get it from her. She was sure of that. It might not be such a bad idea to join up with Kitson. Between the two of them, they would have half a million dollars. He wouldn't be hard to handle and she felt certain he was dependable. It would be safer too. People might wonder how a girl of twenty came to be so rich: a girl on her own was always suspect. It was something to think about.

II

Morgan was the first to arrive.

He pulled up outside Gypo's workshop as the hands on the Buick's dashboard clock stood at ten minutes to eight.

The previous night, he, Bleck and Gypo had worked over the car until they were satisfied that it was one hundred per cent efficient, and Morgan had then taken it back to his place, giving it a try-out.

He found Gypo checking the tools he had

put in the cupboard in the caravan.

He saw immediately that Gypo was pale, and his breathing laboured. When he handled the tools, his hands were shaking.

That should pass, Morgan thought. It had got to pass.

Even he felt strung up now that they were so near to the first step in the plan, and he could excuse Gypo for feeling nervous, but he didn't intend to excuse him if he didn't settle down, and settle down fast.

'Hi, Gypo,' he said. 'You okay?'

'Sure,' Gypo said, not meeting his eyes. 'It's going to be a hot day. Better the sun than the rain, huh?'

Ginny came into the shed, carrying a picnic basket and her suitcase.

Morgan thought the girl looked as if she had slept badly. There were shadows under her eyes and she seemed pale under her make-up.

'Well, this is it,' he said, going over to her. 'Worried?'

She looked at him, her sea-green eyes impersonal and cool.

'No more than you.'

He grinned at her.

'That makes you worried then,' he said.

Kitson came in, followed by Bleck.

Morgan had an immediate suspicion that Bleck had been drinking. His face was flushed, and he walked with a swagger. This gave

Morgan his first twinge of uneasiness.

Kitson seemed nervy, but much more in control of himself than either Gypo or Bleck, and this surprised Morgan.

It was now two minutes to eight, and he saw no point in hanging around stretching nerves that were already too taut.

'Okay, fellows, let's go,' he said curtly. 'Get the caravan out, you three. Ginny, take the M.G. and get over to the Agency.'

He walked with her to the car and watched her get in. He stood over her, looking down at her, thinking how cool she was and admiring her.

'You know what to do, and you'll do it right,' he said. 'Good luck.'

She gave him a ghost of a smile and then started the engine.

Kitson came hurrying over.

'Good luck,' he said. 'Be careful how you drive. That car's fast.'

She looked up at him and nodded.

'Thanks: good luck to you,' and, letting in the clutch, she drove the car out of the workshop.

Five minutes later, the Buick nosed its way out of the workshop, hauling the caravan.

Morgan and Bleck were sitting on the floor of the caravan. Kitson was driving.

Gypo closed the doors of the workshop, then he hung a sign on the padlock that read: *Closed for the Summer Vacation.*

He had a sudden presentiment that he would never see this old ramshackle shed again, where he had spent fifteen idle years of his life. Although he hadn't earned much from the workshop, he had grown to love it as only a sentimental Italian could love a place like this, and there were tears in his eyes as he got into the caravan.

'What's the matter, greaseball?' Bleck demanded savagely. His nerves were crawling. 'What the hell are you so sad about?'

'Cut it out!' Morgan barked, making room for Gypo. His cold, dangerous eyes made Bleck look away. Then punching Gypo lightly on his chest, Morgan said, 'You're going to have something a lot better than this. Your own villa, your own vines and as many cigars as you can smoke. Think of how the women will flock after you when they know you're worth two hundred thousand bucks!'

Gypo nodded, forcing a watery smile.

'I hope so, Frank. It's going to be all right, isn't it?'

'Sure, it'll be all right,' Morgan said. 'You leave it to me. I've always steered you right, haven't I?'

By the time they reached the dirt road leading up to the bottle-neck the three men in the caravan were hot, sore and short-tempered.

They hadn't realized how hot it would be in that confined space with the sun beating down

156

on the caravan; neither had they realized the springs were far from adequate.

Kitson drove fairly fast, and the three men, with nothing to hold on to, were badly shaken as the unsprung wheels of the caravan banged over the rough surfaces of the road.

Gypo was dropped off with one of the diversion signs and a hammer. He obviously disliked being left on his own and yet he was obviously relieved that he had no further part to play in the next operation.

'The greaseball!' Bleck muttered as the Buick, drawing the caravan, moved on up the road. 'If he doesn't bust open that truck, I'll bust him open.'

Morgan reached up and jerked the automatic rifle from the clips screwed to the roof of the caravan. He thrust the rifle into Bleck's hands.

'Concentrate on this,' he said, his voice hard and cold. 'Never mind about Gypo. You look after your job and make sure you shoot straight.'

Bleck took the rifle.

'I could do with a drink! Let's have a shot, Frank. There're a couple of bottles of Scotch in that basket.'

'Later,' Morgan said. 'You do your job first and then we'll celebrate.'

The caravan slowed and then stopped. Kitson opened up the back.

They had reached the bottle-neck.

The two men, Bleck carrying the rifle and Morgan a .45, got out of the caravan. They stood for a moment drawing in deep breaths of the fresh morning air, feeling the sun hot on their faces.

Morgan said to Kitson. 'You know what to do. Listen for the whistle and then come fast.'

Kitson nodded.

'Good luck,' he said, staring first at Bleck and then at Morgan.

'You slay me!' Bleck sneered. 'Don't you imagine you need some luck yourself?'

Kitson shrugged, then shifted into gear and began to drive away when Morgan realized they had forgotten the crowbars.

'Hey! Hey!' he bawled. 'Stop!'

Kitson pulled up and leaned out of the window.

'Goddamn it!' Morgan said, glaring at Bleck. 'Do I have to think of everything? We haven't the crowbars!'

Kitson opened the back of the caravan and Bleck got the crowbars out, then Morgan, his eyes glittering angrily, waved Kitson on. As the Buick and the caravan moved off, Morgan picked up one of the crowbars and carried it to the side of the road.

Bleck followed him.

Morgan had been over the ground around the bottle-neck so often, he knew practically every shrub and bush by heart. He pointed out where Bleck was to lie. He himself went to a position about six yards from Bleck.

Both men lay down and examined the road.

This was a good spot, Bleck thought, bringing the rifle up to his shoulder and squinting through the sights. He was completely hidden, and yet he had a clear field of fire with no obstructions. He began to feel a little less uneasy, but he wished he had had a drink before leaving the caravan. The three shots of Scotch he had had before leaving his apartment were dying on him. Although it was still early, the sun now was making him sweat and his mouth was dry.

'Okay?' Morgan called.

'Great,' Bleck said, and after adjusting the sights of the rifle, he put it down beside him, took out his handkerchief and wiped his hands.

Morgan took off his tie and opened his shirt. He glanced at his watch. The time now was five minutes to eleven. If the truck drove at its usual speed, it would be expected at the bottle-neck at half-past eleven. Ginny should be here, Morgan decided, in a quarter of an hour.

There was time for a cigarette, and taking out his pack, he lit one.

Seeing him smoking, Bleck also lit a cigarette. He put his hand on the rifle, noticing his hand was still shaking and he grimaced. He was feeling tense and his heart was thumping. This hanging about was making him feel bad.

After five minutes of silence, Morgan suddenly lifted his head to listen.

'Sounds like a car coming,' he said.

Bleck scrambled to his feet.

'Get down, you fool!' Morgan snarled. 'It can't be her! Get out of sight!'

Hurriedly, Bleck slid under cover.

A half a mile down the road they saw some vehicle coming in a thick cloud of dust. As it drew nearer they could see it was a military truck. Three soldiers were sitting in the cab. The truck drove past and went on up the road.

'That's the mail run,' Morgan said. 'They're late.'

The hands of his watch crawled on. At twenty minutes past eleven, he began to feel uneasy. Had Ginny met with a smash? Had she lost her nerve and run out on them?

Bleck said, 'Sweet suffering Pete! How much longer is she going to be?'

'Maybe the traffic was bad out of town,' Morgan said, frowning uneasily.

'Suppose they don't let her overtake them?' Bleck said, half sitting up. 'What the hell do we do if they get here before she does?'

'We do nothing. It'll mean we try again tomorrow.'

'But they'll be suspicious if they see her on the road again,' Bleck said. 'It'll box up the whole plan!'

'Pipe down!' Morgan growled. 'There's time yet . . .'

He broke off as he heard in the distance the deep-throated roar of a car coming fast.

'Here she comes!'

A few seconds later they saw the MG flashing along the stretch of straight road a mile from them.

'She's driving like hell!' Bleck exclaimed, scrambling to his feet. 'Look at the way she's coming!'

Morgan, also on his feet, looked down the road.

'Maybe she's got the truck right behind her. Come on! Get those crowbars ready.'

He pulled a length of rag from his pocket and began to twist it into a rope. Then, taking a can of benzine from another pocket, he stepped on to the road.

He heard Ginny change down as she reached the bend in the road, then the next moment he saw the MG as it came through the bottle-neck. He waved, pointing to where he wanted her to stop. She swung the car to the edge of the road and pulled up.

Her face pale and her eyes glittering with anger and excitement, Ginny jumped out of the car.

'The devils wouldn't let me pass! To get past them, I nearly went off the road! Hurry!' Her voice was tense and her face white. 'They're right behind me!'

She snatched a gun from the glove compartment, then picked up the half-gallon jar of pigs' blood that was on the floor of the car.

'Where?'

Morgan pointed to a spot on the road.

As she pulled the cork from the neck of the bottle and began to pour the blood onto the road, Morgan and Bleck pushed the ends of the crowbars under the car and heaved upwards.

The powerful leverage lifted the car easily. It hung for a moment, then crashed over into the ditch.

'Take the crowbars and get under cover,' Morgan said to Bleck, and he pulled off the cap on the gas tank.

Carrying the crowbars, Bleck got back to his place of hiding.

Ginny was splashing the blood on her left arm and over her skirt, grimacing with disgust.

Morgan poured the benzine on the long strip of rag, dipped one end into the gas tank and then laid the six-foot length of rag onto the road.

'They're coming! I can see them!' Bleck shouted. 'Hurry!'

Morgan looked quickly at Ginny.

She was now lying face down in the middle of the puddle of blood, and she looked up at him, her face white and tense.

'Got your gun?' he asked.

'Yes.'

'Take it easy. I'll be with you, kid.'

As he struck a match, he suddenly wondered if the overturned car was too close to her. When it went up, the heat might scorch her, but it was too late now to do anything about that.

'Hurry!' Bleck shouted, panic in his voice.

Morgan touched the end of the rag with the lighted match, then ran past Ginny and dived behind his cover.

The flame ran up the rag and into the gas tank. There was an immediate explosion. A blast of scorching air struck Morgan, making him gasp.

Black smoke and a huge orange-coloured flame engulfed the road.

'She'll be fried!' Bleck yelled, shielding his face against the heat.

Morgan knew there was nothing he could do for Ginny. He switched his mind from her and looked down the road. He caught sight of the truck as it came into the bend to the bottle-neck.

'Here they come!'

Bleck grabbed up the rifle and slammed the butt against his shoulder. The sight weaved before his eyes as he desperately tried to steady the rifle.

The big flame had died down now and the smoke had cleared a little. The car was still burning furiously, and the heat was scorching.

Ginny lay motionless in the middle of the road.

From where Bleck lay, the spectacle looked horribly realistic.

The motionless girl, blood on her arms and her skirt, her long legs spread like those of a sawdust doll and the blazing car built up a convincing picture of a fatal accident.

Morgan cursed himself for not getting the car further away from the girl.

Even where he lay, he found the heat intolerable. She was at least twenty feet closer to the blaze and he was sure she was being scorched alive. But she didn't move nor show the slightest sign that she was suffering.

The truck came through the bottle-neck.

Morgan's fingers gripped the butt of his .45. He could see the driver and the guard. He watched their change of expressions when they saw the blazing car and the girl in the road. The driver slammed on his brakes, stopping the truck fifteen feet or so from where Ginny lay.

What was the next move to be? Morgan wondered. What were these two going to do? Everything now depended on this moment: his hopes and his plans hung in balance.

The guard was leaning forward, staring. The driver was shifting his gear stick into neutral.

Morgan saw both the side windows were open. At least that conformed to his planning.

There was a pause which seemed interminable to Morgan while the guard and the driver stared through the windshield at

Ginny. Then the guard said something to the driver, who nodded.

This badly bothered Morgan. These two were too cool and unflustered by what they were seeing.

Then he saw the guard reach forward and pick up a hand-microphone.

For God's sake! Morgan thought. He's going to radio back for instructions!

He wondered if he should break cover and attempt to take them both. If he had thought they would have done this, he would have had Bleck on the other side of the road so they could come up on either side of the truck, but he dare not try a lone rush against these two.

He wondered how Ginny was feeling, lying there, being slowly scorched, not knowing what was happening, but aware that the truck had stopped within a few feet of her.

Even in this crisis Morgan found time to admire the girl's nerve. To lie there, waiting, not knowing what was happening, in the scorching heat, was a test for the strongest nerves.

He watched the guard talk into the microphone. He could hear his voice, but not what he was saying.

This would mean their escape time would be cut down, Morgan thought. As soon as the truck went off the air, the Agency would know something was wrong and would set off the alarm.

The guard had now ceased talking and had hung up the microphone. He said something to the driver, then opened the truck door and got out.

The driver remained where he was, watching through the windshield.

Morgan wondered what Bleck was doing. From where he lay he couldn't see him.

Bleck was sighting the rifle at the guard as he walked quickly towards Ginny, and he was cursing under his breath because his hands were shaking so badly he couldn't hold the rifle steady, and this threw him into a panic.

By now the guard was within ten feet of Ginny, and Bleck knew any moment Morgan would break cover.

The rifle sight wavered on the guard: on him a moment, off him the next.

Bleck heard a rustle of shrubs as Morgan came out on to the road. He did what he shouldn't have done. He took his eyes off the guard and looked quickly to his right.

Morgan was moving fast and silently up to the on-side window of the truck, his .45 in his hand.

The guard was now bending over Ginny, but not touching her.

Perhaps he had a suspicion that there was something wrong with this set-up. Perhaps he felt he was being watched. He suddenly looked back over his shoulder.

Morgan was now at the window, his gun

pointing at the startled driver, who sat paralysed.

Ginny sat up abruptly.

The guard whipped around and his hand smashed down on her wrist as she was lifting her gun. His movement was unbelievably fast.

With his left hand he hit her across her face, knocking her flat. With his right hand, he whipped his gun out of its holster. The two movements were too quick for the eye to follow.

His breath rasping at the back of his throat, Bleck pulled the trigger of the rifle instead of squeezing it. The rifle sight jerked upwards as the gun went off. The bullet passed harmlessly over the guard's head.

As Bleck fired, the driver who had been sitting motionless in the cab, staring at Morgan, suddenly threw himself sideways, his hand stabbing towards the three buttons on the dashboard.

Morgan shot him in the face.

The guard swung his gun on Morgan. As he fired, Ginny, still dazed by the blow she had received, struck at his arm, shifting his aim, but not enough.

Morgan felt a heavy blow against his ribs and then a burning pain. The shock sent him down on one knee, but he quickly recovered. He took a snap shot at the guard who had Ginny now hanging on his gun arm.

His shot hit the guard in the centre of his

forehead, killing him instantly. His body slumped down on Ginny, flattening her on the road.

Morgan crawled to his feet, the pain in his side making him grit his teeth.

He was in time to see the driver's hand creep towards one of the buttons on the dashboard. Before Morgan could move, the fumbling finger reached the button and pressed it.

Steel shutters, moving like the spring of a released mousetrap, snapped down over the windows and the windshield, turning the truck into a steel box.

Cursing, Morgan staggered upright and slammed his gun-butt against the shutter, covering the driver's window, in a vicious explosion of disappointment. As he stood there, panting, he heard through the shutter a sighing groan from the driver, and then the sound of his body rolling off the seat onto the floor.

Bleck came rushing out from behind his cover, clutching the automatic rifle, his face livid.

Morgan turned and stared at him. There was an expression in his eyes that brought Bleck to an abrupt standstill.

'You yellow rat!' Morgan snarled. 'I've a mind to kill you!'

Bleck dropped the rifle and waved his hands imploringly. 'I tried to hit him!' he cried wildly.

'I got the sights wrong and then the rifle jammed!'

Morgan suddenly realized he was bleeding, and opening his coat, he saw a great patch of blood on his shirt.

Ginny came unsteadily up to him. Her face was red from the heat of the burning car and her hair was singed.

'Is it bad?' she asked anxiously.

'It's nothing,' Morgan said, but he was uneasy, as he was feeling cold and faint. He pushed the whistle into her hand. 'Get Kitson fast.'

She blew the whistle: a long, shrill blast; paused and then blew it again.

'The driver?' she asked as Morgan leaned against the side of the truck, his breathing quick and light.

'I fixed him. He managed to press one of the buttons, but I don't think he touched the others. I heard him fall.'

Bleck had come closer and was standing helplessly near Morgan.

'Frank! You're bleeding!'

'Get away from me, you creep!' Morgan snarled. 'You've bitched up the whole plan. We're sunk now!'

'No!' Ginny said sharply. 'We can still do it! Come over here and sit down! Let me stop the bleeding!'

As soon as he had sat down by the side of the road, she stripped off his coat and shirt.

Bleck stood staring, not knowing what to do.

Morgan shouted at him, 'Get the body out of sight! Do something, can't you?'

Ginny examined the long furrow along Morgan's ribs. It had been a close thing, but the ribs weren't touched. She lifted her skirt and wrenched at the hem of her petticoat, tearing off a long strip of material. Then she picked up Morgan's shirt, tore the part that wasn't blood-stained, made it into a pad and tied the pad tightly to the wound.

'That will hold it for a while,' she said. 'It'll have to be properly fixed as soon as we get to the camp. How does it feel?'

Morgan got slowly to his feet. He put on his coat, grimacing.

'I'm all right. Quit fussing.' He looked across at the truck. 'We're sunk. We can't drive the truck into the caravan now, and time's running out. If we want to save our hides, we'll have to get the hell out of here pronto.'

Just then the Buick, pulling the caravan, came fast down the road and pulled up. Kitson, pale and nervy, got out and looked questioningly at the truck and then at Morgan.

Bleck came out from behind a clump of bushes where he had left the guard's body.

'What happened?' Kitson demanded. 'I heard shooting.'

'We're sunk,' Morgan said. 'We've got to get out of here.'

'Wait!' Ginny said. 'The Buick can push the truck into the caravan. It can be done! We've got to try it! We just can't leave it here!'

Morgan screwed up his eyes, staring at her.

'Yeah . . . what's the matter with me? Of course.' He turned to Kitson. 'Uncouple the caravan and hurry!'

Catching the urgency in his voice, Kitson, bewildered, not knowing what had happened, ran over to the caravan and pulled out the coupling pin.

Morgan yelled at Bleck: 'Help him! Come on! Come on! Get the caravan turned around. You, Ginny, get the Buick behind the truck!'

As Kitson and Bleck manhandled the caravan, Ginny drove the Buick past the truck, then reversed back so the Buick's rear bumper came into contact with the truck's rear bumper.

Kitson and Bleck dragged the caravan close to the front of the truck.

'Block the wheels so it can't shift,' Morgan said. 'Get those crowbars, Ed! Use them to keep the front from tipping.'

Working with desperate speed, Kitson collected several big rocks and piled them against the wheels of the caravan while Bleck dug the end of the crowbars into the road, wedging them against the chassis of the caravan so it couldn't tip forward.

'Okay,' Morgan said, waving to Ginny.

Kitson came to the front of the truck and

171

stood by as Morgan opened the back of the caravan.

'Take it steady,' Morgan called.

Ginny began to move the Buick against the truck. Although the truck's handbrake was on, the steady pressure from the Buick began to shift the truck.

Kitson and Bleck kept kicking the front wheels, steering the truck up the ramp of the caravan. Slowly, the truck moved into the caravan. The front wheels of the Buick mounted the ramp as it pushed the truck right inside.

'Stop!' Morgan called. 'That's got it! Ed, get the crowbars and the rifle. Kitson, couple up the caravan! Hurry! We haven't a minute to waste!'

Ginny manoeuvred the Buick past the caravan, then turned and backed to the coupling pin which Kitson dropped into the slots.

She slid out of the driver's seat and Kitson got in under the wheel. He turned the Buick and the caravan to face down the road.

Morgan and Bleck got into the caravan.

Both men were startled to see how much space the truck took up in the caravan. There was only about eighteen inches of clearance either side and two feet at the back.

They had reckoned on sitting in the cab of the truck and it was obvious that travelling in this small space was going to be uncomfortable. If Kitson took a bend too fast the truck might shift and crush either of them.

'Watch it,' Morgan said as he got in. 'If this damn truck shifts . . .'

Kitson nodded.

'I'll watch it.'

'Hadn't we better block the wheels?' Bleck asked, hesitating at the door.

'Get in, damn you!' Morgan snarled. 'There's no time for that! Get going, Kitson!'

Kitson closed the back of the caravan, then ran to the driver's seat and slid under the wheel.

Ginny had taken off her bloodstained skirt and blouse and was struggling into another grey skirt.

Kitson looked quickly at her, seeing how deadly pale she was. Engaging gear, he drove fast down the road, feeling the sluggish response of the Buick as it dragged the great weight behind it.

As Ginny pulled up the zipper on the side of her skirt, he asked, 'What happened?'

Briefly, her voice unsteady, she told him.

'You mean there's a dead man in the truck?' Kitson asked, horrified.

'If he's not dead,' Ginny said, 'he'll be radioing for help and we'll be in trouble. Morgan said he had killed him.'

'We're going to this caravan camp with him in there?'

'Oh, stop talking!' Ginny said, her voice

173

breaking. She turned away from him and hid her face in her hands.

Inside the caravan, Morgan sat with his back against the wall of the caravan, his feet braced against the rear wheel of the truck.

He was thinking: Well, I've got it! Now I've got to hang on to it. I've killed two men for this. That was their luck. They had a lot of guts. Especially the driver. He knew I'd kill him if he moved and he did move. He had more guts than I've got. I wouldn't have moved. I wouldn't have tried for those buttons, not with a gun within a foot of my face, but he did it and he got the shutters shut. This puts us in a hell of a jam. We're landed with his body. We've got to break into the truck and get him out. I hope he's dead. If he comes to and gets that radio signal working, we'll be sunk.

He stared up at the massive steel truck, thinking that just beyond that steel wall was a million dollars. The nagging, hot pain in his side meant nothing to him beside the excitement he felt as he thought of all that money so close to him now.

On the other side of the truck, out of Morgan's sight, Bleck squatted on the floor watching the truck, uneasy that it might shift and crush him.

He had recovered his nerve now and he had got his second wind.

They had got the truck and he hadn't been forced to kill a man. He had side-stepped the final step in his criminal career, and he realized now it was the thought of this step that had broken up his nerves. Now he was ready to tackle anything. He wasn't after all a man apart, but he knew Morgan wouldn't ever trust him again and he would have to watch him in case he tried to gyp him out of his share.

When Kitson had driven a couple of miles, he saw Gypo walking fast up the road towards the approaching Buick.

Kitson pulled up and Gypo ran towards him.

'Have you got it?' he asked, his eyes round. 'It went all right?'

'Yes,' Kitson said. 'Come on: get in the back!'

He got out and opened the back of the caravan. He went around with Gypo and looked inside.

'Okay?' he said to Morgan, who looked pale, his mouth drawn down with pain.

'Yeah . . . get going!' Morgan growled. 'Come on in, Gypo!'

Gypo stared, coming to an abrupt stop.

'What are you doing there? Why aren't you riding in the truck?'

'Get in!' Morgan snarled. 'We've got to get moving.'

'I'm not getting in like that!' Gypo said, his voice shooting up a note. 'If that truck shifts, you'll be squashed like a fly!'

175

Morgan pulled his .45 from his shoulder holster. As he did so, his coat opened and Gypo could see the blood-stained bandage across his chest.

'Get in!' Morgan said.

Kitson grabbed Gypo and shoved him into the caravan, then he ran around and pulled the lever down, shutting the back.

He got into the driving seat.

The car and the caravan headed fast towards the highway.

CHAPTER SEVEN

I

Gypo stood with his broad back pressed hard against the wall of the swaying caravan, his eyes goggling at the steel wall of the truck that was only a few inches from his protruding stomach.

Bleck had come around the truck and was standing at the back of it, looking down the side where Morgan and Gypo were standing.

The three men were bracing themselves as the caravan swayed and bumped behind the fast-moving Buick.

'Santa Maria!' Gypo exclaimed. 'Then there's a man in there?'

'Yeah, but he won't worry you,' Morgan

said. 'He's dead. Now look, Gypo, you've got to get that shutter open. We've got to be sure he hasn't the radio signal on.'

Bleck came out with his first constructive suggestion since the job began.

'The radio is run from the battery,' he said. 'Can't we get under the truck and cut the leads?'

'That's it!' Morgan said. 'Get under there, Gypo, and find the leads. Get going!'

'I don't want to get under there. The truck might shift and crush me,' Gypo said, his face sagging.

'You heard what I said!' Morgan snarled. 'Hurry!'

Muttering, Gypo opened the cupboard door where he kept his tools, took from it a pair of wire cutters and a screwdriver.

Morgan glanced through the curtain that covered the window on his side.

They were now on the secondary road, and Kitson was driving fast. The caravan was swaying about dangerously. If there was a traffic cop around, he would be after them. There was no way to warn Kitson to slow down. Morgan hoped he would cut his speed before they reached the highway.

Gypo was down on the floor, struggling to get under the truck. It was a tight fit and he was badly scared. He finally got himself under and Morgan handed him a flashlight.

As he edged himself under the truck's

engine, Gypo saw on the floor boards, a few inches from his face, a big patch of red, and even as he recognized it to be blood, some of it dripped down on him, hot and sticky against his neck.

He heaved his body away from it, shuddering, knowing the dead man was only separated from him by the thinness of the boards.

His hands shaking, his body quivering, he strove desperately to locate the battery leads. If it hadn't been for Morgan who was kneeling and peering under the truck at him, Gypo would have declared he had cut the leads, but with Morgan's eyes on him, he didn't dare do that.

Finally he spotted one of the leads, but it was well out of his reach.

'I can't get at it, Frank,' he panted. 'We'll have to do it from the top.'

'The hood's locked,' Morgan said. 'Hang on a moment.'

He went to the tool cupboard and found a pair of long-handled metal shears.

'You'll reach it with this,' he said, pushing the shears under the truck.

Gypo had to put his flashlight down to handle the shears. After some trouble he managed to get them into position, but by then he had lost sight of the lead.

'I've got to have a light,' he panted.

'Get under there and hold the light for him,'

Morgan said to Bleck, making room for him.

Bleck easily slid under the truck. He held the flashlight, grimacing as he saw the blood on the floor boards and on Gypo's panic-stricken face.

Gypo cut the lead.

'That's it,' he said. 'Let me get out of here.'

As Bleck began to slide out from under the truck, he heard a sound that made the hairs on the nape of his neck bristle.

A sighing groan came through the floor boards, followed by a slight scratching sound. He flinched back, half expecting something to touch him.

'Santa Maria!' Gypo gasped. 'Let me out of here!'

He was in such a panic that he started to kick Bleck, trying to get past him.

Snarling, Bleck thumped him in the ribs, making him gasp.

'Cut it out!'

He pulled himself from under the truck and stood up, straightening his coat.

'What's up?' Morgan demanded, seeing how white he was.

Gypo squirmed out, tearing his shirt on the truck as he did so. He stood up, his face ghastly; blood that had dripped down on him making a smear down his cheek and neck.

'He's alive!' he gasped. 'I heard him! He's moving!'

Morgan stiffened.

179

'He can't use the radio now and he can't scramble the lock. Those buttons must work from the battery—they must do! Come on, Gypo, get that shutter open. We've got to get at this guy!'

'Not me!' Gypo said, cringing away. 'He's got a gun, hasn't he? When I open the shutter, he'll kill me!'

Morgan hesitated. He looked out of the window again. They were slowing down at the intersection of the secondary road and the highway. As Kitson brought the Buick to a stop Morgan could see the highway ahead of them, crowded with fast-moving cars.

If that guy in there started to shoot, the shots would be heard.

This was a problem he didn't know how to solve.

Bleck said, 'Better wait, Frank. That highway is always lousy with cops. If there's any shooting . . .'

'Yeah. Okay, we'll wait.'

Gypo drew in a shuddering breath of relief and squatted down, taking out his handkerchief and wiping the blood off his neck and face.

Morgan went up to the truck and, putting his ear against the steel panel guarding the window, he listened. He couldn't hear anything. He remained like that for some moments, then he looked at Bleck.

'Nothing. Are you sure you heard him?'

'Yes, and he was moving.'

'Gypo!' Morgan swung around. 'Don't damn well sit there! Take a look at the back of the truck. The sooner you get working on it the quicker we'll get the dough!'

Gypo dragged himself upright and pushed past Morgan to the back of the truck.

The Buick was on the move again and, peering out of the window, Morgan saw cars overtaking them on the busy six-lane highway. He was relieved to see Kitson wasn't driving faster than thirty miles an hour. The caravan was riding easily over the even surface of the road.

Gypo examined the back of the truck and his heart sank. It was as he thought: this was an expert job. The door fitted so closely there was no hope of blowing it. In the centre of the door was a dial, similar to that fitted to any ordinary safe. By the dial was a tiny window, protected by armoured glass. Gypo could see a number through the glass. He knew if he revolved the dial, the number would change. To open the door he would have to find the exact combination of numbers, and this meant sensitive listening and still more sensitive and above all steady fingers.

'What's it look like?' Morgan asked, coming around to the back of the truck and standing at Gypo's side.

'It's tough all right,' Gypo said. 'To hit on the right combination will take time like I said.'

'Any chance of blowing the door?'

'No. Look at the stuff it's made of. That's not going to blow. Maybe I could cut into it if I had time.'

'Try for the combination,' Morgan said. 'We've got another forty minutes before we reach the caravan camp. Start now.'

Gypo stared at him as if he thought he had gone crazy.

'Now? How can I with all this movement and noise?' he said feverishly. 'I've got to listen. I can't hear a thing with all this traffic.'

Morgan made an impatient gesture, but controlled himself. The pain in his side was getting worse and it worried him. He knew it would be fatal to rush Gypo too soon. His mind moved to the driver in the truck. There were too many complications piling up, he thought as he squatted down on the floor. This job might prove even tougher than he had imagined.

He thumped the steel side of the truck with his clenched fist.

'There's a million bucks in here,' he said. 'Think of it! Just beyond this goddamn wall! A million bucks! Well, we're going to get it! If it's the last thing we do!'

Kitson had been too occupied in holding the Buick to the curves in the road while he was driving fast to the highway to have time to pay any attention to Ginny, but once he had nosed the Buick on to the highway and had the broad straight road under his wheels, he relaxed a little.

Ginny was leaning back, looking out at the faster traffic sweeping past them. She was still very pale, and she kept her hands between her knees to hide the fact that she was trembling.

Kitson kept thinking of the man in the truck. It horrified him to think they would have to get into the truck and get his body out. Had he managed to set off the radio signal? Were they driving straight into a police trap?

'If that guy started his radio signal,' he said, unable to keep this thought silent any longer, 'we could be driving into trouble.'

Ginny hunched her shoulders.

'There's nothing we can do about it.'

'No,' Kitson said, not comforted. 'Well, I'm glad I'm not travelling in the caravan. It must be pretty rugged in there.'

'Listen!' she said sharply.

Kitson felt his heart give a lurch as he heard in the far distance the faint sound of an approaching police siren.

The cars moving on the fast lane automatically switched over to the slower lane, clearing the way.

The noise of the siren grew louder. Then Kitson saw the first police car coming towards them. It was followed by four patrol cops on motor-cycles, then by two more police cars. They blasted their way through the traffic, travelling at well over eighty miles an hour.

Ginny and Kitson exchanged glances.

'I guess we got off that road just in time,' Kitson said huskily.

Ginny nodded.

They drove on. After a few miles they became aware that the steady flow of traffic was slowing down, and far ahead of them they could see a long line of cars coming to a crawl.

'Road block,' Kitson said, his heart beginning to pound. 'This could sink us.'

'Don't lose your nerve,' Ginny said.

The cars ahead of the Buick slowed to a crawl, then finally stopped.

There was a long wait, then they began to move again.

Slowly, Kitson crept the Buick behind the long line of cars, his hands clammy. He could see the road block ahead of him.

There were two police cars across the road, cutting the up traffic into a narrow stream. Six patrol officers stood by the cars. One of them leaned into each car as it came to a stop. He had a brief word with the driver, then waved him on.

Ginny said, 'I'll talk to him. Leave it to me.'

He looked quickly at her, marvelling at her nerve. He wondered what the three in the caravan were thinking. They couldn't see the road block and they must be wondering why they were scarcely moving. Again he was thankful he wasn't back there, and he hoped

Gypo wouldn't do something stupid.

Ten minutes later—minutes that stretched Kitson's nerves to breaking point—they drew up at the road block.

Ginny deliberately pulled her skirt above her knees, crossing her legs. She leaned out of the car window.

The patrol officer who came over to her looked from her face to her knees, and his leathery red face split into an appreciative grin. He didn't even look at Kitson.

'Where have you come from, miss?' he asked, leaning against the side of the Buick, staring at her, admiration in his eyes.

'From Dukas,' Ginny said. 'We're on our honeymoon. What's all the excitement about?'

'Did you see a Welling Armoured truck on the, road?' the officer asked. 'You couldn't have missed it if you had seen it. It has a big sign on the back.'

'Why, no,' Ginny said and, turning she said to Kitson, 'We didn't see any truck, did we, honey?'

Kitson shook his head. His heart was thumping so violently he was scared the cop would hear it.

'Have you lost it?' Ginny said and giggled.

The cop grinned, his eyes on her knees.

'Never mind. You get moving. Have a good honeymoon.' He looked at Kitson and winked. 'I bet you do. Move on, bud.'

Kitson sent the car forward and a moment

185

later they were through the road block and heading down the open road.

'Phew!' Kitson gasped, his hands grippin? the steering-wheel so tightly his knuckles turned white. 'The way you handled that guy!'

Ginny adjusted her skirt, covering her knees and she shrugged her shoulders impatiently.

'Give a man something to look at, and he's just another sucker,' she said. She opened her handbag and took out a pack of cigarettes. 'Do you want one?'

'I guess so.'

She lit the cigarette and gave it to him. There was a smear of lipstick on it, and it gave him an odd satisfaction to know her lips had touched the cigarette before his.

She lit another cigarette for herself.

For the next ten miles they drove in silence, then Ginny said, 'You take the first on your right. It's the road that leads to Fawn Lake.'

Kitson nodded. As he looked ahead, he caught sight of a hover-plane coming towards them, flying not more than three hundred feet above the road.

'Look at that!'

The hover-plane went over the Buick and the caravan with a violent swish of wind.

Ginny said, 'They've moved into action fast enough.'

She looked at her watch. The time was ten minutes after midday. Although only forty-five minutes had elapsed since they had stopped the truck, it seemed to her like a lifetime.

Morgan, Gypo and Bleck also heard the swish of wind from the hover-plane as it passed over them and Gypo cringed down. He knew instinctively the machine was looking for them.

While they had crawled through the road block, the three men had crouched on the floor. Morgan had his gun in his hand, determined to shoot it out with any cop who tried to get into the caravan.

They all relaxed as they felt the Buick pick up speed.

Morgan opened his coat and looked at the pad Ginny had put on his wound. It was saturated with blood and the wound was obviously bleeding again.

Anxious to ingratiate himself once more with Morgan, Bleck got to his feet. Stepping over Gypo's body, he went to one of the bunks and took out the first-aid kit that Morgan had insisted on taking along with them.

'I'll fix it for you, Frank,' he said.

Morgan was feeling faint. He was alarmed at the amount of blood he had lost. He nodded, bracing himself against the side of the caravan.

Gypo stared at him with horror, thinking: If Frank goes, what are we going to do? There's no one like him for handling a tough situation. We'll be sunk if he dies.

Bleck squatted down beside Morgan and

187

got to work. After some minutes he got a pad on that stopped the bleeding.

'You'll be okay now,' he said and rubbed the back of his hand across his mouth. 'How about a drink?'

'Go ahead,' Morgan said bitterly. 'You have every reason to celebrate.'

Bleck made three stiff whiskies and handed the glasses around.

As they were drinking, they felt the Buick swing off the highway and immediately the caravan began to bump and sway as its two wheels bounced over the surface of the dirt road.

The three men hastily finished their drinks. Morgan's mouth drew down into a hard line of pain as he was jerked about on the floor of the caravan.

After a while the Buick slowed down, then finally stopped. There was a pause, then the back of the caravan swung up, and Ginny and Kitson looked in.

'All right?' Kitson asked anxiously. He was shocked to see how white Morgan was.

Morgan looked beyond Kitson and saw they had pulled off the road and were in the shadow of a fir forest. The road, about thirty feet away, was deserted. It twisted uphill, leading, after a six-mile run, directly to Fawn Lake.

Overhead, they could hear the drone of aircraft, a sound that warned Morgan of the danger of remaining here.

'He's still alive,' he said to Kitson and jerked his thumb towards the truck. 'We've got to take him. This is as good a place as any. Shut the caravan and leave it to us. You take the wheel off the Buick as if you've got a flat. If you see a car coming, bang on the side of the caravan. Ginny, you sit by the edge of the road. Take the food basket. Act like you're preparing a picnic. Get moving.'

His face set, Bleck handed out the food basket.

Kitson looked shocked.

'What are you going to do with him?' he asked.

Morgan's mouth moved into a ruthless smile.

'What do you think? Shut the caravan and do what I say!'

'Wait!' Gypo said, his voice shrill. 'I'm getting out of here! I'm not having anything to do with this! This isn't my job! I'm here to open the truck . . .'

'Shut up!' Morgan snarled and his gun jumped into his hand, threatening Gypo. 'You're opening that goddamn shutter! You do what I say or I'll damn well kill you!'

The expression on his face terrified Gypo.

'You wouldn't do that to me, Frank!' His hands waved imploringly. 'Let me out of here!'

Morgan looked at Kitson.

'Do what I tell you! Shut the caravan and

work on that wheel!'

Pale and shaky, Kitson shut the back of the caravan. He was breathing hard and fast as he opened the trunk of the Buick and took out the jack.

Morgan was saying to Gypo in a flat, deadly voice, 'Listen, Gypo, from now on you start to earn your share of the loot. You've had it soft up to now, but from now on, it's going to be rugged, so make up your mind to it! Get that goddamn shutter open!'

His breath whistling through his nose, Gypo approached the shutter and stared at it.

Bleck watched him, his eyes flickering from Gypo to Morgan and back to Gypo again.

Gypo saw the shutter wasn't difficult. It didn't fit tightly: it wasn't in the same class as the door at the back of the truck.

Morgan was also quick to see that.

'Get a tyre lever and a hammer,' he said. 'We can bust this one.'

Gypo flinched. He was thinking of the moment when he had prised open the shutter.

'That guy in there will be waiting,' he said hoarsely. 'As soon as he sees me, he'll shoot me.'

'Get on with it!' Morgan snarled.

Gypo opened the tool cupboard, took a tyre lever and a hammer from one of the racks. His hands were shaking so badly he could scarcely hold the tools.

'Come on! Come on!' Morgan shouted

190

furiously. 'What's scaring you, you fat jelly?'

'If he shoots me, who'll open the truck?' Gypo panted, playing his trump card.

Morgan drew in a long, exasperated breath.

'Give me the tools, you creep!' he snarled. 'But I'll fix you and I'll fix your pal, Ed, too! If you two imagine you're going to get your full share, you've another think coming!'

Right at that moment Gypo would have gladly given up the whole of his share if he could have been transported from this horrifying caravan to his little shed he called his home. He backed away as Morgan snatched the tools out of his hand.

Holding the end of the tyre lever against the gap between the steel shutter and the window, he hammered it home. The lever sank between the frame and the shutter, forcing the shutter back slightly.

Morgan continued to hammer until he had driven four inches of the lever out of sight, then he dropped the hammer and looked at Bleck.

'You going to be yellow too?' he said.

Bleck pulled his .38 from his shoulder holster and moved up close to Morgan.

'When you are ready, I am,' he said, his face set, his eyes determined.

Morgan grinned crookedly at him.

'Trying to save your share?'

'Skip it, Frank. Go ahead. I'm ready to take him.'

As Morgan was about to throw his weight on the lever, there came three quick thumps on the side of the caravan that stopped him dead.

'Someone's coming,' he said. 'Hold it!'

Bleck moved to the window and peered through the curtain.

A car, towing a caravan, had stopped within a few yards of where Ginny was sitting by the side of the road. A middle-aged man whose jolly fat face was burned red by the sun, was getting out of the car. There was a woman and a young boy in the car, looking towards the Buick and the caravan.

Bleck heard the fat man say, 'Hey, miss, can I help? Looks like you've got a flat.'

Ginny smiled at him.

'It's all right, thank you. My husband can manage. Thanks all the same.'

'You're going up to Fawn Lake?' the man asked.

'That's right.'

'So are we. I was there last summer. Have you been there before?'

Ginny shook her head.

'No.'

'You'll like it. It's terrific, and they know how to treat you. My name's Fred Bradford. That's my wife, Millie and Fred junior, my kid. You got any kids?'

Ginny laughed.

Listening to this, Bleck marvelled that her

laugh sounded so natural.

'Well, no, not yet,' she said. 'We're on our honeymoon.'

Bradford smacked his thigh. His good-natured laugh grated on the ears of the listening men.

'Say! That's a good one! Hear that, Millie? They're on their honeymoon, and Bigmouth has to ask if they've got any kids.'

The woman in the car frowned disapprovingly.

'Come on, Fred,' she called sharply. 'You're embarrassing the lady.'

'Yes, I guess I am,' Bradford said, grinning. 'Excuse me, Mrs . . . er . . . did I get your name?'

'Harrison,' Ginny said. 'I'm sorry my husband is so busy.'

'Think nothing of it. Well, maybe we'll see more of you both,' Bradford said. 'Anyway, if we don't, a happy honeymoon.'

'Thanks,' Ginny said.

The man went back to his car, got in and waved; then he drove on up the road.

Morgan and Bleck exchanged uneasy glances.

'If this punk starts shooting,' Bleck said, 'they'll hear the shot.'

'It doesn't matter,' Morgan said, feeling too bad to care. 'They must hunt in these woods. They'll think it's some guy after game.' He took hold of the tyre lever. 'Come on! Let's take him!'

Kitson called through the window.

'What's going on?'

Morgan paused to lift the window an inch.

'Stay right where you are,' he said. 'Just warn us if anyone else comes. We're going to take him now.'

Kitson backed away, feeling suddenly sick.

Morgan shut the window and nodded at Bleck.

'Ready?'

'Yeah.'

As Morgan pulled down on the tyre lever, Gypo hid his face in his hands.

II

Dave Thomas, the driver of the truck, lay on the floor of the truck, suffering the agony of his shattered jaw with the stoic courage of the undefeated.

Morgan's bullet had passed through the lower part of his face, smashing the jaw bone and cutting a furrow across his tongue.

The pain and shock had caused him to go off in a long faint, and it was some time before he came to. He was immediately aware that he was bleeding badly.

He lay only half aware what had happened, and wondering how it was possible for the truck to be moving and yet no one driving it.

He didn't think he had very long to live. No one could lose the amount of blood he was losing and survive, but dying didn't frighten him. He was sure that if a miracle did happen and he did live, there wasn't much they could do about his injuries. He had no wish to go around looking like a freak and perhaps not being able to speak.

What held his concentrated interest was the jolting movement of the truck. He decided finally, and after some thought, that they must have got the truck into some kind of vehicle, and he thought this was a pretty smart move, but not smart enough. He had only to press down the switch on the radio set to send out a continuous signal that would home the police on to the truck, no matter how cleverly hidden it was.

This was something he felt he should do right away, but the radio set was immediately behind and above him and, to get at it, he would have to turn on his side and reach up with his arm above his head.

He knew if he moved over on his side, he would inflict pain on himself when, by lying still, the pain was at least bearable.

So he lay very still, his eyes closed, and he thought about the lean, wolfish face of the man who had shot him. He wondered who the man was. The girl in the sports car was also in it. The whole plan had been pretty smart. That smash had looked convincing, and he was glad

195

that Mike Dirkson, the guard, hadn't been stampeded and had called the Agency and had reported the smash, otherwise the Agency might think they had been taken for a pair of suckers. At least they had had the Agency's permission to investigate, not that that had done them any good then or now.

To think a kid as pretty as that girl, Thomas thought drowsily, could have got mixed up in such a desperate business.

She reminded him a little of Carrie, his thirteen-year-old daughter.

Carrie had the same coloured hair, but she wasn't anything like as pretty as this girl, although she might grow up to be a beauty. One never knew about those things: it was just a matter of luck.

His daughter had always admired him, calling him her hero. She was always telling him how brave he was to drive a truck full of money.

He thought: well, she wouldn't think I'm so damned brave now if she could see me lying here, and not doing anything about saving the truck just because I haven't the guts to turn over on my side. She certainly wouldn't think much of me now.

There were two things he could do to save the truck: one was to set the radio signal going and the other was to press the button to scramble the time lock.

The scrambler button was near the steering

wheel. To get at it, he would have to sit up and lean forward and what that movement would do to his shattered jaw made him sweat just to think of it.

Carrie would expect him to save the truck. His wife, Harriette, wouldn't. She would understand, but Carrie had standards, and he would no longer be a hero to her if he didn't try to save the truck. The Agency too would expect him to save the truck. If he did manage to make the effort, they might prove generous and take care of his wife and Carrie. You couldn't be sure what they would do, of course, but it was pretty certain if these thugs broke into the truck, the Agency would think he hadn't done his duty, and that might make a difference when it came to paying out a pension for Harriette: it might make a hell of a difference.

He thought: well, go on, be brave. The radio signal is the most important. Get that going first. All you have to do is to turn over on your side and reach up. The switch is just above your head. Push that down and, in half an hour or less, there'll be a flock of patrol cars on their way and you'll be a hero. Try it anyway. What's a little pain?

But it took him some minutes to screw up his courage to move, and when he finally did, the flash of pain was so intense that he fainted again, and he lay still, his hand beyond the clutch pedal.

The unexpected sound of hammering brought him to and he opened his eyes.

Facing him was the steel shutter covering the driver's window. He could see a slit of daylight now coming through the shutter. As he focused his eyes, he saw the end of a tyre lever being forced between the shutter and the window frame.

He thought: so they are coming to finish me. Well, that's okay by me, but I'll take one of them with me if they give me a chance. That's the least I can do. Mike wouldn't think much of me unless I hit back for him. I'd like to take two of them, but the way I'm placed I'll be lucky to get one.

Weakly, his hand groped for his gun which he hadn't a chance to draw when Morgan had shot him.

The gun was a .45 Colt automatic, and as it slid out of its holster, it felt very heavy: so heavy that Thomas nearly dropped it.

He made the effort, and got the gun down by his right side, the sight lifted and pointing at the window.

He thought: well, come on, you punk! I've got something for you that'll surprise you. Don't keep me waiting. I'm not going to live much longer, so hurry up!

He heard someone say sharply, 'Someone's coming! Hold it!'

There was a long pause. He felt his consciousness beginning to leave him, and it was only with a tremendous effort of will that he fought off the feeling of faintness.

He muttered under his breath: 'Hurry . . . hurry . . .' Then he heard a man say, 'If this punk starts shooting, they'll hear the shot.'

Another voice said, 'It doesn't matter. They must hunt in these woods. They'll imagine it's some guy after game. Come on! Let's take him!'

The gun in Thomas's hand was growing heavier, and he realized that he could no longer keep the sight on the window. He would have to wait until they opened the door. He would have a good chance for a body-shot then.

He heard the tyre lever creaking as someone on the other side of the shutter bent his weight on it, and he waited, pain making it difficult for him to breathe, but intent and as dangerous and as vicious as a cornered and wounded lion.

'Get another lever,' a voice said, 'and help me.'

Another lever end appeared through the opening. There was more creaking, then a sudden snapping noise and the shutter slid up.

Both Morgan and Bleck kept away from the open window.

They stood either side of the door of the cab and listened. They didn't hear anything and they looked at each other. 'Do you think he's foxing?' Bleck asked, breathing with difficulty.

'He could be,' Morgan said.

Still keeping out of sight, he slid his arm through the open window and groped for the door handle.

Thomas watched him, his eyes half shut, his finger tightening a little on the trigger of his gun, taking in the slack.

Morgan got the door open. It swung Bleck's way, preventing him from looking into the cab.

Morgan looked in quickly, ducked forward and immediately pulled back.

He had a brief glimpse of a man lying huddled on the floor of the cab, his eyes closed, his face the colour of wet clay. Morgan's breath hissed through his teeth.

'It's okay,' he said to Bleck. 'He's dead.'

Thomas thought: not quite, pal. You'll find that out in a moment. Nearly dead, but not quite.

He forced his will to lift his gun hand and he felt the gun, like a ton weight, move slightly as Morgan moved into the open doorway of the truck.

Morgan's gun was pointing at Thomas, but this was merely a precautionary measure. He was quite satisfied that Thomas was dead. No one with that ghastly smashed face and that colour could possibly be alive.

'We'd better get him out of here and bury him,' he said and looked at Bleck, who was leaning forward staring through the window of

200

the door, the door pressed against him, looking at Thomas.

Thomas opened his eyes.

'Look out!' Bleck yelled and tried to get his gun up, but he was handicapped by the door pressing against him.

Thomas squeezed the trigger of his gun as Morgan shot him. The two guns went off simultaneously, sounding like one. Morgan's bullet hit Thomas in the throat, killing him instantly.

Thomas's bullet hit Morgan in the stomach, and he folded at the knees, falling into the cab, his face in Thomas's lap. Gypo gave a long, shuddering cry.

For a long moment Bleck remained frozen. Then he pushed the truck door against Morgan's legs and squeezed himself between the door and the side of the caravan.

He leaned into the cab, pulling Morgan over on to his back.

Morgan looked at him, his eyes glazed.

'It didn't work out,' he muttered, his voice so low Bleck could scarcely hear him. 'Good luck, Ed. You'll need it. You'll all need it . . .'

Bleck straightened. He found himself thinking that if they ever did succeed in breaking into the truck, they would each have two hundred and fifty thousand dollars now, since, instead of five, there were only four left to share the loot.

CHAPTER EIGHT

I

The cabin consisted of a bedroom, a sitting room, a tiny kitchen and a shower cabinet.

It was pleasantly furnished with twin beds in the bedroom, and two lounging chairs and settee in the sitting room. With a little improvisation, it was possible to sleep four there.

It had the advantage of being the most isolated cabin along the lake. It was the honeymoon cabin, the man in charge told Ginny with a knowing smile. They were lucky he could offer it. The last couple who had had it only moved out last night.

The man—his name was Hadfield—had got into the Buick with Ginny and Kitson and had directed them to the cabin.

From time to time he glanced at Kitson, wondering why he looked so tense and why he scarcely spoke a word. He thought the guy was probably nervous, facing his first night as a husband, although why any man should feel nervous with a girl as pretty as this one, Hadfield couldn't understand.

The girl was nervous too, but that was to be expected. All nice girls, Hadfield thought sentimentally, were nervous on their

202

honeymoon and he couldn't do enough for her. He showed her where she could park the caravan, right beside the cabin, and pointed out the boat house where they could hire a boat if they wanted one. He said they wouldn't be disturbed.

'Folks here are pretty sociable, Mrs. Harrison,' he told her after he had unlocked the cabin and had shown her where everything was kept. 'They drop in on each other, but I guess you two would like a little privacy, anyway for a day or two,' and he winked at Kitson, who stared stonily at him. 'I'll pass the word around. You won't be bothered until you are good and ready.'

There had been nothing the four of them could do until dark. That had been the worst period of this eventful day for them. Ginny had gone into the bedroom and had lain down on the bed. After a while she had dropped off into a sleep of exhaustion. Kitson had remained on guard, smoking and keeping an eye on the caravan. Bleck and Gypo had been forced to remain in the caravan with the dead bodies of Morgan and Thomas for company. It had been a bad period.

When it was dark, Bleck and Gypo had come into the cabin.

Gypo was in a bad way. He flopped into an armchair and hid his face in his hands. He had a big bruise on the side of his jaw where Bleck had hit him. There had been a time, when driving up to Fawn Lake, when Gypo had tried to break out of the caravan. He had started to yell and beat on the walls of the caravan. He had behaved as if he had gone off his head.

Bleck had had to hit him pretty hard. There was no other way of controlling him. When Gypo had come to, he had sat on the floor of the caravan, silent and limp. The eight long hours Bleck and he remained in the caravan, waiting for darkness with the windows shut tight to keep out the flies, had been an experience that neither of them was likely to forget.

Bleck and Kitson had gone into the dark wood to find a suitable place to bury Morgan and Thomas. Among the tools that Gypo had brought with him was a shovel, and finally, when they had found the spot, they took it in turns to dig.

They worked in silence and by the light of the moon. It was nervy work, because they could see boats out on the moonlit lake; they could hear voices in the distance, and once they had to crouch down, their hearts pounding, as a couple of lovers passed close to them.

It was after midnight before they patted the ground flat and carefully covered it with leaves and dead branches, and by that time, both of them were so exhausted they could scarcely get back to the cabin.

They found Ginny in an armchair, her .38 in

her lap while she watched Gypo, who had fallen asleep on the settee.

Bleck shut the door. Then he crossed over to the second armchair and dropped into it.

Kitson sat on an upright chair. His face was the colour of cold mutton fat and there was a muscle in his cheek that kept twitching.

'Any trouble?' Bleck asked Ginny.

The girl was pale and there were dark smudges under her eyes. She looked older and less attractive, but her voice was steady when she said, 'No, except he says he wants to go home.'

'As soon as he's opened the truck,' Bleck said, 'he can go to hell for all I care.'

At the sound of the voices, Gypo stirred and opened his eyes. He blinked around, then seeing the three watching him, he swung his legs off the settee and sat up, his face tightening, his hands beginning to shake.

'Ed . . . I'm going to quit,' he said, the words spilling out of his mouth. 'You can have my share of the money. I've been thinking about it. I don't want to have anything more to do with this job. I want you to have my share and let me go. If it hadn't been for Frank, I wouldn't have touched the job. He persuaded me. You three carry on if you want to, but I'm going back to the workshop.'

Bleck studied him.

'I don't think you are.'

Gypo rubbed his hands on his knees, sweat

making his fat face glisten in the shaded light.

'Now, look, Ed, be reasonable. I'm giving you my share. That's a lot of money. I just want to go home.'

'I don't think you're going,' Bleck said in the same flat voice.

Gypo looked imploringly at Kitson.

'Listen, kid, this job's no good. We didn't want to do it. Frank talked us into it. Let's you and me go. These two can have all the money. You and me can work together. We can make a good living. You work with me in the workshop. We'll get along fine together . . . honestly, we will.'

'Skip it,' Bleck said softly. 'You're staying and you're opening the truck.'

Gypo shook his head.

'No, Ed, I've got to go. I haven't the nerve for this job. I'll tell you how to open the truck. You and the girl can do it, once you know how, but I'm not staying. There's five hundred thousand dollars extra for you and for her. I give you my share. The kid will give her his share. We'll go . . .'

Bleck looked at Kitson.

'Do you want to quit?' he asked.

Morgan's violent end had stunned Kitson, but he was now recovering. The nightmare business of burying the two bodies had stiffened his fibre rather than undermined it. He knew he had reached the point of no return. He had everything to gain now and

206

only his life to lose. Whether he wanted to or not, there was no question of quitting.

'No,' he said.

'Listen, kid, you don't know what you are saying,' Gypo said desperately. 'You've got to quit. You've got to come with me. It's no good thinking you're going to get away with this. It's better to quit now. You come with me.'

'I'm not quitting,' Kitson said, his eyes on Ginny.

Gypo drew in a shuddering breath.

'I am going,' he said. 'This is no good. Three men have died. No money is worth that. Frank said he was going to put the world in his pocket. Look what's happened to him. He's in a hole in the ground. Can't you see? Can't any of you see? It's no good.' He got to his feet. 'I'm going home.'

Bleck reached forward and took the .38 that was lying in Ginny's lap. He pointed the gun at Gypo.

'You're going to open the truck, Gypo. If you don't do it, I'll kill you and bury you out there in the wood.'

The final, cold note in his voice convinced Gypo that he meant what he said.

For a long moment Gypo stood there, staring at the gun, then slowly, with a gesture of hopeless despair, he sat down.

'Okay,' he said, his face sagging, 'you force me to stay, but I warn you nothing good will come of this . . . nothing.'

Bleck put the gun down.

'Have you quite finished sounding off?' he asked.

'I have nothing more to say,' Gypo said, hanging his head. 'I have warned you. Remember that. Nothing good will come of it.'

'Well, now,' Bleck said, looking at the other two, 'we've got that settled. We're now four. That means we each will have fifty thousand dollars more than we reckoned to have. We divide Frank's share between us. We go on with the plan. Kitson, you and Ginny, play out the honeymoon angle. Gypo and I work in the caravan. As soon as we get the money, we split up. All agree?'

The other two nodded.

'Okay.' Bleck got to his feet, crossed the room and removed the key from the lock. He put it in his pocket. 'Well, I've had all I want for tonight. I'm going to sleep.' He went over to Gypo and gave him a nudge. 'Take a chair, fatso. I reckon I'm entitled to the settee.' He sat on the settee as Gypo moved wearily to the armchair. As he kicked off his shoes, he said to Kitson, 'There's a second bed in the other room for you, bridegroom. Help yourself.'

Kitson was too exhausted to rise to the bait. He stretched out in the armchair.

Ginny went into the bedroom and shut the door. They heard the key turn.

'Tough luck, bridegroom,' Bleck sneered and turned off the light. 'Looks like she doesn't fancy you.'

'Oh, shut up!' Kitson growled.

II

Soon after seven o'clock the next morning, Ginny came into the sitting room and pulled the blinds, waking the three men.

Cursing, Bleck sat up abruptly, his hand groping for his gun.

Stupefied with sleep, Kitson raised his head and blinked at Ginny, as she walked into the kitchen.

Gypo, groaning with stiffness, leaned forward to nurse his sore jaw.

Ginny called, 'It's time you got under cover. There are people already on the lake.'

Bleck grunted and, getting up, he went into the bathroom. He came out ten minutes later, shaved and showered.

'Go ahead and clean up,' he said to Gypo. 'You begin to smell like a pole-cat.'

Gypo looked dolefully at him and then went into the bathroom.

By the time he had taken a shower, Ginny had carried a breakfast tray of coffee, eggs, ham and orange juice into the sitting room.

'You'd better have it in the caravan,' she said, thrusting the tray into Bleck's hands.

An ugly gleam showed in his eyes.

'Look, baby, I'm giving the orders around

209

here now,' he said, taking the tray. 'I'm in charge of this outfit.'

Her eyes showed contemptuous amusement.

'Nobody's in charge,' she said. 'Even Morgan wasn't. We work according to the plan. It was agreed you and Gypo should only come into the cabin at night, and you were to keep out of sight during the day. If you don't want to stick to the plan, say so.'

'Okay, smartie,' Bleck said. 'So we eat in the caravan. Sounds like you're anxious to be alone with your boy-friend.'

Ginny turned and walked back into the kitchen.

'You lay off her,' Kitson said, getting to his feet.

'Aw, button up!' Bleck snarled, 'go out there and see if anyone's around, then open up the caravan.'

Kitson hesitated, then he went out into the sunshine. He looked to right and left, satisfied himself there was no one watching him, then he called to Bleck and opened the back of the caravan.

Bleck and Gypo got in.

'You're going to have it soft, plough boy,' Bleck said, his eyes glittering. 'You make hay while the sun shines.'

Kitson jerked the lever savagely, shutting the two men in the caravan, then he returned to the cabin.

Ginny was cooking more ham.

He went into the bathroom, took a shower, shaved, then put on a sweat shirt and a pair of cotton jeans.

As he came into the sitting room, Ginny was putting a plate of ham and eggs on the table.

'That looks good,' he said awkwardly. 'Is that for you or—or for me?'

'I don't eat breakfast,' she said curtly, and pouring a cup of coffee, she carried it to the armchair and sat down, her back half turned to him.

Kitson sat down. He found he was hungry, and he began to eat, thinking how well the ham was cooked and the eggs were just as he liked them.

'I guess we'd better get out after this,' he said. 'We might take a boat on the lake or something.'

'Yes.'

He was disappointed that she sounded so curt.

'It's going to be pretty rugged for those two in the caravan,' he said, hoping to get her talking. 'There's not much shade out there. By noon it's going to be hotter than a stove.'

'That's their look out,' she said indifferently.

'Yeah. Do you think Gypo will open the truck?'

She made an impatient movement.

'How should I know?'

'Well, if he doesn't, what are we going to do?'

'Why ask me? Ask Bleck if you can't work it out yourself.'

She got up abruptly, carrying her coffee cup and went into the kitchen.

Kitson felt his face burning. He suddenly didn't want to go on with his breakfast and, grimacing, he finished his coffee, stacked the plates and carried them into the kitchen.

'Look, I didn't mean to get on your nerves,' he said as he laid the things on the table. 'But we've got to be seen around together. Couldn't we be a little less unfriendly? After all . . .' he stopped, floundering.

'For God's sake, go into the other room and let me alone,' she said, her back turned to him; her voice was shaking.

Shocked by her tone, Kitson moved around so he could see her. It was then he realized how pale and drawn she looked. Maybe she wasn't as tough as she made out, he thought. This horrible business of yesterday could have given her a hell of a jolt, as it had him.

'Sure,' he said. 'Sorry,' and he went into the sitting room and sat down, running his fingers through his hair.

After a long moment of silence, he heard her crying. He didn't move. The soft, scarcely heard sound underlined to him the hopelessness of this job. If she could cry over it, there could be no hope.

He sat there waiting and smoking and trying not to listen for some minutes, then abruptly

212

she came out of the kitchen, and before he had a chance of seeing her face, she went into the bedroom.

Again there was a long pause, then she came to the doorway.

'Let's go,' she said curtly.

He glanced at her.

Her make-up was flawless. Only the unnatural glitter in her eyes and the studied way she held herself hinted that she was under a strain.

He got to his feet.

'We'd better get a newspaper,' he said, careful not to look directly at her.

'Yes.'

She walked across the sitting room to the door. She was wearing a light-weight sweater and a pair of bottle-green slacks. The combination showed off her neat, feminine figure as no other get-up could.

Kitson followed her into the sunshine.

As they stepped out of the cabin, the full heat of the morning sun struck them, and both looked across at the caravan that stood in the direct sunlight: both of them realized the heat that must be accumulating in the wooden structure.

They moved on, walking side by side, in silence.

There was a path through the woods that led to Hadfield's office. Next to his office was a grocer store. As they came out of the shadows and into view of the wooden building, Ginny slipped her hand into Kitson's. The feel of her cold flesh sent a tingle up his spine, and he looked quickly at her.

She gave him a ghost of a smile.

'Sorry about the scene,' she said. 'My nerves are bad. I'm all right now.'

'Sure,' he said. 'I know how you must be feeling,' and he tightened his grip on her hand.

Hadfield came out of his office and beamed on them as they came up to him.

'Well, Mr. Harrison,' he said and thrust out his hand. 'I guess you're a happy man. Don't tell me. I can see it on your face. Me . . . I guess if I were Mrs. Harrison's husband, I'd be as happy as you are.'

Ginny laughed as Kitson shook Hadfield's hand awkwardly.

'Why, thanks, Mr. Hadfield. That's a real compliment,' she said. 'We've come for the newspapers. Are there any?'

'Newspapers?' Hadfield lifted his bushy eyebrows. 'Honeymooners shouldn't want to be bothered about newspapers. Sure, I've got this morning's lot. I'll tell you straight away, the only news of interest is this truck robbery.' His good-humoured face split into a grin. 'Between you and me, I hand it to those fellows. They've walked off with a cool million bucks. Imagine! A million bucks in cash! No one knows where they've got to or how they did it, but that's what they've done. That truck

214

with a lock on it the best modern brains could think up, and stuffed with dollars, has just vanished into thin air! It's a knock-out! Nothing like it has ever happened before.' He pushed his hat to the back of his head, grinning at them. 'When I read the account in the papers, I said to myself, that's the smartest thing that's ever happened around these parts for as long as I can remember. Vanished! Imagine! A truck that size with all the police and half the Army searching every road within a hundred miles of here, and still no sign of it.'

He went into his office to get the papers.

Ginny and Kitson exchanged glances.

There was a pause, then Hadfield came out with four newspapers in his hand.

'Maybe you don't want them all,' he said. 'If you want the latest news take the *Herald.*'

'I'll take them all,' Kitson said in a strangled voice. 'What have we got to lose?'

He paid Hadfield for the papers and took them from him.

'You quite happy where you are, Mrs. Harrison?' Hadfield asked. 'Nothing I can do for you?'

'We're fine, thanks,' Ginny said. 'There's nothing.'

While Kitson scanned the headlines, Ginny went into the store.

The front pages of all the newspapers concentrated on the truck robbery. There were pictures of the truck and the guard and the driver. The Army headquarters were offering a thousand-dollar reward for any information that would lead to the finding of the truck.

There was a hint from the police that the driver of the truck might be one of the members of the gang, since there was no trace of him.

While Kitson read, his mouth a little dry, Fred Bradford, the man who had offered help on the road up to Fawn Lake the previous day, came up to get his newspaper.

'Hello there, Mr. Harrison,' he said. 'I see you've got your papers. Well, how do you like it here? Pretty good, huh?'

Kitson nodded.

'It sure is.'

'You reading about this truck robbery? I got it on the radio this morning. They seem to think the truck must be hidden in the woods around here. They're organizing search parties. Every road is being checked from the air, and yet there's still no sign of it.'

'Yeah,' Kitson said, folding the newspapers.

'It slays me to think they could have kept it hidden even as long as this with so many guys hunting for it. Looks like the driver's one of them, doesn't it? That poor guard—what's his name? Dirkson. Well, I reckon they should look after his widow.'

Hadfield, listening, said, 'That smash was a fake so they say. It means a woman is working with the gang. The guard radioed back to the

Agency just before he was killed. They're checking on this guy Thomas, the driver, now to see if there was a woman in his life besides his wife.'

'Well, I wouldn't mind having the reward,' Bradford said. 'My kid says he's going to take a walk through the woods. He kids himself he'll find the truck.' He laughed. 'It'll get him out of the way for a while. I've never known such a restless kid. He drives my good lady nuts.'

Hadfield shook his head.

'They wouldn't bring the truck here,' he said. 'There are too many people using these woods. I reckon if they've hidden it anywhere, it'll be up at Fox Wood. Very few people get up there, and it's well off the beaten track.'

'Yeah, but don't tell my kid that,' Bradford said. 'That's too far for him to go wandering off.'

Ginny came out of the store, carrying a sack of groceries.

'Morning, Mrs. Harrison,' Bradford said, lifting his hat. 'So you got here all right?'

'We got here,' Ginny said smiling. She handed the sack to Kitson, then linked her arm through his, leaning against him, smiling at the two men who looked approvingly at her.

'That's the idea,' Hadfield said. 'Make use of your man, now you've got him. My wife says all a man is fit for is to carry parcels.'

Ginny looked up at Kitson.

'I think you're fit for many more things than

carrying parcels, honey,' she said.

As Kitson flushed, the two men laughed.

'That's what I like to hear,' Hadfield said. 'I'd like my good lady to hear that.'

'Can we take a boat out, Mr. Hadfield?' Ginny asked.

'Why, sure. Just the right time now before it gets too hot. You know where the boat house is? You see Joe there. He'll fix it for you.'

'Well, then I guess we'll get along,' Ginny said.

Bradford said, 'Any time you feel like a little company, Mr. Harrison, we're at cabin 20; about a quarter of a mile from yours. Be glad to see you.'

Hadfield dug his elbow into Bradford's ribs.

'They're on their honeymoon,' he said. 'Whose company do you imagine they want except their own?'

Laughing, Ginny tugged at Kitson's arm, and they moved off down the path, arm-in-arm, her head against his shoulder.

The two men looked after them and then they glanced at each other a little ruefully.

'I guess that guy is lucky,' Hadfield said. 'What a pretty thing she is! Between you and me, I wouldn't mind changing places with him.'

Bradford grinned a little furtively.

'No comment,' he said, 'but I know just what you mean.'

When Kitson and Ginny got back to the

cabin, Ginny left the sack of groceries in the kitchen while Kitson, after making sure no one was around, tapped on the caravan window.

Red faced and sweating, Bleck pushed up the window.

'What is it?' he snarled. 'Is it hot in here! The goddamn flies are driving us crazy! We can't even leave this window open. What do you want?'

'Got the papers for you,' Kitson said and pushed the papers through the window. 'Anything you want?'

'No! Get the hell away from here!' Bleck snapped and slammed down the window.

He went around to the back of the truck where Gypo sat on a stool they had taken from the cabin, his ear pressed to the door of the truck, his fingers on the dial.

The heat in the caravan was insufferable, and Bleck had stripped off his coat and shirt; his hairy chest was running with sweat.

He watched Gypo for a few seconds, then shrugging, he sat on the floor and began to read the papers.

A half an hour later, he threw the papers aside, and got up to see how Gypo was getting on.

Gypo sat still, his face congested, his eyes closed, listening intently, his fingers just moving the dial.

'Sweet suffering Pete!' Bleck exploded. 'Do you reckon to do that for the next ten days?'

Gypo started and opened his eyes.

'Be quiet!' he said angrily. 'How can I work if you keep talking?'

'If I don't get some air soon I'll bust a gut,' Bleck said, wiping his face with the back of his hand. 'Look, can't we fix this curtain to keep the flies out and open the window?'

'You fix it,' Gypo said. 'If you want me to open this truck, leave me alone.'

Bleck glared at him, then he went to the tool cupboard and took out a box of thumb tacks and a hammer. He nailed the curtain tightly to the window frame, then raised the window through the curtain.

He looked out on to the stretch of lake, seeing Ginny and Kitson embarking in a rowing boat. A spurt of jealous anger ran through him as Kitson rowed the boat away from the landing stage.

'That bum's got it easy!' he burst out. 'I should have had that job! There he goes . . .'

Gypo put his head around the side of the truck.

'Will you pipe down!' he said shrilly. 'How can I work . . . ?'

'Okay, okay, okay,' Bleck snarled. 'Quit yelling at me!'

Gypo wiped his aching fingers on the seat of his trousers and stared at the dial. So far he hadn't heard one tumbler fall into place. He could sit there, he thought despairingly, turning the dial for days without getting anywhere: maybe he'd never get anywhere.

'I've got to take a rest. I haven't any more feeling in my hand.'

He came and stood by the open window, drawing in deep breaths of the fresh air that was now beginning to circulate in the caravan.

'Isn't there any other way of opening it?' Bleck demanded, his eyes still on the boat that was now moving through the water quickly under Kitson's powerful strokes.

'I told Frank it would be tough,' Gypo said. 'Maybe I'll never open it.'

'Yeah?' Bleck stared at him. 'You'd better open it, Gypo. You hear me? You'd better open it.'

The menacing gleam in his eyes made Gypo flinch.

'I can't work miracles,' he muttered. 'Maybe no one can open it.'

'You'd better work a miracle,' Bleck said savagely. 'Go on! Get going! The longer you work at it, the quicker you'll be! Get going!'

Gypo went back to the dial, sat down, pressed his ear to the door and began once more to move the dial, listening for a tumbler to fall.

By dusk, Gypo was exhausted. He sat on the stool, leaning against the door, making no attempt to move the dial.

Seeing the distress on his face and how haggard he looked, Bleck let him alone.

Gypo had had only an hour's break in

twelve long, hot hours. He had succeeded in dropping one of the tumblers, and he guessed he had at least another five to find. But he had made a start, and Bleck was feeling more optimistic. Maybe Gypo would find two of the tumblers tomorrow. Maybe they would have the door open by the end of the week.

When it was dark enough, Kitson let them out and they hurried over to the cabin.

Ginny had prepared a meal of pork tenderloins with sweet potatoes and she had baked an apple pie.

The men ate hungrily. Every now and then Bleck shot a scowling glance at Kitson. It infuriated him to see Kitson's face was sunburned, underlining the fact that he had been out in the open all day.

Gypo brightened when he saw what was on his plate, and he ate with gusto. Towards the end of the meal, his fat face lost its look of fatigue and resigned hopelessness.

The meal over, Bleck moved to an armchair, lit a cigarette and looked at the other three.

'Well, we've made some progress today,' he said. 'From now on one of us has to stay with the caravan every night. We can't take the risk of someone seeing the caravan and taking a look through the window or trying to break in. This'll be your job, Kitson. You're having it pretty soft during the day. You can have it a little rough during the night.'

Kitson shrugged. He didn't care.

This day had been a good one for him. Ginny had shown signs of relaxing with him. Although they had kept to impersonal topics she seemed ready to talk to him and she was much less hard. He had rowed her around the lake during the morning and had taken her swimming during the afternoon.

Whenever they met anyone, she always slipped her arm through his, and this pleased him.

During the afternoon when they had been lying side by side in the sun, after a swim, he in trunks and she in a one-piece white costume, she had suddenly moved over to him and had rested her face against his shoulder, her arm across his chest, and for a moment he had thought he had succeeded in breaking down her final reserve only to realize that two other people had come down on to the beach and seeing them lying like that had moved away, leaving them on their own.

He had been careful not to move, hoping she would remain like that, but of course she hadn't. As soon as the two had gone, she lifted her head and looked at him.

'Sorry,' she said. 'I didn't mean to embarrass you.'

'You didn't,' Kitson said. 'I liked it.'

She laughed, sitting up.

'I dare say you did. I'm going to have another swim,' and jumping to her feet, she ran down to the lake side.

Kitson remained where he was, watching her.

Yes, she was relaxing with him all right. He felt then for the first time that he might have a chance with her.

He realized this request of Bleck's for him to guard the caravan at night was a reasonable one. Anyone snooping around in the dark and taking it into his head to break into the caravan could blow their whole plan sky high.

'Okay,' he said, pushing back his chair, 'I'll get out there now.'

Expecting opposition and surprised, Bleck watched him leave. When the door shut behind him, Bleck said, 'Suppose Gypo and me have the beds, baby, and you use the settee? We are the ones doing the work and we need our sleep. That okay with you?'

Ginny shrugged indifferently.

'Oh, sure.'

Bleck stared at her.

'Unless maybe Gypo takes the settee.'

Ginny looked up sharply.

'I'll take the settee, thank you,' she said curtly.

Bleck grinned.

'Suit yourself.' He got up and took a deck of cards from the overmantel and began to shuffle the cards. 'Want a game of gin?'

'No,' Ginny said. 'I'm going for a walk. I'd like this room when I get back.'

Sensing what was in the air, Gypo watched and listened uneasily.

'Sure,' Bleck said, still grinning. 'Hey, Gypo, let's you and me go into the bedroom. We can use the bed for a table.'

Gypo got up and went into the bedroom.

'It's all yours, baby,' Bleck said. 'How did you enjoy your day with the plough boy? Fallen for him yet?'

Ginny leaned back in her chair, her eyes contemptuous.

'Is that what I'm supposed to do?'

'Well, you never know. I suppose there must be a few girls who would fall for him. He's fallen for you.'

She got up and walked over to the cabin door.

Bleck eyed her.

'You and me, baby, could make a team. Why not think about it?' he said as she opened the door.

'Oh, drop dead,' she said without even bothering to look at him. She went out into the darkness and closed the door after her.

An ugly gleam in his eyes, Bleck hesitated. He wanted to go after her and teach her she couldn't talk that way to him, but he knew Kitson would come out of the caravan, and he wasn't ready yet for a show down with him.

Shrugging angrily, he went into the bedroom where Gypo was sitting on the bed, nervously clenching and unclenching his

225

hands.

'Look, Ed,' he said, 'lay off the girl. We've got enough trouble without having woman trouble as well.'

'Aw, shut up!' Bleck snarled, and sitting on the bed, he began to deal the cards.

Around eleven o'clock, they heard Ginny come in, and after a few minutes, the shower running.

Bleck crushed out his cigarette and scooped up the cards on the bed.

'We'll hit the sack,' he said. 'We should be out in that box before light.'

Gypo was ready enough for bed, and within ten minutes, the light out, he began to snore.

Bleck lay staring into the darkness, listening. He could hear Ginny moving about in the sitting room, then after a few minutes he heard the light switch click off.

Bleck believed in direct methods when dealing with women. The gradual approach was in his opinion a waste of time.

He threw aside the sheet, slid silently out of bed, and went to the bedroom door. He paused to satisfy himself that Gypo was heavily asleep, then he turned the door handle gently, stepped into the dark sitting room, then closed the bedroom door behind him.

Almost immediately the light went on, and Ginny half sat up. She was wearing pale blue pyjamas and she looked very desirable to Bleck, who grinned at her as he walked across the room and paused by the side of the settee, looking down at her.

'I thought I'd keep you company, baby,' he said. 'Move over.'

Ginny remained motionless, her sea-green eyes completely expressionless.

'Get out!' she said softly.

'Come on, honey,' Bleck said and sat on the edge of the settee. 'Don't be that way. I've got plans for you and me. When this job's over and we've got the dough, we'll go places together. I'll take you to London and Paris. You'd like that, wouldn't you?'

'I said get out!' the girl repeated, and it angered Bleck that she seemed so calm and unafraid.

'Maybe I can persuade you,' he said and his hands closed over her shoulders, and then he felt something hard dig into his chest.

He looked down quickly and his heart skipped a beat as he saw the .38 automatic pressing into him.

'Take your hands off me slowly,' Ginny said and there was a steely quality in her voice that scared Bleck. 'Slowly or I'll kill you.'

Slowly and cautiously, his mouth dry, Bleck took his hands off her shoulders and lifted them. He had a horrible feeling as he looked into her eyes that he was only a heart beat away from death.

'Now get up,' she went on. 'Slowly; keep your hands like that.'

Slowly, he got up and backed away.

'Get out of here!' she said, the gun sight steady and pointing at his chest. 'The next time you try that little act, I'll kill you. Now get back into your room and stay in there.'

Bleck drew in a long, deep breath.

'Okay, baby,' he said. 'Watch out! I'll fix you for this! Make no mistake about that!'

'Run away, you cheap masher,' Ginny said.

Bleck went into the bedroom and shut the door. He was shaking with rage.

If she imagined, after this, she was going to get her share of the money when the pay-off came, she was mistaken, he thought as he got into his bed.

He'd fix her! He'd teach her to throw a gun on him! She and that bum Kitson! He'd fix them both!

When they got the money from the truck, he'd put a slug through Kitson's head, and as for her—well, that depended. He suddenly grinned viciously in the darkness.

Seven hundred and fifty thousand bucks was a lot better than two hundred and fifty thousand.

He lay for a long time in the darkness, planning what he would do with the money.

Maybe, he decided suddenly, it might be an idea to get rid of Gypo too—to make a clean sweep of them all.

A million was better than seven hundred and fifty thousand.

Talk about the world in your pocket!
With a million in cash, a man was a king!

CHAPTER NINE

I

The next two days followed the same pattern. At dawn, Bleck and Gypo went into the caravan, and Kitson came back to the cabin.

After a few hours sleep, Kitson then went out with Ginny and spent the day with her, swimming and walking or going on the lake.

Bleck sat on the floor of the caravan reading the papers while Gypo toiled at the truck door.

The news as reported in the papers was encouraging. The police and the Army were plainly baffled. Although the search was being continued, there was now a note of helplessness in the police statements to the press. They had finally decided that the truck must have been driven away in another vehicle. There could be no other solution as to how it had vanished so completely. It was thought by now the truck was out of the State. The search had been extended to a five hundred mile radius, and the reward had been raised to five thousand dollars.

Two hundred soldiers and police were combing Fox Wood, and hover planes were still patrolling the roads.

Sooner or later, Army headquarters announced, the truck must be found. It was a physical impossibility for it to vanish the way it had and stay vanished!

If the police and the Army were having their troubles, so too were Bleck and Gypo.

The result of Gypo's two days work had come to nothing.

He had sat on his stool in the broiling heat of the caravan all day, moving the dial, listening, sweating, cursing and listening again, but the second tumbler had refused to fall into place.

With nothing to do but to watch Gypo and read the newspapers, Bleck's nerves by now were crawling out of his skin. Added to the insufferable heat in the caravan and the tension of expecting to hear from Gypo at any second that the second tumbler had dropped, he also had the maddening thought that Ginny and Kitson were out in the open air, enjoying themselves.

Surely even though Kitson was a punch-drunk bum, Bleck argued to himself, he must by now be making an impression on the girl. No man, going around with a woman for three solid days, could fail to make an impression. If he—Bleck—had Ginny on his own for twelve hours, she would have surrendered to his technique by now. So the thought of them alone together added the bite of jealous acid to his already frayed nerves.

Around six o'clock on the third day as the evening sun dropped behind the mountains, shedding an orange-red light over the lake, Gypo cracked.

For three days he had slaved at this lock in almost impossible conditions, and now he felt he was completely defeated.

The second tumbler had refused to fall. He had moved the dial a hair breadth by a hair breadth over the whole circuit, and still it hadn't fallen. It meant he was moving the dial just that much more than it should be moved. It meant that the hand he was so proud of wasn't sensitive enough to control the knob on the dial.

'I can't do it!' he suddenly moaned, slumping against the door of the truck. 'I can't do it, Ed! It's no use! If I try for twenty years, I won't do it! If I don't get out of here I'll go crazy!'

Alarmed by the hysterical note in Gypo's voice, Bleck jumped to his feet and came around the truck, gun in hand.

'Shut up!' he snarled, ramming the gun into Gypo's ribs. 'You're damn well going to open that truck or I'll kill you!'

Gypo began to cry helplessly, his fat body trembling with exhaustion.

'Go ahead,' he gasped. 'Kill me! Do you think I care? I'd rather be dead than work any more on this sonofabitch! Go ahead and kill me! I can't stand any more of it!'

Bleck hit Gypo savagely across his face with the barrel of the gun. Gypo flinched away, blood running from a cut in his fat cheek down his face into his collar. He sagged against the side of the truck, his eyes shut.

'Go ahead!' he cried, his voice shrill and as hysterical as a frightened woman's. 'Kill me! I can't go on! I'm through!'

'Pull yourself together, you creep!' Bleck shouted, alarmed to see how bad Gypo was looking, and thinking if he was going to get out of control, the whole plan would blow up in their faces.

'I tell you I can't do it!' Gypo wailed and collapsed on the stool, hiding his face in his hands.

At that moment there came a gentle tap on the door of the caravan: a sound that made Bleck stiffen and his heart skip a beat.

He had seen Ginny and Kitson go off in the Buick for a shopping trip to town so he knew it couldn't be either of them knocking on the door.

As Gypo started to moan, Bleck grabbed him and shook him, whispering fiercely, 'Shut up! There's someone outside!'

Gypo stiffened and stopped his noise.

The two men waited, listening.

The knock came again.

Bleck signalled to Gypo to remain where he was. His gun in his hand, he crept to the curtained window. Keeping to one side, he peered forward to look through the curtain.

At the door of the caravan was a small boy of about ten, knocking and frowning and staring up at the caravan. In his hand, he held a toy pistol which he pointed at the door.

Bleck watched him, his lips drawn off his teeth in a snarl.

The boy, clad in jeans and a white and red checkered shirt, his feet bare, a battered straw hat on the back of his head, stared curiously at the door of the caravan, his sunburned face puzzled.

There was a long pause as the boy continued to stare at the caravan, then, as if making up his mind, he moved forward and hooked his fingers on the window-sill, preparing to hoist himself up to peer through the window.

Gypo, seeing the sudden murderous, frightened expression on Bleck's face, got up off the stool and joined Bleck at the window. He caught his breath sharply when he saw the boy, and his hand clamped down on Bleck's wrist.

'No!' Gypo hissed. 'Not a kid! Are you crazy?'

Bleck wrenched his wrist free, relaxing as he saw the boy hadn't the strength to pull himself up as far as the window. The boy dropped back, and again stared up at the caravan, his expression frustrated.

After staring at the caravan for some moments, he turned abruptly and hurried off down the path that ran along by the lake side.

'Do you think he heard us?' Bleck asked anxiously.

'I don't know,' Gypo said. The shock of the boy's unexpected appearance had brought him abruptly to his senses.

'He certainly scared me,' Bleck said and wiped his face with his hand. 'Here, you sit down, Gypo, and take it easy. Suppose I try to fix this goddamn lock?'

'You?' Gypo's face wrinkled in disgust. 'No! You could dislodge the first tumbler if you don't have the feel of it. Keep away from it!'

Bleck reached out and took hold of Gypo's shirt front, giving him a hard shake.

'So if I don't do it and you damn well won't do it, how do we open it?' he demanded, his voice thick with rage.

'Don't you understand?' Gypo said. 'We're not going to open it! For three days I've worked on it! Hour after hour after hour! What happens? One tumbler falls, then nothing. That lock has at least six tumblers. I've got five more to find. Okay, maybe in a week I'll find the second one; maybe I won't. If I find it, I've got four more to find. By that time I'll be crazy in the head! No one can work in this heat! No one! I'm quitting! I can't do any more! I've had enough! No money is worth this! You hear me? No money can be worth this!'

'Aw, shut up!' Bleck shouted violently. 'Don't start that again!'

But he was worried. He realized that Gypo was talking sense. The thought of being cooped up in this oven of a caravan for another three or four weeks appalled even him.

Gypo had slumped down on the stool again, holding his hand to his aching face as he stared hopelessly at the dial.

'Could you cut the door open?' Bleck asked.

'Here? Impossible! People would see the flame through the curtain. Then think of the heat! The caravan would catch fire.'

'Suppose we take the caravan up into the mountains? Frank said we might have to do that, and it looks to me that's what we'll have to do,' Bleck said. 'Then you can work with the back of the caravan open. It would be okay like that, wouldn't it?'

Gypo took out his handkerchief and dabbed at his bleeding cheek.

'I've had enough. I want to go home. No one's going to open that sonofabitch—no one!'

'We'll talk to the other two,' Bleck said, a rasp in his voice. 'Where are your guts? There's a million bucks behind that door! A million bucks! Think of it!'

'I wouldn't care if there were twenty million,' Gypo said, his voice shaking. 'I've had enough, I tell you! Can't you understand

English?'

'Relax, will you?' Bleck said, sitting on the floor. 'We'll talk to the other two.'

Unaware of Gypo's crack up, Ginny and Kitson were returning from town, some fifteen miles from the caravan camp, after an afternoon's shopping.

They had decided it would be unsafe to shop any more at the store on the camp. The storekeeper was certain to notice the amount of food they were buying and would know it couldn't have been for two people, so now they did a daily run into town.

During the past two days, Ginny and Kitson had been constantly in each other's company.

Ginny was still trying to make up her mind whether to join up with Kitson when they got the money. She knew he was in love with her and she found that she was growing to like him. Unlike Bleck, there was nothing dangerous about him and she felt safe with him.

As they drove along the highway, heading back to the caravan camp, she kept glancing at him.

Apart from his broken nose, he was quite handsome, she thought, and she had a sudden urge to confide in him.

'Alex . . .'

Kitson glanced at her and then back to the road. When he had her by his side, he was a very careful driver.

'Yeah? Something bothering you?'

'Well, yes.' She lifted her copper-coloured hair off her shoulders and then let it drop back into place. 'You asked me once how I knew about the truck and the payroll. Do you still want to know?'

Kitson was surprised.

'Well, I've wondered, but it's no business of mine,' he said. 'What made you think of that?'

'You've been pretty nice to me,' Ginny said. 'Most men in your place would have been troublesome. I appreciate it. I want you to know I'm not a gangster's moll.'

Kitson shook his head.

'I never thought that.'

'Morgan did. He thought I had stolen the plan from a mob I had been working with and brought it to him for a bigger share. He didn't say so, but I knew that's what he thought.'

Kitson shifted uncomfortably. He knew that was exactly what Frank had thought.

'Well, maybe. I didn't.'

'I knew about the pay roll and the truck because my father was the gate man at the Research Station,' Ginny said quietly.

'He was?' Kitson gave her a quick look. 'Yeah, so you would know about it.'

'I'm not trying to whitewash myself,' Ginny said, leaning her head back against the seat. 'My mother was no good. I guess I have a lot of her badness in me. She left my father when I was ten. She was always talking about money,

237

telling me without it, I'd never do anything. My father was a good man, but he didn't earn much. He was good to me, but that didn't stop me having an itch for money. As I grew up, the itch got worse. It tormented me. I never had any decent clothes. I seldom went to the movies. I used to spend all my time staring into the windows of the luxury shops, envying people who could buy what I saw there and what I wanted. My father often talked about the payroll, and I often dreamed of having all that money. Then the new truck arrived. My father thought they were crazy not to insure the pay roll any longer. He said it wouldn't be so hard to hi-jack the truck. He and I used to discuss it. It was his idea to hide the truck in a caravan. Don't imagine he ever thought of doing such a thing. There was nothing like that about him, but it made me think and the idea of grabbing that truck became an obsession with me.'

Kitson was driving slowly now and listening. He watched the sun, like a red ball of fire, dip behind the mountains.

'My father was a sick man,' Ginny went on, lacing her fingers over one knee. 'He had two years to go before he got his pension, and he tried to hang on, but in the end he had to quit. They gave him time off, but when he wasn't well enough to come back when they thought he should, they sacked him, and away went his pension. I went to see the staff manager to explain, but he wouldn't listen to me. He treated me as if I were a beggar. So, when my father died, I decided I would get even. I would be killing two birds with one stone: I'd settle the score and I'd become rich. I had the plan all worked out in my mind and I had to find someone to help me. I was in a café one night, and I overheard some men talking about Morgan. From what they said, I decided he was the one to go to. So I went to him. That's the story. It was my father's plan, but he would never have used it.'

'I'm sorry for your father,' Kitson said.

'Yes.' He saw her hands suddenly turn into fists. 'I'm sorry I ever started this, Alex. I know I'm hard and bad and money loving. I know all that, but I didn't think it was going to be like this. It's so easy to talk about killing a man. You see it on the movies and it doesn't seem anything, but when it really happens . . .'

'Look, Ginny,' Kitson's voice was suddenly urgent. 'Why don't you and me quit? We could go to Mexico. If we cleared out right now, we stand a chance of getting away with it. Why don't we do that?'

She hesitated, then shook her head.

'No! I'm not going to quit now. The time to have quitted was before we killed the guard and the driver and before Morgan died. I'm going through with this now, Alex. But you quit. I'd like to see you out of this, but I'm going through with it. We still have a chance of getting the money. What have I to lose now? But you quit, Alex. You should never have been in this anyway.' She looked at him. 'Why did you? You didn't want to. I could see that. Why did you vote for it?'

Kitson shrugged his shoulders.

'Because of you,' he said. 'You meant something to me from the moment I saw you.'

'I'm sorry, Alex. I'm really sorry.'

'Look, if we get the money, couldn't we join up together?' Kitson asked, staring hard at the road as it came towards him. 'I love you, Ginny. You're the only girl who has ever meant anything to me.'

'I don't know, Alex. Perhaps.' Let's wait until we get the money. I'm scared of complications. Will you let me think about it?'

Kitson nearly drove off the road, he was so surprised.

'You really mean there's a chance you might, Ginny?'

She patted his arm.

'Let me think about it, Alex.'

It was dark by the time they got back to the caravan camp.

Kitson, elated by the talk he had had with Ginny, dumped the groceries in the kitchen and then went across to the caravan.

The lake side was deserted. It was safe enough to let Bleck and Gypo out.

As he watched them come from the caravan he knew something was wrong.

Gypo walked slowly and heavily, his shoulders hunched. His right cheek was bruised and bleeding slightly.

When Kitson asked him what was the matter, he didn't reply, but entered the cabin and slumped down into an arm chair.

Bleck, his face bleak, an ugly glitter in his eyes, walked to the settee and then reached for the whisky bottle and poured himself a stiff drink. Then he sat down, scowling.

'There was a kid hanging around outside the caravan,' he said as Kitson shut the cabin door and locked it. 'He tried to look in.'

Sensing the atmosphere, Ginny asked, 'What about the lock?'

Bleck shrugged.

'No luck so far,' he said, leaning back and staring at her. 'The second tumbler shows no signs of falling. Gypo has got worked up about it.'

'Worked up!' Gypo exclaimed shrilly. 'I'm quitting! The lock has beaten me! Do you hear? I'm quitting!'

Ginny said quietly, 'But you can't quit. What's the matter?'

'Matter?' Gypo thumped his fists on his knees. 'No one can work in that caravan in that heat! You don't know what it is like! For three days I've tried to bust that lock. It's no good! Now I quit!'

'You told Frank it would take a month,' Ginny said. 'You can't quit after three days.'

241

'Leave him alone,' Bleck said. 'I've been over all this with the jerk until I'm sick of it. The heat in the caravan is sheer hell. We've got to go up to the mountains as Frank said so we can work with the back of the caravan open. We can't go on boxed in; we just can't.'

'It'll be dangerous,' Ginny said. 'Here, we're lost among other caravans, but in the mountains, if we are spotted, they're bound to investigate us.'

'We've got to take that risk,' Bleck said savagely. 'If Gypo can't handle the lock, we'll have to try to cut into the door and we can't do that here.'

'They are still watching the roads,' Kitson said, uneasily. 'We stand a chance of being stopped, Ed. And another thing, we don't know if the Buick will haul that weight up the mountain road. I've been up there. It's bad and part of the road has been broken up by the storm a couple of weeks ago.'

'We've got to chance it,' Bleck said. 'If we leave here tomorrow at noon, we'll be on the mountain road by dark. We'll have to buy a tent and food. It'll mean living rough until Gypo busts the truck.'

'Count me out!' Gypo said violently. 'I'm going home!'

As Bleck started to say something there came a knock on the cabin door.

There was an electrifying pause, then Bleck, gun in hand, stood up.

Gypo, his face white, leaned forward to stare at the door.

Ginny said in a fierce whisper, 'Get into the bedroom, you two!'

Bleck grabbed hold of Gypo, dragged him to his feet and bundled him into the bedroom as Kitson, very tense, crossed the room and opened the cabin door.

Fred Bradford stood just outside.

'Hello there, Mr. Harrison,' he said. 'Pardon me for calling at this time. I guess Mrs. Harrison is getting supper ready.'

'Yes,' Kitson said, blocking the doorway. 'Was there something?'

'I guess so. Could I come in a moment? I won't keep you folks long.'

Seeing Kitson hesitate, Ginny came quickly to the door.

'Why, hello, Mr. Bradford, come right in,' she said, smiling. 'I haven't started supper yet so there s nothing to spoil.'

Bradford moved into the sitting room. He looked self-conscious and a little uneasy.

'Give Mr. Bradford a drink, Alex,' Ginny said.

'No, I don't think I will, thanks,' Bradford said. He sat down, rubbing his knees with the palms of his hands. 'I mustn't take up too much of your time. My kid was around here this afternoon.' Bradford looked directly at Kitson. 'He tells me there were two men in your caravan.'

Kitson felt his heart give a little bounce. He looked over at Ginny, not knowing what to say.

'They were two of our friends,' Ginny said calmly. She smiled at Bradford. 'We promised to lend them the caravan for their vacation and they came down when we were out to look at it.'

Bradford relaxed.

'Well, what do you know? I told my kid it was something like that, but he wouldn't have it. He said they were quarrelling and shouting at each other, and it sort of scared him. He thought they were robbers.'

Ginny laughed.

'I wouldn't go so far as that,' she said, 'but I wouldn't trust them too far in a deal. They're always shouting at each other, but that doesn't stop them planning a vacation together.'

'They certainly scared my kid,' Bradford said. 'I thought I'd better have a word with you. There have been robberies on this lake, Mrs. Harrison. Well, if they're friends of yours . . .'

'Oh, yes. It's nice of you to have bothered. Are you sure you won't have a drink, Mr. Bradford?'

'No, no, thanks. I guess I mustn't keep you.' He pulled at his long nose, frowning. 'You know, for his age, that kid of mine is remarkably smart. He's got an idea about this missing truck. Know what he thinks? He thinks it's hidden in a caravan.'

Kitson's hands turned into fists, and he hastily pushed them out of sight into his trousers' pockets.

Ginny stiffened a little, but her expression remained unchanged.

'In a caravan? What gave him that idea?'

'Oh, I guess it's because he's surrounded by caravans right here,' Bradford said, smiling indulgently. 'But mind you, it's not a bad idea. He says the police would never think of hunting through a place like this for a truck, and he could be right.'

'I suppose he could,' Ginny said. 'He's certainly got imagination.'

'That's a fact. He wants me to go to the police and tell them. He reckons if they find the truck hidden in a caravan, they'll give him the reward. Did you see they've raised the reward now to five thousand? That's quite a slice of money.'

There was a pause, then Ginny said, 'I can't imagine them giving him the reward, can you, Mr. Bradford?' Her smile was a little stiff. 'You know how the police are about rewards.'

'Well, yes,' Bradford said. 'I can't make up my mind whether to go to the police or not. Mind you, I think the kid's got something, but maybe they'll tell me to mind my own business.'

'Since you own a caravan, Mr. Bradford, it wouldn't surprise me if they suspected you had stolen the truck yourself. I remember my father once found some pearls and gave them to the police, claiming the reward. They promptly arrested him, and it took weeks of expense to clear him, and he never got the reward.'

Bradford's eyes opened very wide.

'You don't say! I hadn't thought of that. I guess that settles it. I'll leave well alone. I'm glad I talked to you. I sure hadn't thought of that angle.'

He got to his feet.

'This is goodbye, Mr. Bradford,' Ginny said, smiling at him. 'We are leaving tomorrow.'

'You are? Why, that's a shame! Don't you like it here then?'

'We love it, but we plan to make a long trip. We're heading for Stag Lake, and then we're going on to Deer Lake.'

'That's quite a trip! Well, I wish you happiness.' Bradford shook hands. He stayed talking at the door for several more minutes while Ginny and Kitson stood there willing him to go. Then finally he waved his hand and went off along the moonlit path towards his own cabin.

Ginny shut the door and turned the key.

'Well, as Mr. Bradford says, that settles it. We must go.'

'Yeah,' Kitson said. 'You certainly handled that guy. You were terrific!'

'Okay, okay, plough boy,' Bleck said from the bedroom door. 'Don't get hysterical. That damned kid! I had an idea he heard us.'

Gypo came to the bedroom door and stood, listening.

'Well, tomorrow we go,' Bleck went on. 'We can't take a chance on that kid trying a fast one.' He turned to Kitson. 'Suppose you get out of here and stay with the caravan? That kid might take it into his head to come back and start snooping.'

Kitson nodded. He went to the door, unlocked it and went out into the night.

Gypo said in a flat, final voice, 'Tomorrow, I go home. Understand? I've had enough. Now I'm going to bed.'

He went back into the bedroom and shut the door.

'I'll fix him,' Bleck said, an ugly expression in his eyes. 'I'm getting plenty tired of that creep.'

Ginny went into the kitchen and began preparing supper.

Bleck came to the door and leaned against it.

'You handled that guy pretty well, baby,' he said. 'Have you thought any more about my proposition? I'm smart; you're smart, so that makes us two smart people. How about it?'

She slid two big steaks into the frying pan.

'I wouldn't be interested if you were the last man left alive,' she said, not looking at him.

'Okay, baby,' he said. 'We'll see.'

He was grinning as if he had a secret joke as he wandered over to the armchair and sat down.

Early next morning, Kitson drove into town, leaving Ginny to sit near the caravan on guard while Bleck and Gypo remained in the cabin.

This was taking a risk, but Gypo had been so difficult Bleck didn't feel he could cope with him in the caravan.

Bleck and Kitson had had to tie Gypo to the bed and gag him: that was how bad he had been.

When they had finally fastened him to the bed, Bleck, breathing heavily, a vicious expression in his eyes, waved Kitson out of the room. 'You leave this jerk to me,' he said. 'I'll persuade him to change his mind. By the time you get back, he'll be willing to travel with us.'

Kitson hated leaving Gypo like that, but he knew they couldn't hope to get the truck open without Gypo's skill, and as Gypo seemed to have gone slightly off his head, he was relieved to push the responsibility onto Bleck.

In town, Kitson bought a fair-sized tent and a large stock of canned food. They had discussed the food problem and had decided that it wouldn't be safe to go down to the town to shop once they were up in the mountains and they would have to take enough provisions to last them until Gypo opened the truck.

He returned to the cabin with the trunk of the Buick full of his purchases.

Ginny came over as he got out of the car.

'Anything happen?' he asked.

She shook her head.

'No, but I'm glad you're back. I keep thinking of that kid. The sooner we leave the better.'

They went into the cabin together.

Gypo was sitting in one of the armchairs. His face was white and his eyes sunk deep into his head. He didn't look up when they came in.

Bleck was pacing up and down, smoking.

'All fixed?' he said to Kitson.

'I got everything.'

Kitson looked at Gypo and then at Bleck, his eyes question marks.

'Gypo's okay now,' Bleck said. 'I've talked to him and he's ready to co-operate.'

'You force me to do it,' Gypo said, his voice shaking. 'Nothing good will come of it. I've warned you before. Now I'm warning you again.' He looked up suddenly at Kitson. 'You were my friend. Some friend! You keep away from me! I don't want anything more to do with you!'

'What's the matter then?' Kitson asked, staring at him.

'I had to get a little tough with him,' Bleck said. 'I had to convince him if he didn't co-operate, he would run into a lot of trouble.'

'He said he would break my hands,' Gypo

said in a low, shaking voice. 'How can a man live without his hands?'

Kitson started to say something, but Bleck shook his head at him.

'Come on, let's get going,' Bleck said. 'Anyone around out there?'

Ginny and Kitson went outside.

There were boats on the lake, but no one in the immediate vicinity.

Kitson coupled up the caravan to the Buick, then backed the caravan close to the cabin door.

'You guys ready?'

Bleck came to the door with Gypo.

Kitson opened the back of the caravan, and Bleck and Gypo got in quickly and Kitson shut the back. The move didn't take a couple of seconds.

'I'll stay here while you settle with the office,' Kitson said, giving Ginny his wallet.

While he waited, Kitson lit a cigarette and leaned against the side of the caravan. His nerves were tense now. They were going out into the open. It was asking for trouble, but there seemed no other way if they were going to open the truck.

'Hey, mister!'

Kitson started and looked quickly around.

A small boy, in jeans and a red and white checkered shirt, a straw hat on his head, came from around the other side of the caravan.

'Hello,' Kitson said.

The boy stared at him, his head a little on one side.

'You know my pop,' he said. 'I'm Fred Bradford, junior.'

'Is that right?' Kitson said, trying to sound casual.

The boy frowned at him, then transferred his attention to the caravan.

'That yours?' he asked, jerking his thumb at the caravan.

'That's right,' Kitson said.

The boy studied the caravan.

'I like ours better.'

Kitson didn't say anything. He wished feverishly that Ginny would come back and they could get the hell out of here.

The boy squatted down and stared under the caravan.

'Say! You've got enough steel on her, haven't you?' he said, looking up at Kitson. 'What's the idea? It only adds to the weight, doesn't it?'

'I don't know,' Kitson said, rubbing his jaw uneasily. 'It was like that when I bought it.'

'Pop said two of your friends were in it yesterday. Is that right?'

'Yeah.'

'What was the matter with them?'

'Nothing.'

The boy studied him. Kitson found his young eyes were extraordinarily disconcerting.

'There was something wrong with them. I

251

heard them yelling at each other.'

'They always yell at each other,' Kitson said. 'There's nothing to that.'

The boy stepped back and stared at the caravan.

'Can I see inside, mister?'

'I'm sorry,' Kitson said, turning hot. 'My wife's got the key.'

The boy looked surprised.

'My pop never lets my ma have keys. She always loses them.'

'My wife doesn't.'

The boy squatted down again and began to pull at the grass, scattering the blades right and left.

'Your friends in there now?'

'No.'

'Where are they then?'

'At home.'

'Where's that?'

'St. Lawrence.'

'They live together then?'

'That's right.'

'They were yelling at each other. They scared me.'

Kitson shrugged his shoulders.

'That's nothing. They always yell at each other.'

The boy took off his hat and began to put grass into it.

'One of them called the other a yellow creep because he couldn't do something. What was it he couldn't do?'

'I don't know,' Kitson said, and he lit a cigarette.

'They sounded pretty mad at each other.'

'They're good friends. You don't have to worry about them.'

Having filled the hat with grass, the boy bent forward, dipped his head into the hat and pulled it on.

'This keeps my head cool,' he explained, seeing Kitson staring at him. 'It's my own invention. There could be money in it.'

'Yeah,' Kitson said. 'Look, son, maybe you'd better go home. Your pop may be wondering where you've got to.'

'No, he won't. I told him I was going to look for that truck that's been stolen—the one with all that money in it. He doesn't expect me back for another hour. Did you read about the truck, mister?'

'I read about it.'

'Know what I think?'

'Yeah—your pop told me.'

The boy frowned.

'He shouldn't have done that. If he tells everyone, I could lose the reward.'

Kitson suddenly caught sight of Ginny hurrying along the path towards him.

'I'm going to collect that reward,' the boy went on. 'Five thousand bucks. Do you know what I'm going to do with it when I get it?'

Kitson shook his head.

'I'm not going to give it to my pop: that's what I'm going to do with it.'

Ginny came up.

'This is Bradford, junior,' Kitson said.

'Hello,' Ginny said, and smiled.

'Have you got the key of the caravan?' the boy asked. 'He says I can look inside.'

Ginny and Kitson exchanged glances.

'I'm sorry,' Ginny said to the boy. 'I've packed the key in one of the suitcases. I can't get at it.'

'I bet you've lost it,' the boy said scornfully. 'Well, I've got to go now. Pop says you are leaving.'

'Yes,' Ginny said.

'You're going now?'

'Yes.'

'Well, so long,' the boy said and turning, he walked off down the path, his hands in his trousers pockets, whistling shrilly and out of tune.

'Do you think . . .?' Kitson began, then stopped. 'Well, come on. Let's get out of here.'

They got into the Buick.

As they drove off, Fred Bradford, junior, who had left the path as soon as he had rounded the bend and was out of sight, and had returned through the thickets, stood motionless looking after the departing Buick and caravan. Then he took out a much thumbed notebook and wrote down the licence number of the Buick with a stub of pencil.

254

CHAPTER TEN

I

The broad six-lane highway was full of traffic, including a number of cars hauling trailers. Every now and then a hover-plane would dip down and fly along the highway as if inspecting the traffic, and each time it did so, Kitson flinched inwardly.

From time to time some big truck with a covered top would be stopped and checked by patrol officers, but it seemed the authorities had decided a caravan trailer wouldn't be strong enough to take the truck, for no trailer was being stopped.

All the same it was nervy work, driving, and Kitson had to hold onto himself to keep the car at a steady thirty miles an hour.

For six long hours they kept going.

Ginny, sitting at Kitson's side, had very little to say, and Kitson didn't feel like talking either.

Every time they passed a police car or saw a motorcycle cop, their hearts pounded. It wasn't the trip where conversation came easily.

They reached the road up to the mountains by seven in the evening.

The sun had gone down behind the mountains, and darkness closed in quickly as

Kitson sent the Buick up the first series of hairpin bends.

It was tricky driving. Kitson knew if he misjudged a bend and the caravan ran off the road, there would be no hope of getting it back onto the road again.

He could feel the drag on the Buick and the Buick's sluggish response to the gas pedal. This bothered Kitson as he knew, some twenty miles further up the road, it really got rugged and steep.

He kept glancing at the temperature gauge, seeing the indicator slowly moving from normal to hot.

'She'll be on the boil in a while,' he said to Ginny. 'It's the drag that's doing it. We've still got about twenty miles of this kind of road ahead, then we really strike trouble.'

'Worse than this?' Ginny asked as Kitson swung the wheel and pulled the Buick slowly around a steep sharp bend.

'This is nothing. The bad bit was broken up by a storm a few weeks ago. It's never been fixed. No one ever comes up here anyway. They use the Dukas tunnel through the mountain.'

Three or four miles further up the road and with the indicator of the temperature gauge on boiling point, Kitson slowed and then pulled up.

'We'll give her a few minutes to cool off,' he said and got out, collecting a couple of big rocks to block the back wheels of the car as Ginny opened up the back of the caravan.

Kitson went around and peered in. It was too dark to see Bleck or for Bleck to see him.

Bleck said, 'What's up?'

'We're boiling,' Kitson said. 'I'm letting her cool off.'

Bleck climbed stiffly out of the caravan and moved over to the edge of the road, breathing in the cool mountain air.

'Well, we've got so far. How much farther have we got to the top?'

'About sixteen miles. The worst is to come.'

'Think we're going to do it?'

Kitson shook his head.

'I don't. This is too big a weight to haul. It'll be as much as I can do to get the caravan up there, let alone with the truck.'

Ginny joined them.

'Let's get the truck out and drive it up,' she said. 'We've got the road to ourselves and it's dark enough.'

Bleck hesitated.

'It'll be the only way to get it up there,' Kitson said. 'Even at that it'll be rugged going.'

'Well, okay, but we'll be sunk if anyone spots us.'

Gypo, who had been standing by the caravan, listening, said, 'Where are we going anyway? How much further is it?'

'There's a wood and a lake up at the top,' Kitson said. 'If we can get up there, it'll be the ideal spot for us.'

'If we're going to drive the truck, we'll have to fix that battery lead,' Bleck said. 'Come on, Gypo, do some work instead of standing around like a goddamn ghost.'

By the time they had fixed the battery lead, and they only did it by breaking open the locked bonnet of the truck with one of the crowbars, the Buick had cooled off.

'We could tow it a bit further, couldn't we?' Bleck said, reluctant to bring the truck out of the caravan.

'Better not,' Kitson said. 'The going's getting steeper. We'll only boil again and have another long wait.'

Bleck shrugged. He got into the truck, started the engine and backed it out of the caravan.

'You go on ahead,' he said to Kitson. 'Gypo and me will come after you. I won't use lights. I'll take the direction from your rear lights.'

Kitson nodded and joined Ginny, who was already in the Buick. As he started the Buick moving, Ginny leaned out of the window, looking back, watching the truck.

They started the climb again. The Buick, relieved of the truck's weight, climbed majestically and effortlessly. 'Are they following all right?' Kitson asked.

'Yes,' Ginny said. 'Go a little slower. They're losing you on the bends.'

They kept going for another twenty minutes

258

until they came to the washed-out section of the road.

Kitson flashed on his headlamps and stopped.

'You stay with her,' he said. 'I'm going to take a look.'

He opened up the caravan and explained to Bleck that he was going to examine the road.

They looked at the road in the light of the Buick's headlamps. It went straight up, almost as steep as the side of a house and there were rocks and loose stones scattered about.

'For Pete's sake!' Bleck exclaimed. 'Have we to go up there?'

'That's it.' Kitson shook his head. 'It's going to be rugged. We'll have to shift some of those rocks first.'

He started up the road, pausing to manhandle the biggest stones, rolling them to the side of the road.

It took the three men a half an hour to clear the biggest of the rocks out of the way. The worst part of the road ran for about five hundred yards, then the surface improved.

'I guess that'll do,' Kitson said, panting from his exertions. 'If we get this far, we'll manage the rest.'

The three men started down the road towards the Buick.

'Take it dead slow,' Kitson said to Bleck, 'and keep in bottom gear. You'll have to use your lights. Whatever you do, keep going. If you stop, you won't get enough grip to start again.'

'Okay, okay,' Bleck said irritably. 'You don't have to tell me how to drive. You handle your crate. I'll handle mine.'

'Let me get up to the top before you follow,' Kitson said. 'I may have to have a second shot at it, and I don't want you in my way if I have to back down.'

'Okay. Don't talk so much,' Bleck snarled. 'Get on with it!'

Kitson shrugged and went to the Buick and got in.

With his headlights on, he put the gear lever to 'Low' and then, with a steady pressure on the gas pedal he sent the car up the slope.

He had a lot of power to help him, but the caravan, although empty, was still heavy and it acted as a drag. Every now and then the car's rear wheels spun, throwing stones and loose gravel to right and left.

Ginny was sitting forward, staring ahead, warning Kitson of any big stones before he saw them himself.

They were moving slower now, and Kitson, gripping the wheel, was muttering to himself, squeezing down on the gas pedal, feeling the car juddering.

Any second now, he thought, we'll stop and then we're sunk. He swung sharply to the right, easing the direct drag, then to the left, tacking in the narrow space that needed all his skill to keep the Buick from leaving the road.

The speed picked up.

The water in the radiator began to boil and the inside of the car was unbearably hot.

The headlights picked out the smoother surface of the road just ahead.

'You've nearly done it!' Ginny cried excitedly. 'Only another few yards.'

Kitson had kept a little power in reserve for just this moment. He now pushed the gas pedal to the floor. The rear wheels spun, the back of the car moved to the right, then the tires bit, and the car and the caravan lurched onto the made-up surface of the road and immediately began to gain speed.

Kitson pulled up.

'We've done it!' he exclaimed, grinning. 'Phew! I thought it was going to lick us!'

'Well done, Alex!' Ginny said. 'That was a fine piece of driving.'

He grinned at her, set the parking brake and got out of the car.

Bleck was starting his run up. He hadn't the horse-power that Kitson had had to help him, but neither was he pulling a heavy caravan.

'He's taking it too fast,' Kitson said and began to run down the hill towards the approaching headlights of the truck.

Bleck was rushing the hill, his foot flat on the gas pedal, leaving himself nothing in reserve for an emergency.

The truck bounced and banged over the

uneven surface, throwing Gypo, sitting beside Bleck, heavily against the side of the truck.

'Take it easy,' Gypo gasped. 'You're going too fast!

'Shut up!' Bleck shouted. 'I'm handling this!'

Gypo saw a big stone appear in the headlights of the truck.

'Look out!' he bawled.

Bleck missed seeing the stone and the off-side front wheel of the truck hit it and the truck wrenched to the left. Before Bleck could control the truck, it was sideways on to the hill and the engine had stalled.

Alarmed at the angle the truck was leaning, Gypo yelled, 'It's going over!' and he tried to open the truck door, but the angle was so sharp and the door so solid, he couldn't open it.

'Stay still, you fool!' Bleck shouted. 'You'll have us over!'

Kitson came running up.

He too was alarmed at the angle of the truck, and he jumped on the running-board, adding his weight to the already lifting wheels.

'Start her up and back slowly,' he said to Bleck.

'If I move her, she'll go over,' Bleck snarled, sweat on his face.

'There's no other way. Take it dead slow with a full right lock.'

With an unsteady hand, Bleck thumbed the

starter, then, as the engine came alive, he engaged gear.

'Let the clutch in gently,' Kitson said. 'Don't jerk it. Start pulling her around as soon as she begins to move.'

Cursing under his breath, Bleck began to let the clutch in.

As the truck began to move, he turned the steering wheel.

For one horrible moment he felt the off-side wheels lift clear of the ground and he was sure the truck was going to turn over, but Kitson's weight just balanced it and slowly the truck came around and once more faced towards the steep hill.

As Bleck tried to get into a forward gear, the truck started to run backwards and he had to slam on his foot brake.

The engine stalled.

'Okay,' Kitson said, contempt in his voice. 'Come on out. Let me have her.'

Muttering, Bleck got out. He was glad to give up the wheel. Kitson looked at the angle the truck was now at and he shook his head.

'Get some rocks. We'll have to pack the back wheels,' he said and, going to the side of the road, he caught hold of a large rock and half dragged it, half carried it to the truck and dumped it down into the soft soil behind one of the rear wheels.

Bleck came staggering over with another rock and fixed the other wheel.

Kitson got into the cab of the truck and started the engine.

Leaning out of the window, he said, 'You and Gypo get ready to block the wheels if I stall. I may have to jump her all the way up. The tires won't bite on this.'

'Get on with it!' Bleck snarled, furious with himself for bogging the truck down.

Kitson got the engine running fast, then he released the handbrake, letting the truck settle back on the rocks.

'Here we go!' he shouted and gently let in the clutch.

The truck moved forward, skidded with its rear wheels spinning, throwing dirt and stones back at Bleck and Gypo.

Half blinded, they turned their backs, shielding their faces.

Kitson tried to hold the truck straight, gunning the engine, but the strain was too much, the engine stalled and he had just time to slam on his brakes, having gained a couple of yards.

Even with the brakes on, the truck began to slide back and Kitson yelled to Bleck to block the wheels.

He lost a yard before Bleck and Gypo got rocks against the wheels.

The next time he tried, the other two stood clear and he gained a good four yards before the engine stalled, and Bleck and Gypo rushed up and dumped rocks under the wheels before the truck lost ground.

This went on for a good half hour, Kitson jumping the truck forward while Bleck and Gypo blocked the wheels.

Finally, they were within fifty yards of the Buick, but all three men were so exhausted by their efforts, Bleck called a halt.

'Let the sonofabitch cool off,' he said, leaning against the side of the truck and panting.

Kitson got out of the truck.

'Not far to go now,' he said as Ginny came running down to join them. 'Once off this, she'll be okay.'

'You're doing fine,' Ginny said to him.

He grinned happily at her.

'The tough driver,' Bleck sneered. 'The boy wonder, with a way with cars.'

Ginny looked at him.

'That's something you can't claim, is it?' she said.

Bleck sneered at her.

'Okay, stick up for him,' he said. 'You're the only one.'

He walked away to the edge of the road, where he sat on a rock and lit a cigarette.

There was a long wait, then when Kitson had decided the engine was cool enough, he called to Bleck and got into the truck.

Ten minutes later the truck was standing beside the Buick.

'I can tow her now,' Kitson said. 'Better get

her under cover again.'

He drove the truck into the caravan and Bleck and Gypo got in.

Shutting the back of the caravan, Kitson went to the Buick and slid under the steering wheel.

Ginny said, 'You were fine. If it hadn't been for you, we'd never have made it.'

She leaned forward and her lips brushed his cheek.

II

The sun coming through the chink in the entrance to the tent woke Bleck. He opened his eyes and stared up at the sloping canvas roof, and it took him several puzzled moments to remember where he was.

He closed his eyes, frowning, feeling the stiffness in his bones from lying all night on the hard ground.

Well, at least, they had found a good hiding place, he thought. If they had any luck they could remain up here safely until Gypo opened the truck.

There was a lake with running water, a fair-sized wood that gave them complete cover from the aircraft that patrolled overhead, and they were a good five hundred yards off the road.

No one would believe it possible that the

truck could have been driven up that washed-out road. No one was likely to look for them here.

Now everything depended on Gypo. If he couldn't beat the lock, then he must use the flame.

It maddened Bleck to think that he had had the truck in his possession for four days and still the money was out of his reach.

He opened his eyes and squinted at his watch. The time was five minutes after six. Then, raising his head, he looked across at Ginny who was curled up, her head on a rolled-up coat, a blanket over her, still sleeping.

Kitson lay between the girl and Bleck, and he was sleeping.

There wasn't much room in the tent, but they all had to sleep in there as it was too cold at night to sleep out in the open.

Bleck looked over to see if Gypo was sleeping. Immediately he stiffened and sat up, for Gypo wasn't in the tent.

For a moment, Bleck felt alarmed, then he relaxed a little, thinking Gypo was probably outside, getting the breakfast ready.

But he had to be sure and he threw off the blanket and gave Kitson a hard nudge with his foot, waking him.

'Come on!' he said as Kitson lifted his head to blink at him. 'Gypo's up already. We've got work to do.'

Kitson yawned, then as he was nearest to the exit, he crawled out, blinking in the sunshine.

As Bleck joined him, Ginny sat up, rubbing her eyes and stretching.

'Where's Gypo?' Kitson asked, looking around the small clearing in the wood.

Bleck looked over at the caravan, well hidden under the trees. He looked across at the small lake.

There was no sign of Gypo.

Cupping his hands to his mouth, Bleck bawled, 'Gypo!'at the top of his voice.

There came no answering call and the two men looked at each other.

'The creep's run out on us!' Bleck said furiously. 'I should have watched him. He's gone.'

Ginny came out of the tent.

'What is it?'

'Gypo's gone!' Kitson said.

'He can't have gone far,' Ginny said. 'He was in the tent twenty minutes ago. He was sleeping.'

'We've got to get him back!' Bleck said violently. 'Without him, we're sunk! He must be crazy! It's more than twenty miles to the highway and he'll have to walk every yard of it!'

Kitson ran to the road and Bleck went with him.

They paused at the edge of the grass verge

and looked down the long, steep incline to the narrow zig-zag white road, cut into the face of the mountain that twisted and turned down into a haze of mist, covering the valley.

Kitson suddenly grabbed Bleck's arm, pointing.

'There he goes!'

Bleck screwed up his eyes. He could just make out a tiny figure moving along the road, a mile and a half below.

'We can catch him!' Bleck said. 'I'll make him sorry he was born when I get my hands on him! We'll take the car!'

'No,' Kitson said. 'The road's too narrow. We'd never turn it to come back. We'll go down the hill side. That way we can do two miles to his half.'

He got off the road and started down the steep slope, sliding, jumping when he could, but sliding most of the way.

Bleck hesitated. It looked dangerous to him. He started after Kitson, but at a slower pace.

Kitson reached the road, crossed it, lowered himself over the grass verge and started down the slope again. It was now steeper, and he had to go more slowly. Once he nearly pitched forward, and he only saved himself by throwing himself backwards and then sliding down to land with a flurry of dislodged stones onto the road again.

Recovering, he paused to look down.

He could now see Gypo clearly.

Gypo was jogging along downhill, covering the ground at quite a pace.

Bleck joined Kitson.

'There he goes!' Kitson said.

Snarling, Bleck pulled his gun.

'What do you think you're going to do?' Kitson said, grabbing Bleck's wrist. 'He's the only one who can open the truck, isn't he?'

Bleck's face was streaming with sweat and he was gasping for breath. Savagely, he wrenched his wrist free and shoved the gun back into its holster. Then he started down the next slope.

As Kitson was about to follow, he saw Gypo suddenly pause, stop and stare up the mountain side. For a moment, Gypo stood motionless. Then he started to run.

'He's seen us!' Kitson bawled to Bleck. Then raising his voice, he yelled, 'Gypo! Stop! Come back!'

But Gypo didn't stop. He ran on doggedly. His legs felt like lead and his lungs seemed to be bursting.

He now realized the futility of this attempt to escape.

He had woken in the tent and seeing the other three were sleeping soundly, he had suddenly decided to go home.

He hadn't thought that he would succeed in getting out of the tent without one of them waking, but he was urged to try.

He had squirmed out of his blanket, then,

crouching, he had undone the flap of the tent, stepped over Kitson's sleeping body and was out in the sunshine, scarcely believing it had been so easy and simple.

He hesitated then. He knew he had over twenty miles of lonely road to cover before he reached the highway where he could get a lift back to his workshop.

The time was five minutes past six. The chances were those three would sleep on until seven or even eight. That would give him an hour's start—two with any luck—before they realized he was gone.

That decided him, and he set off at a fast walk down the road.

He had been walking a little over half an hour and had covered nearly two miles when he heard the sound of falling rocks, far above him.

Looking up, he saw Bleck and Kitson coming down the hill side, sliding and nearly falling, but coming at an alarming pace.

The sight of them filled Gypo with terror.

He heard Kitson yell, 'Gypo! Stop! Come back!'

He began to run blindly.

He hadn't run more than a few hundred yards before he realized he could never keep up this pace. Again he looked back.

Bleck was slithering down the slope and, as he watched, he gained the road. Kitson was coming down in a cloud of dust, sliding on his

271

heels, sending a shower of stones before him.

Like a frightened, hunted animal, Gypo left the road and began to rush madly down the slope. In a few seconds, he lost his balance and fell face forward. His hands took the shock and he began to roll over and over.

He came to a gasping halt near the road. Desperately he scrambled to his feet and looked back over his shoulder.

At the level he was now on, he realized neither Bleck nor Kitson could see him, owing to the overhanging rocks that screened him from their view. Although he couldn't see them, and he had a feeling of momentary safety, he could hear them, and the sound of their movements sounded alarmingly close.

He looked around wildly, sure that in a few minutes, they would catch up with him.

To his right was a wide stretch of short thick shrubs that grew on the mountainside. His one panic-stricken thought was now to hide, and he bolted headlong into the shrubs, wading thigh-deep through the close undergrowth, tearing his trousers against the stiff little shrubs, but not caring, until he reached the centre of the thicket, then he threw himself down, and stretched out flat, the shrubs closing over him like the covering of a protective blanket.

Trying to control his breathing, he lay motionless, listening.

Kitson was the first to reach the road. He came to an abrupt stop and looked to right and left, surprised and startled to see no sign of Gypo.

Panting and cursing, Bleck joined him.

'Where is he?' Bleck gasped.

'Looks like he's gone to ground,' Kitson said.

Both men looked towards the stretch of shrubs. It was the obvious and only place where anyone could hide on this bare mountain slope.

'That's where he is!' Bleck said, pointing, then raising his voice, he bawled, 'Gypo! Come on out of there! We know you're in there!'

Gypo flinched at the sound of Bleck's voice, but he flattened himself further into the sandy soil, holding his breath and waited.

Bleck turned to Kitson.

'Let's get after the creep! You go in at the top and I'll go in here!'

He walked to the shrub patch and pushed his way in, but he had only forced his way forward for about ten yards or so before he stopped, realizing the labour and the time it would take to cover the whole vast patch of ground. Unless he was lucky enough to walk right on to Gypo he would probably never find him.

Kitson, too, moving into the dense tangle of shrubs, also realized the difficulty of the task and he also came to a stop.

The two men looked at each other over the sea of green, tightly growing shrubs.

'Gypo!' Bleck shouted, his voice shaking with rage. 'This is your last chance! If you don't come out I'll give you a beating you'll live to remember! Come on out!'

Hearing the rage and despair in Bleck's voice, Gypo remained motionless. He realized that if he only kept his nerve and remained right where he was, he stood a good chance of getting away.

Bleck began to move forward again, but without much hope, and Gypo heard him forcing his way through the shrubs, going away from him. He could also hear Kitson crashing through the undergrowth, and also going away from him.

He waited, getting his breath back while his pounding heart slowly returned to a more normal beat.

After some minutes, the noise of the two men searching for him began to fade into the distance, and Gypo decided it would be safe to make a move.

If they were going to cover the whole of the ground, it would be safer for him to keep shifting his position.

He started off, pulling himself over the sandy ground, manoeuvering his body past the short thick stems of the shrubs, careful not to disturb the head of the shrubs that now formed a screen above his crawling body.

He had been crawling forward for some thirty or forty yards, almost relaxed in his feeling of safety, when he saw the snake.

He had just put his right hand out, his arm fully extended, his fingers digging into the soft soil to pull himself forward, when he glanced ahead, and there was the snake, coiled, its flat, diamond head within a few inches of his hand.

Gypo sucked in his breath in a hiss of terror. His reflexes became paralysed. It was as if he were turned to stone. Fear chilled his blood and sent his heart pounding so violently that he felt suffocated.

The snake, too, remained motionless.

Several agonizing seconds passed, then with his breath whistling through his clenched teeth, Gypo snatched his hand back. As he did so, the snake struck.

Gypo felt the sharp stab of pain in the heel of his hand. He sprang to his feet with a wild, terrified scream, and started a blind, blundering rush through the shrubs.

Bleck and Kitson had reached the end of the shrub patch and were turning to come back at another level.

Gypo's scream made both men stiffen and pause.

Then they saw Gypo running, his arms thrashing the air, and they heard his blood-chilling yells.

'The lug's gone crazy!' Bleck said, and breaking into a run, he started to crash through the shrubs after Gypo, followed by Kitson.

Gypo's panic-stricken run carried him clear of the shrubs, then when he reached the steep slope of the mountainside, he fell and began to roll down the hill, setting up a cloud of dust and dislodging stones as he rolled helplessly down the slope.

Kitson, racing ahead of Bleck, was the first to reach him. He dropped down on his knees beside Gypo, who had come to rest on his back, wedged against a rock.

'Gypo!' Kitson panted. 'It's okay. I won't let him touch you! What's the matter?'

He was shocked to see that Gypo's face was livid and his eyes were like holes in a grey-white sheet.

'The snake . . .' Gypo managed to gasp.

Bleck came blundering up, his breath rasping at the back of his throat.

'You yellow rat!' he snarled. 'I'll kill you for this!'

He aimed a kick at Gypo's prostrated body, but Kitson blocked his swinging foot with his arm.

'Cut it out!' Kitson said. 'Can't you see there's something wrong with him?'

'The snake . . .' Gypo sobbed and tried to lift his paralysed right arm to show Kitson.

Kitson leaned forward and saw how red and swollen Gypo's hand was. He touched the swollen flesh, and Gypo gave a squeal of pain that sent a chill up Kitson's spine.

'What happened?' Kitson asked, squatting

down beside Gypo.

'The snake . . .' Gypo panted. 'I . . . crawled right . . . on to it.'

Kitson saw the two telltale punctures in the inflamed flesh.

'Take it easy, Gypo,' he said. 'I'll fix it. Don't get scared.'

'Get me . . . to hospital,' Gypo moaned. 'I don't want . . . to die the way . . . my brother died.'

Kitson took out his handkerchief, and twisted it into a cord, then he tied it around Gypo's wrist.

'You mean he's been bitten by a snake?' Bleck said, grabbing Kitson by his shoulder. 'Then how the hell are we going to open the truck?'

Kitson shook him off. He took out a penknife from his pocket and opened one of the blades.

'This is going to hurt, Gypo,' he said, catching hold of Gypo's wrist. 'But it'll fix it.'

He dug the point of the knife into Gypo's hot, swollen hand and cut down.

Gypo screamed, hitting Kitson with his left hand feebly and trying to pull free.

The wound Kitson had made began to bleed. Still keeping his grip, Kitson tried to squeeze out the snake poison. He was alarmed at Gypo's pallor: he looked as if he were dying.

'Alex,' Gypo gasped, 'you are . . . my friend. I didn't mean what I said. Get . . . me to . . .

hospital . . .'

'I'll get you there. Take it easy,' Kitson said. He tightened the handkerchief around Gypo's wrist, then stood up. 'I'll get the Buick.'

Bleck said, 'You'll do—what?'

'I'm getting the car and I'm taking Gypo to hospital,' Kitson said. 'Look at him! He's in a bad way.' He turned and started up the hill towards the road.

'Kitson!' The snap in Bleck's voice made Kitson pause and turn.

'What is it?'

'Come back here!' Bleck shouted. 'Have you gone nuts? Look up there!' He pointed to an aircraft that was slowly circling the mountains. 'You bring the car out of cover and they'll spot it. How long do you think it'll be before the cops come up here to investigate?'

'So what?' Kitson said angrily. 'We've got to get him to hospital, otherwise he'll die. Can't you see that?'

'You're not to bring the car out of cover,' Bleck said.

'It's thirty miles to the hospital,' Kitson said. 'What do you expect me to do—carry him?'

I don't give a damn!' Bleck snarled. 'You're not bringing the car out on this road in daylight. He'll have to take his chance!'

'Oh, go to hell!' Kitson said and, turning, he started up the side of the mountain towards the road.

'Kitson!'

The threat in Bleck's voice made Kitson pause and he looked back.

Bleck had his gun out and it was pointing at him.

'Come back here!' Bleck said.

'He's dying!' Kitson said. 'Can't you see that?'

'You come back here!' Bleck said, his voice vicious. 'You're not getting the car. Come back here and fast! I'm not telling you again, plough boy!'

Aware that his heart was beginning to thump, Kitson came slowly back down the slope. This was it! he thought. This is where I take this punk. I've got to watch out for his right hand. This is the show down. I'm not going to let Gypo die.

'We've got to do something for him,' he said as he approached Bleck. 'We just can't stand here and watch him die! We've got to get him to hospital.'

'Look at him, you fool!' Bleck said. 'By the time you get up there, get the car, bring it down here, load him in and get him to hospital, he'll be dead.'

'We've got to do something for him,' Kitson said and, not looking at Bleck, he moved past him, his muscles tense, and out of the corner of his eye, he saw Bleck lower the gun.

Kitson swung around, his fist coming down in a chopping blow on Bleck's wrist.

The gun shot out of Bleck's hand and

dropped into the shrubs. Bleck jumped back and faced Kitson.

There was a pause as they looked at each other, then Bleck grinned.

'Okay, you bum,' he said softly. 'You've been asking for it. I've always wanted to take you, now I'll show you what fighting means.'

Kitson waited, his hands in fists, his eyes narrowed.

Bleck moved forward, weaving a little, his chin tucked down, his hands held low.

Kitson shot out a probing left, but Bleck's head shifted and Kitson's fist scraped past his ear. Bleck ducked under Kitson's right-hand counter and his right thudded into Kitson's ribs; a thump that made Kitson give ground and gasp.

As Bleck moved in, Kitson caught him with a left and a right to the head that staggered Bleck.

The two men shifted away, then came in simultaneously, slugging at each other, shifting from the heavier blows, taking the lighter ones, moving in and out, cautious and watchful.

Kitson thought he saw an opening and he slammed in a hard left, but Bleck weaved away and Kitson's left slid over his shoulder. His lips peeling off his teeth, Bleck let go with his right that took Kitson solidly under his heart.

It was a devastating punch and its solid impact brought Kitson down to his knees.

Still grinning, Bleck moved forward and

clubbed Kitson on the side of his neck and Kitson dropped face down, his mind blacked out.

Bleck stood back.

Kitson managed to heave himself up on his hands and knees, shaking his head. He saw Bleck moving forward, and he threw himself at Bleck's knees, his arms wrapping themselves around Bleck's legs.

As Bleck fell, he thumped Kitson on the top of his head.

The two men sprawled on the ground. Still dazed, Kitson tried to get a grip on Bleck's throat, but Bleck hit him on the side of his head, and then rolled clear.

As Bleck got to his feet, Kitson pushed himself upright. He was a little late in getting his hands up, and he took Bleck's right-hand punch, high up on his cheekbone. He sagged under the force of the punch. Lurching forward, he tied up Bleck's arm, and for a long moment, the two men wrestled, Bleck trying to break Kitson's hold, and Kitson frantically trying to hold on until his head cleared.

Bleck finally broke free and let go a long, raking left that Kitson just managed to avoid. He sank a right-hand punch into Bleck's ribs and he saw Bleck's face contort with pain.

Encouraged, Kitson crowded forward. He slammed a right and a left to Bleck's head.

Grunting and snarling, Bleck backed away.

Kitson tossed over a left swing that landed

high up on Bleck's head. Bleck staggered and threw up his hands. Kitson sank his right into Bleck's belly. Bleck reeled back, gasping.

Intent now on the kill, Kitson moved forward recklessly. He started a punch, but realized a shade too late that Bleck was throwing his right hand.

Kitson felt the thud against his jaw, then something white and hot exploded inside his head. He knew as he fell he had walked into Bleck's special punch, but there was nothing he could do about it. He fell face down, his face coming into contact with sharp stones, and, grunting with pain, he rolled over, his cut face upturned to the hot sun.

He lay there, stunned, for some moments, then he made the effort and raised his head.

Bleck was bending over Gypo, staring down at him.

Kitson shook his head, then he got unsteadily to his feet. He came staggering over to Bleck, who looked over his shoulder at him, his face set and hard.

'He's dead,' Bleck said in a cold, flat voice. 'The creep would pull a stunt like this on us.'

Kitson knelt by Gypo's side and took his cold, damp hand between his hands.

Gypo looked relaxed, his mouth open, his dark, small eyes stared fixedly up at the blue sky.

Regardless of the pain that moved through his beaten body, Kitson thought: with Gypo dead, what hope have we now of opening the truck? The million dollar take is now a mirage. The world in our pockets! Morgan certainly picked the wrong one this time.

'Leave him,' Bleck said. 'He's dead. There's nothing we can do for him.'

Kitson didn't say anything. He held on to Gypo's hand, looking down at the dead man.

Shrugging, Bleck started the long walk back to where the truck was hidden.

CHAPTER ELEVEN

I

Two men came down the path by the lake and walked to where Fred Bradford was sitting, reading the morning's newspaper.

He had just had breakfast, and having sent his wife and son down to the lake, he was enjoying a little relaxation before joining them.

He looked towards the approaching men, wondering who they were.

One of them was wearing the uniform of an Army major; the other wore a cheap, ready-made suit with a pork-pie hat set squarely on his head.

The major was a small, fair man with a military moustache, and a brown, lean face. His blue eyes were hard and direct.

His companion was tall and bulky. His red, weather-beaten face was coarse featured, and Bradford guessed he was a police officer in plain clothes.

'Mr. Bradford?' the major asked, coming to rest in front of the sitting man.

'Why, sure,' Bradford said, getting to his feet. 'You want me?'

'Fred Bradford, junior?' the major asked.

Bradford stared at him.

'Why, no. That's my son.' He folded the newspaper nervously and dropped it into his chair. 'What do you want with him?'

'I'm Major Delaney, Field Security,' the major said and, waving his hand to his companion, 'this is Lieutenant Cooper, City Police.'

Bradford looked uneasily at the two men.

'I'm glad to know you gentlemen.' He paused, then went on, 'You don't want my boy, do you?'

'Where is he?' Cooper asked.

'He's down by the lake with his mother,' Bradford said. 'What is this all about?'

'We would like to talk to him, Mr. Bradford,' Delaney said. 'There's nothing to worry about.'

At this moment, Fred Bradford, junior, came wandering up the path, whistling shrilly. He stopped whistling when he saw the two men, and he approached more slowly, a sudden wary expression on his face.

'Here he is now,' Bradford said. Turning to his son, he said, 'Hey, junior, come here. Where's your mother?'

'She's fooling down by the lake,' the boy said, a scornful note in his voice.

'Are you Fred Bradford, junior?' Delaney asked. 'That's right,' the boy said, looking up at the two men.

'Did you write this?' Delaney asked, taking an envelope from his pocket and extracting a sheet of notepaper.

Bradford recognized his son's sprawling handwriting that covered the paper.

'That's right,' the boy said.

He squatted down on his haunches, took off his battered straw hat and began to fill it with grass.

Bradford said blankly, 'My son wrote to you?'

'He wrote to police headquarters,' Delaney said. 'He claims to know where this missing truck is.'

Bradford gaped at his son.

'Junior! What have you been doing? You know you don't know where it is!'

The boy looked up at his father scornfully, then went on filling his hat with grass. When he had filled the hat, he bent forward and dipped his head into the hat, pulled the hat on and then straightened up.

'I have to do it that way,' he said to no one in particular, 'otherwise the grass falls out. It

285

keeps my head cool. It's my own invention.'

Delaney and Cooper exchanged glances, then Delaney said kindly, 'Where is the truck, son?'

The boy sat down and crossed his legs. He adjusted his hat, pulling it more firmly down on his head.

'I know where it is,' he announced solemnly.

'Well, that's fine,' Delaney said, restraining his impatience with an effort, 'Where is it?'

'How about the reward?' the boy asked, looking up sharply; his eyes fixed disconcertingly on the major's face.

'Look, junior,' Bradford said, sweating with embarrassment, 'you know you don't know where the truck is. You'll get into serious trouble wasting these gentlemen's time.'

'I know where it is all right,' the boy said calmly, 'but I'm not telling until I get the reward.'

'Come on, son,' Delaney said, his voice sharpening. 'If you know something, trot it out. Your father's right: you could get into serious trouble if you're wasting our time.'

'The truck's hidden in a caravan,' the boy said.

'Now look,' Bradford said, 'we've been over all that. You know as well as I do . . .'

'Just a moment, Mr. Bradford,' Delaney broke in, 'I'll do the talking, if you please.' He turned to the boy. 'What makes you think the truck is in a caravan, son?'

286

'I've seen it,' the boy said. 'They have two big steel girders bolted to the bottom of the caravan so the truck can't fall through.'

'They? Who do you mean?'

'The guys who stole the truck, of course.'

Delaney and Cooper looked at each other. Delaney was faintly excited.

'You've actually seen the truck?'

The boy nodded, then, frowning, he took off his hat.

'It's cool enough when I first put it on,' he said seriously, 'but after a while, the grass seems to heat up.' He emptied the grass out of his hat. 'I guess I'll have to keep putting fresh grass in if it's going to work at all.'

He began to fill the hat with grass again.

'Where did you see the truck?' Delaney asked, his voice thin with exasperation.

The boy continued to tear up handfuls of grass which he dropped into the hat.

'Did you hear what I said?' Delaney barked.

'What was that?' the boy asked, pausing for a moment to look up at Delaney.

'I asked you where the truck is,' Delaney said.

The boy began to put more grass into his hat.

'My father says the police wouldn't give me the reward,' he said. 'He says they'll keep it for themselves.'

Bradford shifted uneasily.

'I never said any such thing!' he said angrily.

'You should be ashamed of yourself talking that way.'

The boy stared at him, then he blew a long stream of air from his lips, making a noise like the ripping of calico.

'What a wopper!' he said when he had finished making the noise. 'You said if you told them the truck was hidden in a caravan, they'd think you had stolen it. You said all cops were crooks.'

'Okay, okay,' Cooper growled. 'Never mind what your old man said. Where did you see the truck?'

Very slowly and very carefully, the boy bent over the hat, dipped his head into it and pulled it down on his head.

'I'm not telling you until I get the reward,' he said, straightening and staring up at the lieutenant.

'Yeah? Well, we'll see about that,' Cooper said, his face hardening. 'You two can come down to headquarters, and if you've been wasting our time . . .'

'I'll handle this,' Delaney said quietly.

'Now, listen, son,' he said, 'anyone who gives us information that will help us find the truck, gets the reward. It doesn't matter who it is. If your information helps us find the truck, then you'll get the reward.'

The boy studied the major for several seconds.

'Honest?'

The major nodded.

'Honest.'

'You won't give the reward to my father? You'll give it to me?'

'I'll give it to you.'

'Five thousand?'

'That's right.'

The boy brooded for a long moment while the three men watched him.

'No fooling?' he asked, staring at the major. 'You'll give me the reward if I tell you?'

The major nodded, his smile very wide and very sincere. 'No fooling, son. When the Army says something, the Army means just what it says.'

Again the boy brooded, then finally he said, 'Well, then I'll tell you. There are four of them: three men and a girl. Two of the men stayed in the caravan all day. They only left at night. I saw them leave after it got dark. I have the number of the car. They said they were going to Stag Lake, but they were lying. They took the road to the highway and that's no way to go to Stag Lake. The caravan is white with a blue top.' He took from his pocket a much thumbed notebook and tore out a page. 'That's the car number.'

'But how do you know the truck is in the caravan?' Delaney asked, carefully putting the scrap of paper into his wallet.

'I saw it when the two men got into the caravan in the morning,' the boy said. 'I got up

289

specially early to watch.'

'But how did you know it was the truck?'

The boy regarded the major patiently.

'I read the description in the papers. It was the truck all right.'

'When did they leave?'

'Yesterday midday. I saw them go. They didn't take the road to Stag Lake. They were heading for the mountains.'

'We've lost a lot of time,' Delaney said, frowning. 'Why didn't you get your father to telephone us?'

'I asked him. He wouldn't let me and he wouldn't do it himself, that's why I wrote,' the boy said. He said all cops were crooks.'

Delaney and Cooper stared hard at Bradford for a long moment.

'I was just fooling,' Bradford said in a small voice, his face red. 'I didn't really think . . .'

'Can you give me a description of these people?' Delaney said, turning to the boy.

'Sure,' the boy said and gave an accurate description of Kitson, Ginny, Gypo and Bleck.

Cooper wrote down the descriptions in his notebook.

'That's fine, son,' Delaney said. 'You've done a swell job. I'll certainly recommend you for the reward if we find the truck.'

'You'll find it all right,' the boy said. He took off his hat and shook out the grass. 'There's something wrong with this idea. It gets hot too quickly.'

Cooper said with a grin, 'Try putting some ice in it. That'll cool you off.'

The boy's look was withering.

'That's a dumb idea,' he said. 'The ice would melt.'

Delaney patted the boy on his shoulder.

'I'll tell you how to fix it,' he said. 'Cut the top off the hat: that'll let the air in and it'll also start a new fashion.'

The boy considered this, then he nodded.

'That's quite smart,' he said. 'I'll try it. There could be money in it.'

As the two men walked back to their car, Delaney said, 'Up in the mountains: that's the one spot we haven't checked. They could be up there.'

'No, they couldn't,' Cooper said. 'If I thought they could have got up there, I'd have checked before now, but no one could get up there. The road is washed out. You could never get the truck up that bit of road.'

'They might have been lucky,' Delaney said. 'There is nowhere else to look. I'm going to check.'

Cooper got into the car and started the engine.

'Are you really going to recommend that kid for the reward?' he asked.

Delaney settled himself beside Cooper. There was a far away expression in his eyes as he said, 'What is a kid of ten going to do with five thousand bucks? His father would only grab it.' He glanced at Cooper and his smile appeared very sincere. 'We know who is going to get the reward, don't we? It is stated whoever finds the truck gets the reward. I guess you and me will find it so we will get the reward.'

Cooper blew out his cheeks.

'The way you talked to that kid had me worried.'

Delaney nodded.

'I know how to handle kids,' he said. 'You've got to be goddamn sincere with them, otherwise they don't trust you. I've always been a pretty sincere man,' and he laughed.

II

It was a little after nine o'clock when Kitson came back to the camp. He carried Gypo's shovel on his shoulder and his shirt was plastered with sweat.

Ginny was sitting on a rock in the shade of a tree, her face very white and her eyes full of unshed tears.

Bleck had got the truck out of the caravan. He was leaning against the door, his ear to the lock, his right hand moving the dial very slowly and carefully while he listened.

Kitson put down the shovel, then went over to join Ginny. He sat down at her feet and lit a cigarette, his hands unsteady.

She reached out and put her hand on his shoulder.

'What a way to die,' Kitson said, reaching up and covering her hand with his. 'There was nothing I could do for him. He died while that rat and I were fighting, but even at that, I could never have got him to hospital in time.'

'Don't talk about it, Alex.'

'And burying him like that: the way you bury a dog. He was a good guy, Ginny. I ought to have listened to him. He didn't want this job. He tried to talk me into quitting. I wish I had listened to him.'

'Yes.'

'He said nothing good would come of it. He was right. Let's get out of here, Ginny. You and me. As soon as it's dark, we'll go.'

'Yes,' Ginny said. 'It's all my fault. I'll never forgive myself. I started it. When you went down to bury him, I sat here, thinking. I can see how wrong and how bad I've been. Even if we open the truck right now I wouldn't touch any of the money. I must have been out of my mind!'

'You mean you will come with me?' Kitson said, not looking at her. 'We could start a new life, Ginny. Would you marry me?'

'If that's what you want,' she said. 'But you don't really imagine we are going to get away with this, do you? Sooner or later, they'll get onto us.'

Kitson stubbed out his cigarette and threw it

293

away.

'We might be lucky. It's worth a try. We'll take the Buick and make for the Mexican border. They haven't got our descriptions. If we once get to Mexico . . .'

Bleck yelled, 'Hey, Kitson! Come over here! What do you imagine you are doing? Come here and give me a hand!'

Kitson and Ginny exchanged glances, then Kitson got to his feet. He walked over to the truck.

'Can you handle a flame?' Bleck asked. His face was set and tense, his eyes wild-looking.

'No.'

'Well, now's the time to learn. We're going to burn our way into this godamn box! Come on—give me a hand with the cylinders.'

'Not me,' Kitson said quietly.

Bleck glared at him.

'What do you mean? We've got to get this truck open, haven't we?'

'I haven't,' Kitson said. 'I'm through. I shouldn't have touched this job. You open it. The money's all yours if you can get at it. I'm quitting.'

Bleck drew in a long slow breath.

'Listen, you creep, I can't handle it on my own! Give me a hand with the cylinders and stop shooting off with your mouth!'

'As soon as it gets dark,' Kitson said, 'Ginny and me are leaving. You can please yourself what you do, but we're leaving.'

'So that's it,' Bleck snarled. 'You two . . . well, what do you know? So you finally made it, plough boy. And you're walking out on a million dollars. You're crazy!'

'That's what we're doing,' Kitson said quietly.

'You've got a long walk ahead of you,' Bleck sneered.

'We're taking the Buick.'

'That's what you think. I'm using the Buick and I'm not ready to go yet.' He thumped the side of the truck. 'I'm busting open this truck if it's the last thing I do! Neither you, you yellow-gutted monkey nor your floozie is going to stop me! If you want to quit, then damn well quit, but you'll quit on your flat feet. You're not taking the car!'

Out of the corner of his eye, Bleck saw Ginny suddenly get to her feet and begin to move towards him.

He realized this was two against one. He guessed Ginny had a gun.

Kitson was saying quietly, 'We're leaving tonight, and we're leaving in the car. You can come with us to the highway if you want to, but after that you're on your own. Suit yourself.'

Bleck hesitated, then he looked towards Ginny, who was still now, her right hand held out of sight by her side.

If he didn't play this right, these two would kill him, he thought.

Shrugging his shoulders, he said to Kitson,

'Well, okay, if that's the way you want it. We've got until dark to work on the truck. That's twelve hours. In that time we could be lucky. You're not just going to sit around and do nothing all that time, are you? Give me a hand with the cylinders!'

Surprised by this sudden climb down, Kitson hesitated.

'Okay,' he said, 'but it's not going to get you anywhere. You're not going to burn a hole in that truck if you try for twenty years.'

'We'll see.' Bleck glanced over at Ginny. She was still watching him, but she had relaxed. 'You talk too much, plough boy. Come on and give me a hand.'

As Kitson moved past Bleck to the caravan, Bleck pulled his gun and rammed it into Kitson's ribs.

'Drop that gun!' he yelled at Ginny, 'or I'll blast a hole in your boy friend!'

Ginny let go of the gun she held in her hand. It dropped onto the grass.

Bleck backed away, covering them both.

'Get away from it,' he snarled.

Ginny moved to Kitson.

Bleck circled them, picked up Ginny's gun and threw it into the lake.

'Now you two listen to me,' he said. 'We're busting this truck. Don't kid yourselves I can't handle you both. We're not going to move from here until we've opened the truck and got the dough. If you don't want it, I do, and

I'm going to have it.' He waved his gun at Kitson. 'Get in there and get the cylinders out.'

Shrugging, Kitson went over to the caravan and Bleck followed him.

'I'm not going to manage this on my own,' Kitson said. 'Gypo and I put them up. I know what they weigh. You'd better get hold of the other end.'

Bleck grinned. He put his gun in its holster.

'Don't start anything funny, plough boy,' he said. 'I can handle you any time.'

Kitson reached up and jerked the cylinder out of its bracket. Bleck eased his end out and got it on his shoulder. The two men slowly backed out of the caravan.

As Kitson got clear of the caravan, he suddenly let go of his end of the cylinder. The unexpected shock as the cylinder thudded to the ground threw Bleck off balance.

Kitson jumped forward. His right fist thudded into the side of Bleck's neck, flattening him.

Cursing, Bleck tugged at his gun, but Kitson's thirteen stone of bone and muscle came down on him.

For several seconds the two men fought like animals, then Bleck drove his knee into Kitson's chest and threw him off. He got his gun out as Kitson reached him.

Kitson's hand grabbed Bleck's wrist and at the same time he jolted his left into Bleck's face.

Bleck grunted and let go of the gun.

Kitson was on his feet and covering Bleck with the gun before he could shake off the effect of the punch.

Bleck half sat up, blood running down his face from a cut under his eye, his lips drawn off his teeth in a snarl.

'I'll fix you for this!' he said viciously.

'Your fixing days are over,' Kitson said, breathing heavily.

Then suddenly, without warning, there came a roar of an aircraft engine and a swish of air as a small military training plane flew over their heads, flattening the grass with its slipstream as it banked steeply and flew on across the valley. Bleck staggered to his feet, staring after the aircraft.

'They saw us!' he gasped. 'They couldn't fail to have seen us! They'll be up here and after us!'

The three stood motionless, watching the aircraft bank in a tight circle and head back towards them.

'Get under cover!' Bleck yelled and he made a frantic rush towards the woods.

The other two scattered, also running towards the woods, but the aircraft was already on them.

Flying not more than a hundred feet above them, the aircraft swept over them with a roar and a rush of wind. They could see two men leaning out of the open cockpits, looking directly down at them, then the aircraft banked and went away.

Ginny and Kitson looked at each other; their eyes frightened.

Bleck bawled, 'Get under cover, you fools! Don't stand out there!'

Ignoring him, Kitson said, 'They saw us. They'll be up here, Ginny.'

'Yes. I said they would get on to us.'

Kitson moved quickly to the road, crossed it and, crouching, he looked over the grass verge down the long zig-zag road that was now clearly to be seen right down into the valley.

About ten miles down the road he saw three cars coming fast, spreading a cloud of dust as they raced into the twisting bends in the road.

He felt a little knock of fear at his heart as he ran back to Ginny.

'They're coming now!'

Bleck came out of the wood, cursing.

'Can you see them?'

'Yes. They'll be here in ten minutes at the rate they are coming.'

'We've got a chance,' Bleck said, his voice shaking. 'Get the Buick. If we can get over the top of the mountain we stand a chance.'

'A mile further up the road peters out,' Kitson said. 'We might climb . . .'

Bleck ran to the caravan and came back carrying the automatic rifle.

'They're not taking me alive,' he said, his eyes glittering. 'No death cell for me.'

Kitson opened the Buick door and Ginny slid in beside him.

He could feel her trembling and he patted her knee. 'Take it easy,' he said. 'We still have a chance.'

As Bleck got in beside Ginny, Kitson eased the car over the rough grass and onto the road.

The three of them looked back at the truck, standing under the trees.

'The punks said it was the safest truck in the world,' Bleck said savagely. 'They weren't bluffing.'

Kitson sent the car banging and bouncing up the road.

Bleck leaned out of the window to get his last look at the truck. There's more than a million dollars in that truck, he was thinking. There's my future and my life locked up in there too.

Kitson drove fast, skidding into the bends, his face tense, his eyes fixed on the road ahead.

They came to the first hairpin bend, and he slowed to take it, but misjudged it. He had to stop and reverse while Bleck cursed him.

As they began to climb again, the aircraft, like a worrying sheep dog, circled above them.

'If I could get a shot at that punk!' Bleck snarled, staring up at the circling plane.

In the distance they heard the wailing note of a police siren. Ginny shivered, her hands turning into fists.

Kitson was now having trouble in holding the car to the road, which was full of potholes and loose stones washed down the mountain from the past storm.

On their left was the side of the mountain that went straight up like a granite wall. On the right side was a sheer drop into the valley.

'We're not going to get much further,' Kitson said, slowing down. 'This is about where the road packs up.'

As he turned into the next hairpin bend, he stopped abruptly. A fall of rocks and shrubs blocked the road. There was no way of getting the Buick past the obstruction.

Holding the automatic rifle in his hand, Bleck got out of the car. He paid no attention to the other two, but ran forward and began to climb the obstruction.

Kitson paused to look up.

High above them, he could see the snow-covered mountain peak. He hesitated a moment, then, catching Ginny by her arm, he pointed upwards.

'We'll go that way, Ginny,' he said. 'We stand a chance of hiding up there. If we stick with Bleck, we're bound to be caught.'

Ginny flinched as she looked at the face of the mountain.

'I couldn't climb up there,' she said. 'You go, Alex.'

He was pushing her along now.

'We go together,' he said and started up the

face of the mountain. The first hundred yards was easy enough and Ginny followed him. Every now and then Kitson paused, reached down and hoisted her up beside him.

They could hear the siren much closer now.

The climb became harder and their progress slower.

They both felt horribly exposed against the bare face of the mountain, but fifty feet higher up was a mass of rocks behind which they could hide and Kitson kept urging Ginny to climb faster.

Once, in her panic, Ginny slipped, but Kitson grabbed her, not letting her pause, but pulling her up and forcing her on.

They reached the mass of rock as they heard the cars come to a halt below them.

They lay side by side, gasping for breath and peered down.

There was an overhanging rock that hid the lower part of the road from their view, but, looking to his right, Kitson caught sight of Bleck running frantically up the road, beating the air with his free hand and looking back from time to time.

He lost sight of Bleck as he rounded the bend in the road.

Kitson looked upwards, planning his next move.

Far above him, still sheltered from the road, was a broad ledge, screened by shrubs. He reckoned if they could get up there they could hide until the police got tired of looking for them.

He touched Ginny's arm.

'Feel like going on up?'

She nodded.

'Yes, all right.'

He smiled at her. Their faces were close and she moved forward, pressing her lips on his.

'I'm sorry, Alex,' she said. 'This is all my fault.'

'I had the choice,' he said. 'It just didn't work out.'

They could hear men's voices below, talking excitedly.

'They've found the Buick,' Kitson whispered. 'Come on, let's go.'

They began to climb again.

It was a nightmare business for Ginny, and she would never have made it without Kitson to pull her over the difficult places.

As they neared the ledge, she suddenly stopped climbing. Her foot rested on the root of a shrub, her hands gripped the pointed end of a rock. She was pressed against the mountain side and her eyes were closed.

'Go on, Alex,' she panted. 'I can't go any further. Leave me. I just can't do it.'

Kitson looked up. They were only a few feet from the ledge.

Then as he looked down at Ginny, just below him, he saw beyond her the long drop into the valley and a wave of dizziness swept over him.

He shut his eyes, hanging onto a shrub, feeling sweat start out on his face.

Looking up, Ginny saw him clinging just above her and she thought he was going to fall.

'Alex!'

'It's okay,' he gasped. 'I'm just dizzy. Don't look down, Ginny. Just hang on a moment.'

They remained there like two flies on a wall, then, very cautiously, Kitson began to move again. He found a better foothold, then he reached down towards Ginny.

'Give me your hand,' he said. 'Come on. Don't be scared. I wont let you go!'

'No, Alex! You'll never get me up there. I'll fall . . .'

'Give me your hand!'

'Oh, Alex, I'm scared! I'm going to let go! I can't hang on . . .'

He grabbed hold of her wrist as she released her grip. Her choked scream was whipped away by the wind. She dangled at the end of her arms, her skirts billowing out, her long, slim legs moving as if she were walking.

Kitson hung on, taking her weight.

'Ginny! You've got to help,' he panted. 'I'll swing you against the side. Try to get your feet on something, then I'll lift you.'

He swung her and her toes scrabbled frantically for a hold, found one and he felt her weight come off his arm.

Holding her, he looked down at her.

'That's fine,' he said. 'Give me a moment.'

They remained like that. A long minute crawled by, then he said, 'Okay. Now!' and he heaved upwards.

She slid up and over the projecting ledge and collapsed limply at his side.

Then they heard a shot. The sound was very loud and set up an echo.

Ginny stiffened and her hand closed tightly on Kitson's wrist.

The shot had come from below and to their right.

Cautiously, Kitson leaned forward and peered down. He had a clear view of the road below. He could see the Buick and, nearby, three police cars.

Moving very cautiously up the road, just beyond the obstruction, were ten soldiers and three police officers.

About fifty yards further up the road and just around one of the bends lay Bleck. He was sheltering behind two small boulders, the barrel of his automatic rifle pushed forward between them.

Another fifty yards up the road, just out of Bleck's view, stood a jeep with three soldiers by it.

Kitson realized that the jeep must have come up the other side of the mountain and Bleck was trapped. He felt a surge of relief that he had gone up the mountain instead of following Bleck.

By the upper bend in the road, a soldier lay face down in the road, blood running from a wound in his head.

The soldiers coming up the road, paused at the bend, keeping out of Bleck's sight. They were only twenty feet from him.

A major, short, dapper, and blond, peered cautiously around the bend in the road, spotted the dead soldier and hurriedly drew back.

Raising his voice, he shouted, 'We know you're there! Come on out with your hands in the air! Come on! You've got no chance! Come on out!'

Kitson could see Bleck pressing himself further into the ground.

Ginny joined Kitson and looked down.

Although they were two hundred feet above the soldiers, the men seemed alarmingly close to them.

'Are you coming or do we come and get you?' the major shouted.

'Come and get me, punks!' Bleck yelled, a savage, frightened note in his voice. 'Come and get me, and see what you get!'

The major said something to one of the police officers, who nodded.

The major then walked over to a soldier and spoke to him. There was a brief consultation. The soldier handed his rifle to another soldier, then took out a small object from one of his pouch pockets and started forward cautiously.

Kitson watched, his heart pounding.

When the soldier reached the bend in the road, he paused.

'This is your last chance!' the major shouted. 'Come on out!'

Bleck's reply was profane and obscene.

The major shouted, 'Okay, let him have it!'

The soldier tossed the object high into the air. It rose, turned lazily and began its fall.

Ginny hid her face against Kitson's shoulder.

Kitson started to yell a warning to Bleck, then stopped, knowing if he made a sound, he would give away his own hiding place.

The grenade dropped squarely in front of the two boulders behind which Bleck was sheltering.

Kitson shut his eyes.

The *Krrrump!* of the exploding grenade was unbelievably loud, and Kitson heard the rattle of stones and the whistling of flying splinters.

He moved back, not looking down and put his arms around Ginny.

She clung to him, shivering, and they remained like that.

A man suddenly shouted, 'There's only one here. Where are the other two? Where's the girl?'

'They won't find us,' Kitson said, his fingers running through Ginny's copper-coloured hair. 'They'll never think of looking for us up here.'

Then he heard the aircraft coming.

From above he knew they must be completely exposed to view.

They looked at each other, then Ginny tried to burrow against him, making herself as small as possible.

The cold clutch of fear at his heart, Kitson watched the aircraft coming.

It swished out of the sun, flying just above them and, looking up, he could see the pilot peering down at him.

The pilot waggled the wings of the aircraft, as if to tell Kitson he had seen him, then the aircraft banked, and Kitson could imagine the pilot yelling excitedly into his mike, telling those down on the road what he had seen.

'Ginny! Listen to me,' Kitson said, lifting her face and looking into her terrified eyes. 'Bleck was right. I'm not going into any death cell. You could beat this rap. The most they would give you if you were unlucky would be ten years. You're only a kid. The jury would be kind to you. Ten years is nothing. You could make a new start in life when you come out. You stay here and let them bring you down.'

'And you?' Ginny said, her fingers gripping his arm.

Kitson forced a grin.

'I'm taking a dive. It's quick and it's my way out. I'm not going into the death cell.'

Ginny drew in a deep breath.

'We'll go together, Alex. I'm not scared, but I would be, to be shut away for ten years.

That's something I couldn't take. We'll go together.'

A voice over a loudspeaker system suddenly bawled, 'Hey, you two up there! Come on down! We know you're up there. We don't want any shooting. Come on down!'

'You stay, Ginny . . .'

'No. I mean it.'

Kitson bent and kissed her, holding her close.

'Remember what Frank said? The world in our pockets? Well, maybe this could be it, but not this world; some other world. Let's go and find out.'

He put his hand in hers and they both stood up.

They looked directly down onto the road where the soldiers and police had spread out, ready to dive for cover, their rifles pointing up at the two figures on the ledge.

'Okay,' Kitson shouted. His voice sounded thin and weak to the listening men below. 'We're coming.'

He looked at Ginny.

'Are you ready?'

She tightened her hold on his hand.

'Try not to let go of me, Alex,' she said. 'Yes, I'm ready.'

The watching men saw them suddenly step off the ledge and come hurtling down towards them.

We hope you have enjoyed this Large Print book. Other Chivers Press or Thorndike Press Large Print books are available at your library or directly from the publishers.

For more information about current and forthcoming titles, please call or write, without obligation, to:

Chivers Large Print
published by BBC Audiobooks Ltd
St James House, The Square
Lower Bristol Road
Bath BA2 3BH
UK
email: bbcaudiobooks@bbc.co.uk
www.bbcaudiobooks.co.uk

OR

Thorndike Press
295 Kennedy Memorial Drive
Waterville
Maine 04901
USA
www.gale.com/thorndike
www.gale.com/wheeler

All our Large Print titles are designed for easy reading, and all our books are made to last.